The Journey of Niels Klim to the
World Underground

The Journey of Niels Klim to the **WORLD UNDERGROUND**

By Ludvig Holberg

Introduced and edited by
James I. Mc Nelis, Jr.

A Bison Book
University of Nebraska Press
Lincoln

Contents

Contents

INTRODUCTION

... except for ... Kierkegaard, Hans Christian Andersen, and Karen Blixen, Danish literature as a whole has about as much reality in the world of letters as that philosophic prop, the falling tree in the woodland vastness. Its sound falls on appreciative Danish ears, but who else apprehends its power and stature? Who else hears it at all?[1]

Who in this country today ever hears of Baron Holberg's *Journey of Niels Klim to the World Underground,* in spite of the fact that since the book appeared in 1741, it has been translated into thirteen languages and published in more than sixty editions? The present edition, the eighth in English, is based on the first English translation of 1742, and is the first new edition in English since that published in Boston in 1845. Even though *Klim* is one of the best examples of the imaginary voyage—only Cyrano de Bergerac's *Histoire Comique de la Lune* and Swift's *Gulliver's Travels* are more famous—the author's name is unfamiliar to most students of eighteenth-century English literature. To students of dramatic literature, however, Holberg is known as the "Molière of the North," and some of his plays have been published in this country as recently as 1950.

Ludvig Holberg was born in Bergen, Norway, on December

3, 1684. His father, a Norwegian army officer, died when Ludvig was an infant, and his mother when he was ten. The custom then was to pay officers' sons an allowance intended to cover the cost of their education, and to begin their military training early. Accordingly, the young "corporal," as these boys were called, was appointed to a regiment and sent to one of the midland districts of Norway, rather far from his birthplace. There at Fron, in the valley of Gudbrandsdalen, he studied for two years, until 1698, under a teacher who made up for his own intellectual short-comings by a generous application of the birch. Holberg's anti-militaristic feelings, expressed in his later writings, must have had an early start.

Returning to Bergen to continue his studies, he found that, because of a reform in the grammar school, Latin was more than ever the most important subject, and that debates on abstruse theological and metaphysical topics were conducted in that tongue as a means of attaining proficiency in its use. At the University of Copenhagen, where he went to take his B.A. degree after the fire in Bergen in 1702, it was much the same story. Holberg later satirized this method of learning in *Klim*, and sided with the Moderns in the Ancients and Moderns controversy by travestying classical poetry in his mock-epic poem, *Peder Paars*. Latin was not, of course, a dead language—"Polite Danes were wont to say that a man wrote Latin to his friends, talked French to the ladies, called his dogs in German, and only used Danish to swear at his servants."[2] For Holberg, who, like a true eighteenth-century gentleman, had a deep distrust of the *vulgus mobile,* the mob, Latin was a valuable instrument. He wrote *Klim* in Latin, and declares in his *Memoirs* that he delayed the Danish translation because "many of the moral precepts in this work were of a paradoxical character, which I considered it inexpedient to expose to the judgment of the less instructed portion of the community."[3]

He spent the next two years as a teacher and a sometime preacher in Voss, Norway, where, it is said, the brevity of his sermons made him quite popular with the congregation. During this period he took time out to return to Copenhagen,* where he passed the examinations in philosophy and theology, the only ones given, for an advanced degree. In 1704 he embarked on the first of five journeys about Europe and England, from which he was to bring back the light of modern learning to those dark degrees of northern latitude. He went to Germany and then on to the Netherlands, considered the intellectual center of the continent, but Amsterdam, he decided, was not for the literary man; rather it was a place where "trade occupies every man's thought, where even men like Grotius and Almasius have to give way to shipowners and merchants."⁴ About a year later he returned to Norway, exhausted and penniless, and through the aid of a friend, Christian Brix, managed to find employment as a teacher, chiefly of French. Apparently the Norwegians who hired him were not of a critical nature, for once in Paris he overheard a chambermaid remark that he spoke French like a German horse.

In the spring of 1706 he embarked at Christianssand for England, never to return to Norway again. Many Norwegians had been drawn to England by the increased trade resulting from the need for timber in rebuilding London after the great fire of 1666. There was a considerable colony of the Northerners in London, mainly seamen and merchants. Danes and Norwegians were also drawn to Oxford. From 1602 to 1683 the *Liber Peregrinorum* shows 112 students registered from these two countries.

---

* Norway and Denmark were politically unified under Danish kings from 1442 until 1812, when Norway acquired its independence. Holberg, consequently, figures prominently in the literature of both countries. Norway claims him because he was born in Bergen; Denmark claims him because all his mature life was spent in Copenhagen.

From 1683 to 1708 there were 60, of whom 46 were Danes and 14 Norwegians.[5] An ambitious and energetic traveller, Holberg loved to stroll about big cities, take the high road from country to country, and "Expatiate free o'er all this scene of man." With his friend Christian Brix he covered the ground on foot from Gravesend to London and from London to Oxford. Again there was the difficulty of too little money, but with some help from his friend and with money earned from giving lessons in languages and the flute, he managed to subsist at Magdalen College for eighteen months. He must have regarded it as time well spent; at any rate, he later remarked that he had many reasons for considering himself under great obligations to the Oxonians.[6] It was at Oxford that he planned his first literary work, *Introduction to the History of the European Kingdoms* (1711). The most that can be said for it is that it is more forthright and less ostentatiously learned than other histories of its time. It was dedicated to the king, who appointed him professor extraordinary to the University of Copenhagen. Despite this impressive title, Holberg had no money; his new post paid no salary, and furthermore it prevented him from giving private lessons. Finally in 1714 he was granted a travelling stipend and spent most of two years in France and Italy. At last, after two more poverty-stricken years in Copenhagen, he was appointed to the chair in metaphysics. He was a philosopher in spite of himself and most assuredly found the occupation distasteful. It has been suggested that this is the main cause of the irony which thenceforth pervaded his soul.

Inspired apparently by Boileau's *Le Lutrin*, Holberg's mock-epic *Peder Paars* was published in 1719 in four books of 6,000 lines. For all its richness of imagination, humor, and irony it is still rather intellectual than poetic, being in this respect no different from the work it imitated. Holberg's purpose was two-fold: to ridicule the devices of classical poetry, particularly those in Homer and Virgil, and to call Denmark back to its senses from an atmosphere of humbug, pedantry, and hypocrisy. Peder Paars is a simple Danish citizen, but like Odysseus and Aeneas, he has enemies among the immortal gods. On his way to visit his sweetheart he is shipwrecked and washed ashore on the smallest of the Danish islands. After adventures there among individuals of types common to contemporary Denmark, he is rescued by the goddess of love and arrives in Jutland, where, among other misfortunes, he is put in a madhouse. After his release he is conscripted into the army, and to regain his freedom and his citizenship is compelled to surrender all his possessions. Here the poem ends, unfinished. It is more than a masterpiece; it marks the beginning of a new era in Scandinavian literature.

As well as displaying Holberg's humor and satire, *Peder Paars* also shows a considerable dramatic ability. Since foreign acting groups pleased neither the public nor the king, an ardent theatergoer, Holberg was asked to try his hand at drama. His first five comedies were enthusiastically received, and between 1722 and 1728 he wrote, in all, twenty-eight plays. The number itself is impressive, but the soundness of the plays themselves and their variety of character and action make the feat unexampled in all literature. Since the first play is as competently constructed as the last, Holberg appears to have undergone no apprenticeship in this art, although he obviously learned much from the dramatic performances he witnessed during his travels in England, France, and Italy, and especially from Molière, whom he admired immensely. The motto of the Danish National Theater, "Not merely for pleasure," describes Holberg's own approach to the writing of plays; they were a form of entertainment which offered the author a means of delivering a morally worthwhile message.

Not long before the furious fire in Copenhagen in 1728, the theater went bankrupt. In 1730 Christian VI ascended the throne, and the puritanical atmosphere of the court precluded any revival of the drama. The theater did not reopen until 1747, under the more relaxed reign of Frederick V. Holberg wrote another six plays between 1747 and his death. His dramatic achievement was magnificent; he had solidly established the beginnings of a national theater.

In 1730 he finally had been appointed professor of history. From then on he devoted his energies mainly (with the exception of the time spent on *Klim*) to history and to essays devoted to social, ethical, philosophical, metaphysical, and religious questions. *The History of Denmark* is his most mature historical work; his most popular were the *History of Heroes* and *History of Heroines,* written in the manner of Plutarch. Other important historical works of this period were *Descriptions of Denmark and Norway, Description of Bergen,* and *General History of the Church.* He was not an Addison or a Steele, but his *Moral Reflections (Morale Tansker,* 2 volumes) appealed to the taste of the Danes just as similar works appealed to the English. The *Epistles (Epistler,* 5 volumes) show Holberg at his ripest and best and most intimate.

> He tells us as willingly why he prefers a cat to a dog, and what a real shoemaker ought to know—as he tells us his opinion on God and eternity; the destination of man and the supposed greatness of the popular heroes of history whom . . . he is more inclined to consider as the mischief makers of mankind and the squanderers of its economic wealth.[7]

Official recognition of Holberg's achievements came in 1747, when he was made a baron by Frederick V. His last years were active to the end. In 1753, aware that he had contracted a serious lung ailment, he faced death with equanimity: "It is enough for me to know that I have sought all my life long to be a useful citizen of my country. I will therefore die willingly, and all the more so because I perceive my mental powers are likely to fail me."[8] Death came on January 28, 1754, when Holberg was sixty-nine.

The imaginary voyage as a literary form was first studied by Ralph E. Tieje in *The Prose Voyage Imaginaire before 1800* (1917). Philip B. Gove, in *The Imaginary Voyage in Prose Fiction* (1941), has supplied invaluable aids to the student by defining and describing the genre and by providing an annotated list of two hundred and fifteen such works published between 1700 and 1800.

By the end of the eighteenth century the development of the form was complete; it was a story and it had verisimilitude. The uses to which it could be put were manifold. It could be used to depict a utopian world, or as an instrument of moral, philosophic, political, or social satire. More often than not the utopian and satiric were combined, for the imaginary voyage as a narrative form always had an "ulterior purpose." Swift chose to prove in *Gulliver's Travels* that man has the capacity for reason but is not reasonable. Holberg intended that *Klim* correct popular errors and help the reader in distinguishing the "semblance of virtue and vice from the reality."[9]

Julius Paludan's *Om Holbergs Niels Klim* (1878) still remains, as Gove observes, the best analysis of the complex literary beginnings of the genre. He traces the development from mythical geographic sagas, sea stories, and utopias, such as Homer's *Odyssey* and Plato's descriptions of Atlantis (in the *Timaeus* and in the *Critias*), right up to the appearance of Holberg's *Klim*. Following works of the Greek and Roman period there were the medieval fabulous tales of Alexander, various Icelandic sagas, and legends of missionary monks such as Saints Brandan and Patrick. Later came Marco Polo, Mandeville, and Rabelais with his pervasive influence on Cyrano de Bergerac, Swift, Holberg, and a host of others. The utopias of More, Bacon, and Campanella reinforce the recurrent utopian theme to be found in most of the imaginary voyages. There were also the books of travel and geographical discovery, and the *Relations* of the Jesuits about far-off countries. From these accounts of real lands the writers of imaginary voyages gained an appreciation of the use of detail and the value of credibility, or "realism," in their fictional creations. Lemuel Gulliver referred to a famous voyager of the seventeenth century as his "Cousin Dampier."

The effect of the "new science" upon the literary imagination, particularly as it was reflected in imaginary voyages, was tremendous. Professor Marjorie Nicolson's *Science and Imagination* (1956) and *Voyages to the Moon* (1948) amply describe and demonstrate its impact. The discovery of the telescope and Galileo's triumphant *Siderius Nuntius* (1610) reminded mankind that this planet was not the whole "Book of God's Works" but that the "Book" included the rest of the universe as well. Men reasoned that if existence were a good thing and if God's goodness and creativity were infinite, then it was necessary that the planets in outer space contain some sort of life: God would not leave so many worlds untenanted. In the wake of such speculations, there appeared a number of moon-voyages, the most entertaining being Cyrano de Bergerac's. The discovery of the microscope recalled man's gaze from the indefinite vastness of the universe to the "myriads in the peopled grass." Man seemed to find himself suddenly on an "isthmus of a middle state," between the infinitely small and great, between animals and angels. Ideas derived from the use of the telescope and microscope are dramatized in the Lilliputian and Brobdingnagian worlds of *Gulliver.*

The earth itself had its share of imaginary voyagers. Australia, *terra Australis inconnu,* was a popular setting for a utopian romance or satire. Among the most interesting of these are D'Alais's *Histoire des Sévarambes* and Foigny's *Avantures de*

Jacques Sadeur, both from seventeenth-century France. The world underground was also a subject for the writers of imaginary ˈvoyages, though not so popular a locale as the surface of the earth or of the moon. The most famous subterranean voyage to antedate Holberg's is Athanasius Kircher's *Mundus Subterraneus* (1665). Others are *Relation d'un Voyage du Pôle Arctique, au Pôle Antarctique, Par le Centre du Monde* (anonymous, 1721) and the Chevalier Mouhy's *Lamékis, ou Voyages Extraordinaires d'un Egyptien dans la terre intérieure* (1735-37).

The foregoing has been an extremely summary account of those works which contributed to the formation of the imaginary-voyage genre, and of some of the sources of *Klim.* Holberg in turn influenced other authors, a number of imitations of *Klim* appearing soon after its publication, and the underground theme being revived more than a century later in Jules Verne's *Journey to the Center of the Earth* (1864). Casanova states that in writing his *Jcosameron* he was inspired in part by *Klim,* and Edgar Allen Poe mentions *Klim* in *The Fall of the House of Usher* as "in strict keeping with the character of phantasm."

There have been a number of efforts made to describe, or define, the genre of imaginary voyages as it was in the seventeenth and eighteenth centuries. Geoffroy Atkinson in *The Extraordinary Voyage in French Literature from 1700 to 1720* (Paris, 1922) distinguishes five kinds of imaginary voyages: the Extraordinary, the Fantastic or Marvelous, the Extra-terrestrial, the Satirical or Allegorical, and the Subterranean. The Extraordinary Voyage, he writes, is

> a fictitious narrative, purporting to be the veritable account of a real voyage made by one or more Europeans to an existent but little known country—or to several such countries—together with a description of the happy condition of society found there, and a supplementary account of the traveler's return to Europe.[10]

The Fantastic or Marvelous eschews any realistic authentication and treats of dreams, witchcraft, or supernatural agencies. The Extra-terrestrial—for example, Godwin's moon-voyage or Cyrano de Bergerac's travels to the sun and moon—is self-explanatory. The Allegorical or Satirical is frankly imaginary: in this type the hero travels to a Utopia of Dogs, the Land of the Jansenists, or a Land of Love. The Subterranean, of which *Klim* is the exemplar, is also self-explanatory. The obvious drawback to this system of categorization is that the categories are not mutually exclusive: any particular voyage might be classified in two or three ways. Cyrano de Bergerac's *Histoire Comique de la Lune* might be classified as either Extra-terrestrial, Satiric, or Fantastic; *Gulliver* as Extraordinary or Satiric; and *Klim* as Subterranean or Satiric or Fantastic.

William A. Eddy introduces the term *Philosophic Voyage,* "a didactic treatise in which the author's criticism of society is set forth in the parable form of an Imaginary Voyage made by one or more Europeans."[11] The intention is to eliminate from the genre all real travels and all others intended as pure entertainment. Eddy divides the Philosophic Voyage into the Fantastic and Realistic. The Realistic are those which were credible when written, such as *Histoire des Sévarambes*. The Fantastic are subdivided into the Extra-terrestrial (Cyrano de Bergerac), Subterrestrial (Holberg), and Terrestrial (Swift).

What the imaginary voyage is and how it came to be are two questions; why it was so popular is a third. From the beginning of the seventeenth century extends a period of intense scientific, philosophical, and religious inquiry, and, more often than not, intense controversy. The "Book of God's Works" and the "Book of God's Words" were the subjects of close discussion and analysis; the studies of the curious ranged from comparative anatomy to comparative theology, from school curricula to city planning. The age might be called most properly one of re-examination. Donne put it simply: "The new philosophy calls all in doubt."

The welter of new ideas, theories, and projects—their constant intrusion into printed works probably provoked Swift's sarcastic reference to "the great modern improvement of digressions"—was best ordered in the imaginary voyage. Voyage after voyage in the literature bears this out. The author sends his hero off to some strange land, celestial, terrestrial, or subterranean, where he looks about and describes what he beholds. Religion, society, science, government, education, manners, and morals are all seen through the hero's eyes; and no matter whether the point of view is satirical or utopian, the narrative always comprises a critical re-examination of the the ways of our world. The author might cherish an impassioned belief in progress and the superiority of the Moderns; or he might agree with Donne that this world is a poor thing, and revere the Ancients: in either case he would find in the imaginary voyage the form best suited to his complex needs.

Holberg's purpose—"to correct popular errors and to distinguish the semblance of virtue and vice from the reality"[12]— entitles him to range, within the limits of the fable, over all human affairs and institutions. He uses Potu, the land of the reasonable trees, to make a variety of points. For example, Holberg is a feminist—rather like Defoe in this respect—and holds that it is stupid to discriminate against women of intelligence and ability. In Potu, women have exactly the same opportunities as men; in fact the highest judge in the city of Keba is a woman. Holberg disapproves of the European university system, particularly the debates in Latin over philosophic and theological subtleties. In Potu such debates are relegated to the sporting arena and bets are laid on the outcome. More than a century before Samuel Butler's *Erewhon* Holberg anticipates a relationship between bad moral behavior and a poor physical condition; Klim is cupped for affronting the sheriff's wife. Ships on the planet Nazar are propelled by some mechanical means—and such examples could easily be multiplied. The imaginary voyage was the best remedy for "the itch of digressions," because any sort of observation, any criticism of human kind and its activities could find therein its appropriate place; or, to put it another way, it was the ideal form to order the multiplicity of notions, observations, and projects which the intense critical atmosphere generated. One cannot help thinking of the turmoil of the present time, and of the proliferation of science-fiction, which is the contemporary form of the imaginary voyage, serving the same purposes and possessing the same advantages—although, unlike their predecessors, the modern writers for the most part look at their new worlds without optimism, and see mankind as the victim of scientific progress. The imminent possibility of interplanetary travel enhances the present-day reader's enjoyment of Klim's observations as he moves, a satellite with a satellite, around Nazar, as one of the first human beings in orbit.

As the genre developed, the story or fable was improved by the authors' efforts to achieve verisimilitude. To secure the desired effect there were two main requirements. First, the author "documented" his book—he incorporated letters and journals and other documentary evidence purporting to prove that the hero had been an actual, living person. Similarly, he supplied a quantity of concrete, realistic detail which would (almost) persuade the reader that the imaginary countries did in fact exist. But all this documentation and circumstantial detail, no matter how ingeniously contrived, availed little unless the author could fulfill the second requirement—that of depicting his protagonist as a thoroughly believable human being.

Robinson Crusoe and *Gulliver* are triumphant examples of the success of this method. *Gulliver*, for example, begins with a letter from Captain Gulliver to his Cousin Sympson in which he complains of inaccuracies in his journal, which Sympson had talked him into publishing. This is followed by a short note from Sympson, explaining why he edited the work as he did. Gulliver, says Sympson, was distinguished for his veracity. "The author of these travels, Mr. Lemuel Gulliver, is my ancient and intimate friend; there is likewise some relation between us by the mother's side." *Klim* begins with the "Apologetic Preface," a document signed by supposed real people testifying that the published Latin version differs in no respect from the manuscript found among Klim's papers after his death. Klim's account starts with a brief description of his activities after he had passed his examinations at the University of Copenhagen and returned, an impecunious student, to his native city, Bergen. Without prospects or employment he passes his time trying to clear up some points in natural philosophy, and finally decides to explore a large and deep cave upon the top of a mountain. The expedition, he writes, "was undertaken in the year of our Lord 1665, Hans Munthe and Lars Sorensen being consuls of Bergen, and Christian Bertelsen and Lars Sand being senators." The journal ends with an appendix written by Master Abeline, giving a short account of Klim's last days.* He declares that Klim's manuscript of his travels was left with him and that he had not published it earlier for very important reasons.

These devices assist the reader in the initial suspension of disbelief, but whether or not the narrative will continue to hold him depends upon the characterization and the presentation of realistic detail about the hero's character, adventures, and the strange countries themselves. Gulliver and Klim differ considerably, but they are both credible.

Holberg's work echoes much that went before, but like all

* Caspar W. Smith, in *Om Holbergs Levnet* (1858), mentions the fact that there had really been a sexton in Bergen named Niels Klim who died about the time that Holberg's Klim was supposed to have died.

successful artists he has used his sources with such originality that the work is unquestionably his own. Even so, not a little of the pleasure of reading *Klim* comes from detecting themes and devices which appear to have their origin as far back as Homer and Plato. Holberg's Potuans, reasonable beings in the shape of trees, remind the reader of Lucian's *True History*, in which sailors driven by a great tempest of two months' duration finally land on a delightful island where the rivers are of wine and the trees are women from the waist upward. Members of the crew who attempt gallantries remain forever transfixed. Potu suggests the barren wood in Canto XIII of the *Inferno*; Dante plucks a twig from a great thorn tree and it cries, "Why dost thou tear me?" and sheds dark blood. The Potuans are, however, not so forbidding. Klim, immediately after his arrival in Potu, leaps into a tree to avoid a charging bull, and finds to his dismay that he has leaped into the arms of the sheriff's wife. Other beings who speak *a posteriori* are reminiscent of Rabelais's humor. The country where the young rule the old recalls Cyrano de Bergerac's *Histoire Comique de la Lune*. Lucian condemns the too-long life; Holberg's Spelekans desire an early death to escape the misfortunes of poverty or sickness. Swift's Struldbrugs represent some of the same ideas. One cannot, however, be precise about the exact source of many of the themes and ideas. While it may very well be, as Professor Eddy wrote, that many ideas from Plato, Lucian, and Bishop Godwin came to Holberg by way of Cyrano de Bergerac, it would be unwise, as Paludan demonstrates, to confine so learned a man as Holberg to too narrow a range of sources. John Colin Dunlop finds it "impossible not to perceive imitations of Gulliver, of Rabelais's Vie de Gargantua, Cyrano de Bergerac, Doni, Machiavelli, and even, perhaps, the early Greek Romances."[13] In addition Dunlop observes that there is some evidence of a national strain to be found in the sagas of King Hading's visit to the land of the

dead and the living, King Gorm's and Thorkild's journey north
in Saxo's eighth book, and the saga of Erik Vidforle, who, after
converting Greece to Christianity, goes to seek a paradise in
India. The closest relationship, however, is with *Gulliver*. Ever
since the publication of Seyer Olrog's translation of *Gulliver* in
1768, Danish scholars have been investigating Swift's influence.
Some of their modern work is marred, just as English scholar-
ship had been, by a mistaken emphasis upon Swift's rather than
Gulliver's misanthropy. Whatever Holberg's indebtedness to
Swift may have been, he, according to the best tradition of the
past, makes no mention of it in his *Memoirs* when he discusses
the composition of *Klim*.

Holberg wrote that he was reluctant to publish his *Klim*
because he was unwilling "to be again exposed to the animad-
versions of those morose judges who detest every thing humorous
or facetious, and view a joke in the light of an offence of which
no Christian should be guilty."[14] The censors in the clergy were
not all that deterred him. He was growing old and did not want
to be thought a buffoon; he dreaded the misconceptions which
are usually put upon moral tales and pieces of pleasantry. But
again, according to the old gentlemanly tradition, his friends
and a publisher prevailed on him to allow publication. His
reasons for permitting it remind one of Swift's satire upon just
such excuses in *A Tale of a Tub*—"a great dearth of foreign
news, a tedious fit of rainy weather." Like Swift's *Tale*, *Klim*
was honored by the immediate publication of a key to the work.
Holberg thought no more of key-searchers than had Swift and
referred to them as "the mystical class of persons"; nevertheless,
he promised to give unreservedly "the whole key to the work."
Klim first appeared in Germany in Latin in 1741. Not much
later an edition in German came out in Denmark and caused
some commotion, but at length, in Holberg's words, "the majority

of the public saw that there was nothing in the book to excite alarm, or to call for such intemperate abuse."

The idea for Klim's underground journey came to Holberg from the accounts of those persons in his country "who speak confidently of their intercourse with fairies and supernatural beings, and who are ready to take their corporal oaths that they have been carried away by subterranean spirits to hills and mountain caves." Although the gullible and the superstitious are deservedly ridiculed, that one objective is a trifle, in Holberg's opinion, compared to the story's vastly more important burden of moral precepts and reflections. The characters scattered through the work are "so numerous and various that they may be said to illustrate a complete system of ethics, hence a key would be required for almost every page."

Holberg is somewhat reluctant to call the work a satire. While he does admit that it has the "air of satire" because of the way vice is animadverted upon, he prefers the term "philosophical romance." Swift wrote in *A Tale of a Tub* that one might inveigh against foppery and fornication, pride and dissimulation, bribery, rapine, and injustice, but in truth " 'Tis but a ball bandied to and fro, and every man carries a racket about him to strike it from himself among the rest of the company." Holberg also appreciated the fact that to satirize what is general is less dangerous than to satirize what is individual. "Thus there is less danger in attacking mankind generally, than a whole nation, and a whole nation than a particular family; and even a particular family may be more safely made the subject of animadversion than a single individual." His experience after the publication of *Peder Paars* tended to reinforce this notion: it is said that some persons who were offended by the poem threatened his life. Holberg does not say which sort of satire he thought most effective; he obviously knew which was most dangerous. In tones that remind one of Lemuel Gulliver, he declares his disgust and resignation: "No encomiums or persuasions shall ever induce me to attempt again this kind of writing; I leave such enterprises to others whose shoulders are stronger than mine, and I will endeavour to efface the stain of my former industry by a virtuous abstinence from all such pursuits for the future."

Gulliver and Klim were competent enough reporters of what they observed, but were blind to their own shortcomings (which, nonetheless, are plainly visible to the reader). Gulliver in Brobdingnag and Klim in Potu are alike in being incapacitated by their own pride and incapable of profiting from their experiences. Gulliver, frustrated by his physical insignificance in comparison to the Brobdingnagian giants, tries to salve his ego by asserting the greatness of his native country. "I would hide the frailties and deformities of my political mother, and place her virtues in the most advantageous light." All to no avail. He tries to ingratiate himself by offering to teach the king how to make cannon with which to destroy his enemies; the king is repelled. After long discussions he finally concludes that Gulliver's species is "the most pernicious race of little odious vermin that nature ever suffered to crawl upon the surface of the earth." Klim shows no patriotic feeling, but he does have pride and more than average ambition. The Potuans, who carefully evaluate his capacities, have trouble deciding whether or not Klim is a rational being, just as the birds on the sun had trouble making up their minds about Cyrano and the Houhyhnhnms about Gulliver. Klim is finally assigned a job as messenger, in accordance with their appraisal of his intelligence and because, as he can move more rapidly than they, he can perform the job most efficiently. Klim's pride is hurt. He is a university graduate. He prides himself on the speed of his perceptions. However, as the Potuans soon discover, although he grasps things quickly, his understanding of them is superficial. Klim, like most of mankind, wants something more than justice and will not be content with his lot. According to Potuan custom, any citizen who suggests a change in the laws is led to the market place, where he stands on a gallows with a rope about his neck while the proposal is considered. If it is rejected, he is hanged; if it is accepted, he is accorded all the honors of a public hero. Klim, impelled by ambition, proposes that all women be removed from public office—an innovation which fails to win approval. Through the graciousness of the king his death sentence is commuted to exile to the Firmament, the underside of the earth. His exit from the planet Nazar is the same as that of Gulliver from Brobdingnag and as of Foigny's Sadeur to and from Australia: he is carried off by a gigantic bird.

Klim profited no more from his experience in Potu than did Gulliver in Brobdingnag, and neither one faced up to the true state of affairs during his later adventures. In Houyhnhnmland Gulliver learns to consider all mankind as another kind of Yahoo. Forced to return home, he avoids human society and prefers the company of his horses in the barn. He disregards the example of Christian kindness set him by his rescuer, Captain Pedro de Mendez, whom he "at last . . . descended to treat . . . like an animal which had some little portion of reason," and spends the rest of his life, we can assume, in a bitter and dreary misanthropy. Klim's pride and ambition are almost satisfied when he lands in Quama, a country whose inhabitants are human beings living in a primitive state, and who treat him as a god. Resolving to improve their lot, he raises and trains an army, teaches them to use pikes and javelins and to make guns and powder, and finally leads them to victory over their enemy neighbors. But Klim is not satisfied until he subjugates all the countries of the "Firmament"; he usurps the Quamitic throne and becomes emperor. When the Quamites rebel against his tyranny, Klim is forced to flee. He creeps into a cave, falls through a hole, and finds himself in Norway whence he came. Klim's shortcomings are of a more palpable sort than Gulliver's and he repents, but too late.

The rough similarity in characterization is paralleled in the structure of the two works. The first half of *Gulliver* is devoted to the protagonist's adventures in the small and great worlds of Lilliput and Brobdingnag, and is divided into two books, the first ending with Gulliver's return home after Lilliput. The voyages to Lilliput and Brobdingnag are equivalent to Klim's adventures in Potu, Utop(ia) in reverse, and its surrounding countries. In both works the utopian theme is an important part of this half. The third book of *Gulliver*, narrating his adventures in Laputa, Balnibarbi, Luggnagg, Glubbdubdrib, and Japan, corresponds generally to Klim's stay in Martinia and his visits to other countries on the way to Quama. In this third section the authors indulge their fantasies more freely than in any other. Klim's adventures in Quama and Gulliver's in Houyhnhnmland take up approximately the last quarter of both works.

The extent of Holberg's indebtedness to Swift is clearly perceived when we proceed from the general similarity in structure and characterization to more particular borrowings. While a complete listing of all these resemblances is outside the scope of this Introduction, some are important enough to warrant examination here. In Potu, Klim is harassed by monkeys who think he is one of them, much to the amusement of the Potuans. After a monkey invades Klim's room one night, the king orders that Klim be bedecked with branches so that the monkeys will take him thereafter for a Potuan and leave him alone. In this instance, Holberg, who, like most of Swift's readers, was impressed by the Yahoos, has combined the Yahoos of Book IV with the monkey episode of Brobdingnag in Book II. The monkey or Yahoo theme reappears in Klim's adventures in Martinia, a land of more or less rational monkeys, where it is related to Holberg's disgust, similar to Swift's, with the innovating or projecting spirit. The Martinians are in a continual frenzy of activity, shifting from fad to fad, fashion to fashion, project to project. Klim is outfitted with a tail, and becomes a national hero when he introduces the wearing of wigs. Holberg also has his land of natural philosophers or scientific projectors, much like Swift's Balnibarbi. Here agriculture is neglected and the country exists on the edge of ruin while the populace occupies itself with scientific projects. An abstracted philosopher urinates against Klim's back and soundly thrashes him when he objects. Rescued by other philosophers, he learns from the neglected wife of one of them that they plan to dissect him to discover some new phenomena in anatomy.

Holberg has some variations on the theme of the Struldbrugs, Swift's immortals in Book III. Struldbrugs are designated at birth by a red circular spot directly over the left eyebrow. The spot changes color at various periods of life until the Struldbrug turns forty-five, when it becomes coal black permanently. The Holbergian variant is a class of rational trees, born with marks on their foreheads which indicate how long they will live. But the knowledge that death can not come unexpectedly does not make their lives better or happier; instead they brood about their approaching dissolution and postpone repentance for their sins until the last hour. In the kingdom of Cambara, the trees live only four years; they mature in one year and spend the remaining three preparing for death. To Klim their kingdom seems a land of saints and angels. In Spelek the trees live to be four hundred, and since death is so far away that it is seldom thought of, the Spelekans live lives of falsehood, lasciviousness, and bad manners. In a similar fashion, Holberg dramatizes other pairs of extremes, in each case showing that the supposed advantage or disadvantage is counterbalanced by an opposite effect. The Struldbrugs, too, paid dearly for the gift of immortality.

Holberg's technique here does not differ from Swift's. In Potu, Klim is thought to be a blockhead because of the quickness of his perceptions; in Martinia he is despised because of his slowness. Swift superimposes the giant world of Brobdingnag upon the tiny world of Lilliput, and in doing so impresses the reader not with the importance of physical size but with the significance of moral virtue.

Parallels might also be noted in Swift's and Holberg's treatment of such subjects as the education of women, the relativity of perceptions, war, medicine, government, knowledge, and many other subjects. There are, however, some striking differences. The main one, and the one which caused Holberg the most trouble, pertains to religion. Except for the Little- and Big-Endian controversy in Lilliput, which is a comment on religious controversy, not religion, Swift avoided the subject in *Gulliver*. Holberg's attitude toward religion is clearly the same as the Potuans'. In that country religious controversy is not permitted. The holy books may not be explained, and anyone daring to dispute about the being and nature of the deity is bled and sent to the madhouse. All are agreed that there is a God who created and who maintains all things; that God in His being is inconceivable to man; and that therefore it is foolish and vain to argue about Him. For the rest, they believe in a hereafter where all will be rewarded for their virtues and punished for their vices. The Potuan theological creed is so short that it can be written on two pages. Holberg's position is deistic and similar in many respects to Pierre Bayle's; aside from a few principles, all other theological differences were of no concern to him. Considering the prevailing pietism of his country, Holberg was surely courageous in speaking out as he did. He wrote in his *Memoirs* that he discovered "There are no men who bear so ill to be told of their vices as those who thunder against vice in public."

Holberg's approach to his subject and his choice of images

result in more exposition and fewer dramatic incidents than are to be found in *Gulliver*.* Gulliver's adjustments to the small world of Lilliput and to the great world of Brobdingnag are in themselves highly dramatic and amusing. Can the reader ever forget the invisible thread in Lilliput or the rats as big as mastiffs in Brobdingnag? Of necessity, Gulliver's position, to be convincing, demanded just such dramatic situations and precise realistic detail, particularly when it meant a shift in the proportions of the world. The triviality of human affairs is satirized simply by reports of the actions, attitudes, and opinions of the tiny Lilliputians. Gulliver's own smallness of character is exposed by the Brobdingnagian king's reaction to his slanted reports about his native land. Klim describes the rational trees and gives us a clear account of their society, religion, and government, but much of the information is pure reporting—it has no connection with his own situation. His adjustment to life among the Potuans, in so far as it concerns physical details, is scarcely dwelt upon.

Rational trees as images are markedly different from tiny Lilliputians and gigantic Brobdingnagians. A straightforward account of Lilliputian affairs emphasizes, without other comment, the triviality of human affairs. The physical side of human life is magnified in all its horror by a description of the monstrous breast of the Brobdingnagian nurse and of the immense louse burrowing into the flesh of a beggar. Swift's senses were abnormally keen, and he loathed the dirt and stink of his time, when people made little use of soap and water. Holberg expressed no such passionate regard for cleanliness; he might see the filthy fop as a monkey, but not as a Yahoo. His images do not lend themselves to that sort of savage satire. A society of rational trees might be presented as better than ours, but because

* In its expository tone, *Klim* is much like Samuel Butler's *Erewhon*.

the reader does not identify himself emotionally and physically with the trees as he does with Swift's images, he finds Holberg's satire more genial and intellectual.

Holberg's satirical object, European society, is the same as Swift's, but Holberg is not preoccupied by man in his physical being. Swift concentrates on man, Holberg on society. This difference accounts for the fact that Holberg distinguishes one society from another on a national basis, while Swift does not. Paludan suggests that Potu probably represents Holland in the slowness of its governmental processes and in the utilitarianism and soundness of reasoning of its citizens. Hammer, however, sees Potu as an idealized picture of England. Holberg explicitly satirizes the customs and characteristic differences of the nations of Europe in the manuscript written by one of the Subterraneans who had visited there; Klim finds the manuscript in Quama. In this document France is said to be much like Martinia, and England, which Holberg obviously admired, is treated with more consideration than any other country.

Holberg himself was probably aware that *Klim,* in spite of its immediate popularity and widespread audience, was not so effective as *Gulliver.* The reason he gives in the following quotation (without, of course, mentioning *Gulliver,* but certainly with it in mind) is the greater freedom writers enjoyed in England, not his own choice of a primarily expository method and of less vivid images.

> Thus much only I will venture to say by way of admonition, that if any one, upon comparing this little production with some other celebrated moral tales, should think it tame and feeble, he should call to mind the different circumstances in which the author was placed from those of more fortunate writers. In Germany, in France, and especially in England, where no shackles are imposed upon genius, and where every thought that can occur to the human mind may be freely published, it is far easier to display the strength of the judg-

ment and the imagination, than in our northern kingdom, where the force and spirit of a writer are checked and blunted by a most rigid censorship. From this cause, even if poets and philosophers were to arise in our country capable of rivalling the poets and philosophers of England, they would scarcely come to maturity.

English writers, Swift particularly, would not have agreed with the ideal picture Holberg drew of conditions in their country, though they were surely better than in his own.

Holberg's was "a mind ambitious of glory" and he would have been pleased at the place history has accorded him in literature.

Holberg was not only the founder of Danish literature and the greatest of Danish authors, but he was, with the exception of Voltaire, the first writer in Europe during his own generation. Neither Pope nor Swift, who perhaps excelled him in particular branches of literary production, approached him in range of genius, or in encyclopedic versatility.[15]

JAMES I. MC NELIS, JR.

---

[1] Richard B. Vowles, Review of *A History of Danish Literature* by P. M. Mitchell, *The American Scandinavian Review*, XLVI (1958), 391.

[2] Edmund Gosse, "Holberg," *Encyclopaedia Britannica*, XI (1956), 637.

[3] Lewis Holberg, *Memoirs* (London: Hunt and Clarke, 1827), pp. 180-181.

[4] S. C. Hammer, *Ludvig Holberg, the Founder of Norwegian Literature and an Oxford Student* (Oxford: B. H. Blackwell, 1920), p. 9.

[5] *Ibid.*, pp. 13-14.

[6] *Ibid.*, p. 16.

[7] *Ibid.*, p. 30.

[8] William Morton Payne, "Ludvig Holberg," *Library of the World's Best Literature, Ancient and Modern*, ed. Charles Dudley Warner, XIII (New York: R. S. Peale and J. A. Hill, 1897), p. 1753.

[9] Holberg, *Memoirs*, p. 174.

[10] Geoffroy Atkinson, *The Extraordinary Voyage in French Literature from 1700 to 1720* (Paris: Librairie Ancienne Honoré Champion, Édouard Champion, 1922), p. 7.

[11] William A. Eddy, *Gulliver's Travels, a Critical Study* (Princeton: Princeton University Press, 1923), p. 8.

[12] Holberg, *Memoirs,* p. 174.

[13] John Colin Dunlop, *History of Prose Fiction* (London: George Bell and Sons, 1888), p. 621.

[14] Holberg, *Memoirs,* p. 170. All the quotations from here to the end of the introduction, except the final one, may be found in the same source, pp. 171-176.

[15] Gosse, "Holberg," p. 637.

APOLOGETIC PREFACE

Peter Klim and Andreas Klim,
Sons of Thomas Klim, and Grandsons of
Klim the Great

to

the Courteous Reader.

Since it has come to our ears that the truth of this history has been called into question by some persons, and that the publishers of *The Journey of Niels Klim* have fallen into ill repute in several places, we have deemed it advisable to prefix to this new edition an attestation signed by certain citizens whose testimony is above all criticism. The two first subscribing witnesses were contemporaries of our hero, and the others lived soon after, all being universally known for their strict virtue and integrity, and who would never allow anything to be palmed off upon them, nor suffer themselves to be sent on a sleeveless errand. With the evidence, then, of such reputable men, signed with their own hands and sealed with their own seals, we shut the mouths of our critics and jeerers and bring them to acknowledge their incredulity to be

1

unfounded, and to retract their injudicious accusations. The attestation, addressed to myself and my brother, reads thus:

We the undersigned, at the request of the two respectable and very worthy young men and brothers Peter Klim and Andreas Klim, do hereby certify that we, on examining the books and papers of the late illustrious Niels Klim, found among them a manuscript entitled *The Journey of Niels Klim,* to which was attached a Subterranean grammar, together with a dictionary in two languages, Danish and Quamitic. That on comparing the admirable Latin translation of the renowned and highly praiseworthy Abeline, which at this present moment is in almost everybody's hands, with the original writing, we discovered that the said translation was a faithful one and did not deviate from the original. In witness whereof we have hereunto set our hands and affixed our respective seals.

ADRIAN PETERSEN, by my own hand
JENS THORLAKSEN, by my own hand
SVEND KLAK, by my own hand
JOKUM BRANDER, by my own hand
JENS GAD, for self and brother, by my own hand
HIERONYMUS GIBBS, a Scot, by my own hand

We hope that with such forcible and authentic evidence every doubt will now be entirely removed. But should there, nevertheless, be found any critics stubborn enough to persist in their disbelief, such power of incredulity we must endeavour to overcome with other weapons. It is a well-known fact that in that part of Norway called Finnmark there are people so profoundly skilled in the magic of nature (a science into which the learned of other nations have scarcely ever pried) as to be able to raise a storm at pleasure, and again appease it; to transform themselves into wolves; to speak several languages which are entirely unknown in our world; and to travel from the North Pole to the South Pole in less time than an hour. One of these Finns whose name was Peyvis had recently come to Bergen, where, at the request of the sheriff, he gave so many surprising and miraculous proofs of his art and learning that all the spectators pronounced him perfectly worthy of a doctor's cap. Just at that time there issued from the press a severe critique upon *The Journey of Niels Klim,* wherein the censor relegated it to tales of the nursery. This circumstance was the occasion of orders being given to the said Peyvis, while endeavours were still making to vindicate the honour of the Klims, to concentrate all the powers of his art, and attempt a voyage to the regions below the earth. He promised to comply with the sheriff's commands, expatiating on his own peculiar faculty, promptness, and dexterity in nearly the following words:

> What wilt thou, then? Say!
> The strongest, the greatest, the mightiest on earth,
> From the South to the North,
> My word must obey.
> I rend in twain the rainbow,
> And sun, and moon, and stars I headlong hurl below;
> By moonlight make the thunder roar and lightning glow:
> The whirlwinds and the raging storms my voice do know,
> And from the impenetrable rock I make sweet honey flow;
> The North Sea's roaring waves I bid at once recoil;
> I freeze the hedgerow fields and make the icebergs boil.
> What wilt thou, then? Say!
> What's there found in the ocean, what is there on earth,
> In the fire, in the air, from the South to the North,
> That my word does not obey?[1]

All shuddered with fear and were filled with amazement on hearing him pronounce such strange-sounding and incredible words. The Finn, however, immediately and undauntedly prepared himself for the voyage, stripped himself to the skin, and (O, wonderful to behold!) suddenly transformed himself into an eagle, soared into the atmosphere, and vanished in an instant. After a whole month's absence, early one Friday morning a little before sunrise, our metamorphosing doctor entered the sheriff's room completely exhausted and breathless, very similar to a horse that has been driven hard up an acclivity. His strength had entirely left him; he swooned, while the sweat poured from his forehead in continual streams. It was not long before he came to himself again, when, after breathing a little, and taking a gulp or two of brandy to revive his spirits, he gave us a full description of his adventures, describing with a brilliancy of acumen all that had befallen him in his aerial voyage and in his travels in the Subterranean regions. He related also that, after divers bloody combats in which the Klimites had always triumphed, the reins of government were again in the hands of our Niels's son, who held the sceptre for a long time under the guardianship of his mother, but grown old himself and become illustrious through numerous and brilliant exploits, he now reigned far and wide in the Subterranean world under the name and title of Niels the Second.

Every circumstance which this learned man related was immediately penned down word for word and will prove an extremely important, and at the same time interesting, appendix to the annals of which the literati of Bergen have announced the publication under the title, *A Continuation of the History of the Fifth Monarchy*. Besides the annals already spoken of, there will appear at the same time a grammar of the Quamitic language, which to the present age will perhaps not prove of any particular advantage, but will become so much the more important to posterity as our country (without boasting), which is really fertile in projectful heads, will certainly not fail to embrace every possible opportunity, both night and day, of establishing a commercial intercourse with the Quamites, a people who have invented machines with which they are enabled, without the aid of witchcraft, to sail with perfect safety to the regions below the earth.

APOLOGETIC PREFACE

Shame on you now, ye incredulous mortals! and learn hereafter to act with more prudence in important matters! Shame
upon you, ye railers and jesters! and beg pardon for your unfounded accusations! Lastly, shame upon you, ye critics and
censors! and in order that the republic of letters may not again
have to endure your slanders, stifle them for the future.

[1]Holberg's Latin version:

> "Quicquid in orbe vides, paret mihi. Florida tellus,
> Cum volo, spissatis arescit languida succis;
> Cum volo, fundit opes; scopulique ac horrida saxa
> Limosas iaculantur aquas. Mihi Pontus inertes
> Submittit fluctus; Zephyrique tacentia ponunt
> Ante meos sua flabra pedes; mihi flumina parent."

"Petronii Satir. cap. 134 vs. 1 sqq. (Ex recensione Fr. Buecheleri, Berolini
1862):

> "Quicquid in orbe vides, paret mihi. Florida tellus,
> Quum volo, spissatis arescit languida sucis,
> Quum volo, fundit opes, scopulique atque horrida saxa
> Niliacas iaculantur aquas. Mihi pontus inertes
> Summittit fluctus, Zephyrique tacentia ponunt
> Ante meos sua flabra pedes. Mihi flumina parent . . ."

Ludovicus Holbergius, Nicolai Klimii Iter Subterraneum (Copenhagen:
Sumptibus Societatis ad Promovendas Litteras Danicas Conditae, 1866), pp.
5-6.

CHAPTER I

The Author's Descent to the Subterranean World

In the year 1664, after I had passed my several examinations in the University of Copenhagen, and had deservedly obtained the character, which is there called laudable, by the votes of my judges, as well philosophers as divines, I prepared for my return into my native country, and accordingly put myself aboard a ship bound for Bergen in Norway, dignified indeed with various marks of honour from the gentlemen of the several faculties, but in my fortunes quite impoverished. This was an evil that attended myself as well as several of the Norwegian students, who returned from the study of the arts and sciences into their own country stripped of all they were worth. As we had a pretty brisk gale, after a voyage of six days we arrived at Bergen harbour. Being thus restored to my country, something wiser indeed, though by no means richer, I was supported for a time at the expense of my near relations, and led a precarious sort of life, yet not altogether indolent and inactive. For in order to clear up by experience some points of natural philosophy, the study I had devoted myself to, I rambled over every corner of the province with an insatiable curiosity to explore the nature of the Earth, and to search into the very bowels of our mountains. No rock so steep but I climbed it, no cavern so hideous and deep but I made a descent into it, to try if haply I could discover anything curious and worth the inquiry of a philosopher. For there are a multitude of things in our country of Norway hardly ever seen or heard of, which if France, Italy, Germany, or any other country so fruitful of the marvelous could boast of, nothing would be more talked of, nothing more sifted and examined.

Among those things which to me appeared most worthy of observation there was a large and deep cave upon the top of that mountain which the natives call Floïen. And because the mouth of the cave used to send forth a gentle murmuring sound, and that too by intervals, as if by its frequent sighs its jaws were now shut, and now opened; hence the literati of Bergen, and particularly the celebrated Master Abeline, and Master Edvard, one of our first geniuses in astronomy and natural philosophy, imagined this affair highly worthy of a philosophical inquiry; and since they themselves were too old for such an enterprise, they excited the younger inhabitants to a closer examination of the nature of the cavern; especially as at stated intervals, after the manner of human respiration, the sound being sometime withheld, issued out with a certain proportional force.

What with these discourses, and what with my own natural inclination, I formed a design of entering into this cavern, and communicated my intention to some of my friends. But they by no means approved of it, plainly declaring that it was a wild and frantic undertaking. But all they could say, so far was it from extinguishing, that it did not even damp the ardour of my mind; and their advice, instead of weakening, administered fuel to my curiosity. For that eagerness with which I pursued the study of nature inspired me to face every danger, and the straitness of my private circumstances gave a spur to my natural inclination. For my own substance was quite wasted, and it seemed to me the greatest hardship to live in a state of dependence in a country where all hopes of preferment were cut off, where I beheld myself condemned to poverty, and every avenue to honour and advantage entirely stopped, unless I would make my way by some flagrant act of dishonour or immorality.

Thus resolved, and having got together what was requisite

for such an exploit, upon a Thursday morning, when the heavens were all serene and cloudless, I left the city soon after twilight, to the end that having finished my observations, I might return again that same day; because, being ignorant of futurity, it was not possible I should foresee that I, like another Phaeton, should be flung upon another world, not to revisit my native soil till after a ten years' peregrination.

This expedition was undertaken in the year of our Lord 1665, Hans Munthe and Lars Sorensen being consuls of Bergen, and Christian Bertelsen and Lars Sand being senators. I went out attended by four fellows I had hired, who brought with them such ropes and iron crooks as would be necessary to descend by. We went directly to Sandvik, the most commodious way to climb the mountain. Having with difficulty reached the top, we came to the place where was the fatal cave, and being tired with so troublesome a journey, we all sat down to breakfast.

'Twas then my mind, foreboding as it were the approaching evil, first began to be dismayed. Therefore, turning to my companions, "Will anyone," says I, "undertake this task?" But no reply being made, my ardour, that had languished, kindled anew. I ordered them to fasten the rope about me, and thus equipped, I commended my soul to Almighty God. Being now just ready to be let down, I gave my companions to understand what I would have done, viz., that they should continue letting down the rope till they heard me cry out, upon which signal they should stop, and if I persisted to cry out, that then they should immediately draw me up again. In my right hand I held my harpoon, or iron hook, an instrument that might be of use to me to remove whatever might obstruct my passage, and also to keep my body suspended equally between the sides of the cavern. But scarce had I descended so low as about ten or twelve cubits, when the rope broke. This accident was discovered to me by the sudden outcries of the men I had hired. But their noise soon died away; for with an amazing velocity I was hurried down into the abyss, like a second Pluto, allowing my harpoon to be a sceptre.

For about the fourth part of an hour (as near as I could guess, considering the great consternation I must be in) I was in total darkness, and in the very bosom of night; when at length a thin small light, like twilight, broke in upon me, and I beheld at last a bright serene firmament. I ignorantly thought, therefore, that either by the repercussion or opposite action of the subterranean air, or that by the force of some contrary wind, I had been thrown back, and that the cave had vomited me up again. But neither the sun which I then surveyed, nor the heavens, nor heavenly bodies were at all known to me, since they were considerably less than those of ours. I concluded therefore that either all that whole mass of new heavens existed solely in imagination, excited by the vertigo my head had undergone, or else that I was arrived at the mansions of the Blessed. But this last opinion I soon rejected with scorn, since I viewed myself armed with a harpoon, and dragging a mighty length of rope after me, knowing full well that a man just going to Paradise has no occasion for a rope or a harpoon, and that the celestial inhabitants could not possibly be pleased with a dress which looked as if I intended, after the example of the Titans, to take Heaven by violence, and to expel them from their divine abodes. At last, after the maturest consideration, I fell to imagining that I was sunk into the subterranean world, and that the conjectures of those men are right who hold the Earth to be hollow, and that within the shell or outward crust there is another lesser globe, and another firmament adorned with lesser sun, stars, and planets. And the event discovered that this conjecture was right.

That violence with which I was hurried headlong had now continued for some time, when at length I perceived that it languished gradually in proportion to my approach towards a certain planet, which was the first thing I met with. That same planet increased so sensibly in bulk or magnitude that at last, without much difficulty, I could plainly distinguish mountains, valleys, and seas through that thicker atmosphere with which it was surrounded.

Then I perceived that I did not only swim in a celestial matter or ether, but that my motion which had hitherto been perpendicular was now altered into a circular one. At this my hair stood on end, for I was full of apprehension lest I should be transformed into a planet, or into a satellite of the neighbouring planet, and so be whirled about in an everlasting rotation. But when I reflected that by this metamorphosis my dignity would suffer no great diminution, and that a heavenly body, or at least an attendant upon a heavenly body, would surely move with equal solemnity to a famished philosopher, I took courage again, especially when I found from the benefit of that pure celestial ether that I was no longer pressed by hunger or thirst. Yet upon recollecting that I had in my pocket some of that sort of bread which the people of Bergen call *bolken,* and which is of an oval or oblong figure, I resolved to take it out and make an experiment whether in this situation I had any appetite. But at the first bite perceiving it was quite nauseous, I threw it away as a thing to all intents and purposes useless. The bread thus cast away was not only suspended in air, but (what was very marvelous to behold) it described a little circular motion round my own body. And from thence I learned the true laws of motion, by which it comes to pass that all bodies placed in equilibrium naturally affect a circular motion. Upon this, instead of deploring my wretchedness, as I had done, for being thus the sport of Fortune, I began to plume a little, finding that I was not only a simple planet, but such a planet as would have a perpetual attendant conforming itself to my motions, insomuch that I should have the honour to be reckoned in the number

11

of the greater heavenly bodies or stars of the first magnitude. And to confess my weakness, so elated was I that if I had then met any of our consuls or senators of Bergen, I should have received them with a supercilious air, should have regarded them as atoms, and accounted them unworthy to be saluted or honoured with a touch of my harpoon.

For almost three days I remained in this condition. For as without any intermission I was whirled about the planet that was next me, I could distinguish day from night; and observing the subterranean sun to rise, and set, and retire gradually out of my sight, I could easily perceive when it was night, though it was not altogether such as it is with us. For at sunset the whole face of the firmament appeared of a bright purple, not unlike the countenance of our moon sometimes. This I took to be occasioned by the inner surface of our Earth, which borrowed that light from the subterranean sun, which sun was placed in the center. This hypothesis I framed to myself, being not altogether a stranger to the study of astronomy.

But while I was thus amused with the thoughts of being in the neighbourhood of the gods, and was congratulating myself as a new constellation, together with my satellite that surrounded me, and hoped in a short time to be inserted in the catalogue of stars by the astronomers of the neighbouring planet, behold! an enormous winged monster hovered near me, sometimes on this side, now on that side, and by and by over my head. At first view I took it for one of the twelve heavenly signs in this new world, and accordingly hoped that, if the conjecture was right, it would be that of Virgo, since out of the whole number of the twelve signs, that alone could yield me, in my unhappy solitude, some delight and comfort. But when the figure approached nearer to me, it appeared to be a grim, huge griffin. So great was my terror that, unmindful of my starry dignity to which I was newly advanced, in that disorder of my soul I drew

12

out my university testimonial, which I happened to have in my pocket, to signify to this terrible adversary that I had passed my academical examination, that I was a graduate student, and could plead the privilege of my university against anyone that should attack me.

But my disorder beginning to cool, when I came to myself, I could not but condemn my folly. For it was yet a matter of doubt to what purpose this griffin should approach me, whether as an enemy or a friend; or, what is more likely, whether, led by the sole novelty of the thing, he had only a mind to feast his curiosity. For the sight of a human creature whirling about in air, bearing in his right hand a harpoon, and drawing after him a great length of rope like a tail, was really a phenomenon which might excite even a brute creature to behold the spectacle. For the unusual figure I then exhibited gave to the inhabitants of the globe round which I revolved an occasion of divers conjectures and conversations concerning me, as I afterwards learned; for the philosophers and mathematicians would have me to be a comet, being positive that my rope was the tail; and some there were who, from the appearance of so rare a meteor, prognosticated some impending misfortune, a plague, a famine, or some other such extraordinary catastrophe; some also went further, and delineated my figure, such as it appeared to them at that distance, in very accurate drawings; so that I was described, defined, painted, and engraved before ever I touched their globe. All this I afterward heard with no small pleasure, and even laughter, when I was conveyed to that planet, and had learned their language.

It must be noted that sometimes there appear new stars, which the Subterraneans call *sciscisi,* or blazing stars, which they describe as something looking horrid with fiery hair, and after the manner of our comets, bushy on the top, so as that it projects in form of a long beard; and these, as in our world, so in that, are reckoned ominous.

But to resume my history. The griffin advanced so near at last as to incommode me by the flapping of his wings, and even did not scruple to attack my leg with his teeth, so that now it openly appeared with what disposition he pursued me. Upon this I began to attack this troublesome animal with arms, and grasping my harpoon with both my hands, I soon curbed the insolence of my foe, obliging him to look about for a way to escape; and at last, since he persisted to annoy me, I darted my harpoon with such a force into the back of the animal between his wings, that I could not pull it out again. The wounded griffin, setting up a horrible cry, fell headlong upon the planet. As for myself, quite weary of this starry station, this new dignity, which I saw exposed to infinite hazards and evils, *I held to the harpoon and fell with him.*[1] And now this circular motion I had described altered once more into a perpendicular one. And being for some time agitated and tossed with great violence by the opposite motions of a thicker air, at length by an easy, gentle descent, I alighted upon the aforesaid planet, together with the griffin, who soon after died of his wound.

It was night when I was conveyed to that planet. This I could gather from the sole absence of the sun, and not from the darkness; for there still remained so much light that I could distinctly read my university testimonial by it. That light by night arises from the inward surface of our Earth, whose surface reflects a light like that of the moon among us. And hence, with respect to light alone, there is little difference between the nights and days, only that the sun is absent, and his absence makes the nights a little colder.

[1]Holberg's Latin version:

> *"Arbitrio volucris rapior, quoque impetus egit*
> *Huc sine lege ruo, longoque per aera tractu*
> *In terram feror, ut de coelo stella sereno,*
> *Etsi non cecidit, potuit cecidisse videri."*

Book II, lines 203-204, in Ovid, *Metamorphoses,* vol. 1 (Cambridge, Mass.: Harvard University Press, 1951), p. 74:

> *"ignotes regionis sunt, quaque inpetus egit,*
> *hac sine lege ruunt altoque sub aethere fixis"*

Ibid., vol. 1, p. 82, lines 320-322:

> *"volvitur in praeceps longoque per aera tractu*
> *fertur, ut interdum de caelo stella sereno*
> *etsi non cecidit, potuit cecidisse videri."*

CHAPTER II

His Descent upon the Planet Nazar

Having thus finished this airy voyage, and being set down upon the planet without the least hurt, I lay for a considerable time without motion, waiting till daybreak for the event. 'Twas then I found the usual infirmities of nature return, and that I stood in great need of sleep as well as food, insomuch that I repented I had so rashly discarded my loaf of bread.

My mind thus oppressed with various anxieties, at length I fell into a profound sleep, and had slept (as near as I could guess) two hours, when a horrible bellowing interrupting my sleep, at length entirely dispelled it. A strange variety of notions had filled my brain during this sleep. I thought I was returned into Norway and holding forth among the students according to custom; and at one time I imagined I heard the voice of the deacon Niels Andreas chanting in the church of Fanoë, just out of the city, and that it was the noise of his voice which according to custom had so cruelly wounded my ears. And agreeably to this, when I awoke, I really thought it was his horrid voice that had disturbed me. But when I saw a bull standing near me, then indeed I concluded my rest had been broken by his bellowing.

Presently throwing my eyes around me, the sun now rising, I beheld everywhere green, fertile plains and fields; some trees also appeared, but (what was most amazing) they moved; though such was the silence and stillness of the air at that time that it would not have moved the lightest feather from its place. Immediately the bull came roaring at me, and I in my terror and consternation seeing a tree just by me, attempted to climb it. But when I got up into it, it uttered a fine small voice, though something shrill, and not unlike an angry lady's; and presently I received, as it were from the swiftest hand, such a blow as quite stunned me, and laid me prostrate on the ground. I was almost expiring with this thunderbolt of a stroke, when I heard certain confused murmurings round me, like those in great markets, or upon full 'Change. Having opened my eyes, I beheld all about me a whole grove of trees, all in motion, all animated, and the plain overspread with trees and shrubs, though just before there were not above six or seven.

'Tis not to be expressed what disorders this produced in my understanding, and how much my mind was shocked with these delusions. Sometimes I thought I must certainly dream; sometimes I thought I was haunted by spectres and evil spirits, and twenty absurder things did I imagine; but I had no time to examine these machines, or to inquire into their causes; for presently another tree advancing to me, let down one of its branches, which had at the extremity of it six large buds in the manner of fingers. With these the tree took me up from the ground and carried me off, attended by a multitude of other trees of various kinds and different sizes, all which kept muttering certain sounds, articulately indeed, but in a tone too foreign for my ears, so that I could not possibly retain anything of them, except these two words, *pikel emi,* which I heard them very often repeat. By these words (as I afterward understood) was meant "a monkey of an odd shape," because from the make of my body, and manner of dress, they conjectured I was a monkey, though of a species different from the monkeys of that country. Others took me for an inhabitant of the firmament, and that some great bird had transported me hither, a thing that had once before happened, as the history or annals of that globe can testify. But all

17

these things I understood not till after the space of some months, in which time I became acquainted with the Subterranean language.

For in my present circumstances, what through fear and what through the disorder of my intellect, I was quite regardless of myself, nor could conceive how there could be any such thing as living and speaking trees, nor to what purpose was this procession, which was very slow and solemn. But yet the voices and murmurs with which all the plains echoed seemed to indicate anger and indignation; and in good truth it was not without ample reason that they had conceived this resentment against me; for that very tree, which I climbed up in my flight from the bull, was the wife of the sheriff, or principal magistrate of the next city; and so the quality of the person injured aggravated the crime; for it looked as if I had a mind to violate not a female of mean and plebeian birth, but a matron of prime rank, which was a most detested spectacle to a people of so venerable a modesty as these were.

At length we arrived at the city to which I was led captive. This city was equally remarkable for its stately edifices, and for the elegant order and proportion of the streets and highways; so lofty were the houses, that they resembled so many towers. The streets too were full of walking trees, which by letting down their branches saluted each other as they met, and the greater number of branches or boughs they dropped, the greater was the compliment. Thus when an oak went out of one of the most eminent houses, the rest of the trees drew back at his approach, and let down every one of their branches; from whence it was easy to infer that that oak was far above the vulgar sort; and indeed I soon understood that it was the sheriff himself, and the very person whose wife I was said to have so highly affronted. Forthwith they hurried me to the sheriff's house, upon my entrance into which the doors were immediately locked and bolted upon me, so that I looked upon myself as one condemned to a jail. What greatly contributed to this fear was that there were three guards placed without, like sentinels, each of them armed with six axes, according to the number of their branches; for as many branches as they had, so many arms they had; and as many buds at the extremities, so many fingers. I observed that on the top of the trunks or bodies of the trees their heads were placed, not at all unlike human heads; and instead of roots, I saw two feet, and those very short, by reason of which the pace they used was almost as slow as that of a tortoise; so that had I been at liberty, it had been very easy for me to have escaped their hands, since my motion was perfect flying compared to theirs.

To be short, I now plainly perceived that the inhabitants of this globe were trees, and that they were endowed with reason; and I was left in wonder at that variety in which nature wantons in the formation of her creatures. These trees do by no means equal ours in height, scarce any of them exceeding the common and ordinary stature of a man; some indeed were less; these one would call flowers or shrubs; and such I conjectured were youths and infants.

Words cannot express into what a labyrinth of thought these strange appearances threw me, how many sighs they extorted from me, and how passionately I longed after the dear place of my nativity. For although these trees seemed to me to be sociable creatures, to enjoy the benefit of language, and to be endowed with a certain degree or portion of reason, insomuch that they had a right to be inserted in the class of rational animals, yet I much doubted whether they could be compared to men; I could not bring myself to think that justice, mercy, and the other moral virtues had any residence among them. Racked with these thoughts, my bowels yearned, and rivers of tears flowed down my cheeks. But while I was thus indulging my grief, and pouring

19

out my silent complaints in such unmanly sorrows, the guards entered my chamber, whom I looked upon as so many Roman lictors, considering the axes they bore. These marching before me, I was led through the city to a very lofty dome in the center of the Forum, or great market place. I seemed to myself to be greater than a Roman consul, and to have obtained the honour of a dictator; for there were but twelve axes attended the consuls, whereas I was attended by eighteen. On the folding doors of the dome, to which I was led, a figure of Justice was carved, holding a pair of scales with her branches or arms. This image had a virgin air, an earnest look, a piercing sight, with a certain venerable dejection that made her appear not too proud, nor yet too humble. This place I clearly perceived was the Senate House. Being introduced into court, the floor of which shone with marble of tessellated or mosaic workmanship, I there beheld a tree seated on a golden tribunal, with twelve associates sitting on either hand on so many benches in the most exact and elegant order. The President of the Tribunal was a palm tree, of a middling stature, but easily distinguished from the rest of the assistants by the great variety of her leaves, which were of various dyes. The inferior officers, to the number of twenty-four, guarded each side, all armed with six axes apiece. A most tremendous prospect! since from so much armour it was natural to infer they were a people that delighted in blood.

The senators, at my entrance, extended their branches toward the skies; which ceremony being ended, they sat down again; and being all seated, I was brought to the bar between two trees, whose trunks or bodies were covered with sheepskins. I suspected they were lawyers, and such in good truth they were. Before they began to plead, the President wrapped her head in a garment of a dark colour. One of these advocates made a very short speech, which he thrice repeated; to which the other advocate replied with equal brevity. These pleadings were followed by a silence of half an hour. Then the President, removing the covering from her head, rose up, and again extending her branches toward the sky, pronounced certain words, which I supposed contained my sentence; for at the end of the speech I was dismissed back to my old prison, and confined there, as I guessed, to be in readiness to be brought forth to punishment.

Being left alone, and resolving in my memory everything that had happened, I could not forbear smiling at the stupidity of this people; for they seemed rather to be acting a play than exercising justice, and everything I had seen, their gesture, their dress, and method of proceeding seemed to savour more of the buffoonery of the stage than the awful tribunal of justice. Then I congratulated the happiness of our world, and the superiority of the Europeans to all others. But though I arraigned the folly and dullness of this subterranean nation, yet I was forced to own that they ought to be distinguished from the brute creation; for the elegance of the city, the symmetry of the buildings, with several other particulars, loudly proclaimed that these trees were not devoid of reason, nor altogether ignorant of the arts, especially mechanics; but then it was in this alone that I thought all their virtues, all their whole perfection consisted.

While I was holding this silent conference with myself, a tree enters holding a lancet in his hand, who, unbuttoning my bosom and making bare my arm, opened the middle vein quite like an artist. When he had drawn as much blood as he thought sufficient, he bound up my arm with equal dexterity. This being performed, he inspected the blood with the deepest attention; and being perfectly satisfied, he walked away in a kind of silent admiration. All this confirmed me in the opinion I had entertained of the stupidity of this nation. But as soon as I had thoroughly learned the Subterranean language, and all these things had been explained to me, my disdain was turned into admiration. The proceedings at law, which I had so rashly condemned, were thus explained. From the make of my body, they inferred I was an inhabitant of the Firmament. I appeared to have attempted the chastity of an honourable matron, and one of prime quality. For this crime I was dragged to the bar of justice. One of the advocates or lawyers aggravated the crime, demanding the punishment due by law; the other requested not that the punishment should be remitted, but only that it should be deferred till it could be discovered what and who I was, and of what country; whether a brute animal, or a rational one. Moreover, I learned that the action of the judges' extending their branches towards heaven was the ordinary ceremony of religion before they proceeded to trial. The lawyers were all covered with sheepskins, as emblems of innocence and impartiality in the management of their causes; and indeed all the lawyers here were men of probity; which shows that in a well-constituted government it is not impossible, but that there may be honest lawyers. So severe were the laws against knavish advocates that fraud and foul play could not escape detection, perfidiousness could find no shelter, slander no mercy, impudence no countenance, and deceit no impunity.

The threefold repetition of words was made use of to assist the slowness of their perception, in which the natives of this globe were distinguished from all others; for very few could comprehend what they had only cursorily read, or understand what they had only once heard. Those whose forward capacities took a thing presently were deemed defective in judgment, and therefore it was seldom that such were admitted to any weighty posts or offices; for they had learned by experience that the government had been endangered when in the hands of those who were quick of apprehension and who were commonly styled great geniuses; but that those of slower capacities had restored to order what the others had thrown into confusion. These things were paradoxes to me, yet upon a more serious recollection, they seemed not altogether absurd.

But the history of the President filled me with the greatest astonishment. She was a virgin, and a native of that city, and by the then reigning sovereign was appointed *Kaki,* or supreme judge in the city; for among these people there was no difference of sexes observed in the distribution of public posts; but an election being made, the affairs of the republic were committed to the wisest and most worthy. And in order to form a right judgment of the proficiency or of the intellectual endowments of everyone, there were proper seminaries instituted, the chief directors of which were styled *karatti* (a word that strictly signifies examiners). It was their office to inspect into everyone's abilities, to inquire nicely into the genius of the youth, and after such inquiry to transmit annually to their prince an account or list of such as were to be admitted to all duties and posts of government, and to point out at the same time, in what particular every one of them was most likely to be of service to the state. The Prince upon the receipt of such catalogue ordered their names to be inscribed in a book, that he might never be at a loss what sort of persons to prefer to the vacant posts.

The aforesaid virgin four years before had obtained a most honourable testimonial from the karatti, and upon that account was by the sovereign appointed President of the Senate of the city in which she was born. This rule they observe constantly and inviolably, because they believe that the welfare of any place will be best consulted and pursued by those who are natives of it. Palmka (that was the name of the virgin) for the space of three years governed this truly Spartan commonwealth with the highest applause, and was esteemed the wisest tree in all the city; for so great was her dullness of apprehension that she hardly ever conceived a thing without its being three or four times repeated. But what she once apprehended she thoroughly understood, and with such acumen solved every difficulty in it that her decrees were deemed so many oracles.

And hence there were no judicial decrees of hers during her administration of justice which were not confirmed and applauded by the High Court of Justice at Potu, the capital of the empire; therefore the institution in favour of the weaker sex, which at first view I had condemned, had nothing absurd in it upon a more accurate review. Bless me! thought I, what if the wife of our mayor of Bergen were to sit in judgment instead of her husband? What if the daughter of Counsellor Sorensen, that all-accomplished young lady, were to plead at the bar instead of her stupid father? Our laws would never receive the least dishonour from them, nor would justice be so often violated. Moreover, I was of opinion, since in the European courts of law causes were so soon determined, that such sudden and hasty determinations, were they to undergo a strict scrutiny, would by no means pass without censure.

To proceed to explain some other things. The reason of the venesection or letting blood I understood to be this: when anyone was convicted of a crime, instead of whipping, maiming, or capital punishments, he was condemned to the venesection, that is, to have a vein opened, by which it should appear whether his crime proceeded from malice, or from the vitiated blood, and whether by such an operation he could be cured. So that these courts of justice regarded the amendment rather than the punishment of the offender. Yet the very method of amendment had a sort of punishment in it, because it was a mark of ignominy to undergo this operation by judicial sentence. If anyone fell a second time into the same crime, he was deemed an unworthy member of the state, and as such was to be banished to the Firmament, where all were received without distinction. But of this sort of exile we shall enlarge hereafter. Then as to the reason why upon the opening of my vein the surgeon was so astonished

24

at the sight of my blood, it was this, namely, that the natives of this globe had a white fluid juice in their veins. And the whiter this was, so much the greater mark it bore of innocence and probity.

All these things, when I had perfectly learned the Subterranean tongue, I thoroughly understood, and thenceforward began to form a milder judgment of a people I had too hastily censured. And though at first I was of opinion that these trees were excessively stupid and brutish, yet I soon found reason to think that they were not altogether destitute of humanity, and that therefore I was in no danger of my life. And what confirmed me in this was that twice a day I saw my food duly brought me. This food consisted of fruits, herbs, and pulse, and my drink was a liquor the most delicious and grateful I ever tasted.

The sheriff, in whose custody I was, soon sent advice to the sovereign of the empire, who resided at Potu (not far from this city), that a certain rational animal, of a very unusual make, had fallen into his hands. The sovereign, excited by the novelty of the thing, gave orders that I should be instructed in their language and then sent to court. Hereupon I had a language master appointed me, under whose care in the space of six months I made so great a proficiency that I was enabled to converse pretty readily with the natives. After having passed through this first exercise, a new order arrived from court concerning my farther instruction, by which I was commanded to be entered into the seminary, that the natural powers of my understanding might be inquired into by the karatti, and in what kind of learning I gave the most hopeful promises of success. All this was done with great exactness. While I was performing my exercises here, they were as careful of my body as they were of my mind, and particularly, they used their utmost art to bring me into their own shape, and accordingly they skillfully fitted artificial branches to my body.

During this, the sheriff, at whose house I lodged, every evening as I returned from the seminary entered into various conferences with me. He heard me with the utmost pleasure descanting on those things that had occurred to me in this subterranean tour. But he was above measure amazed at the description I gave him of our Earth, and of that immense heaven that surrounded it, studded with infinite stars. All this he heard with the utmost avidity. But it kindled his blushes when I told him of the trees of our globe, which were lifeless, immovable, and fastened by the roots to the ground; nay, he beheld me with some resentment when I attested that our trees were cut down for fuel to heat our furnaces and dress our provisions. But considering the thing more gravely, his indignation subsided, and extending his five branches to the skies (for so many he had) he adored the wisdom of the great Creator, whose ways are past finding out; and henceforward he heard me with still greater attention. His wife, who had hitherto avoided me, when she learned the true reason for which I was brought to judgment, and that I was deceived in the appearance of a tree, which in our country 'twas a customary thing to climb, now laid aside all suspicion, and was entirely reconciled. But yet, that I might not at the beginning of our reconciliation open an old wound, I declined all conversation with her, unless in the presence and at the express command of her husband.

CHAPTER III

A Description of the City of Keba

In the meanwhile, and during the course of this discipline under the karatti, my host walked me about the city to show me whatever was curious and observable. We walked up and down without any molestation, and what was more to be admired, without any crowding or jostling; quite otherwise than it is with us, where people flock in heaps to anything that is new and uncommon, that they may feast their curiosity. For the inhabitants of this planet have very little taste for novelty and pursue only solid things. The name of this city is Keba, and it is the second in dignity of the whole Potuan Empire. The inhabitants are so sedate and grave, you would swear they were all senators. Age is particularly honourable here; nor is there a profounder deference and veneration anywhere paid it; for it carries authority not only in its sentiments, but in its looks and nods.

But I much wondered that a nation so sober, so modest as this should be delighted with comedies and certain ludicrous shows and spectacles that were there exhibited. This did not seem to suit with so much gravity. Which my host perceiving, "Through all these dominions," says he, "the subjects divide their time between things serious and things of a gayer turn." For among other laudable institutions of this empire, there is an indulgence of innocent pleasures, by which it is believed the soul is strengthened and prepared to sustain the more arduous duties, and by which those black clouds of melancholy are dispelled which are thought to be the sources of riots, seditions, and pernicious counsels. Therefore they chequer the severer toils with sports and plays, so happily tempering seriousness with pleasantry, that the first cannot degenerate into sourness, nor the latter into impertinence. But it was not without indignation I observed that school disputations do there make a part of the shows and theatrical performances. For at set times of the year, wagers being laid, and a reward assigned to the conquerors, the disputants engage like a couple of gladiators, and much upon the same terms that fighting cocks or any such battling animals do among us. Hence it was a custom among the great to maintain a set of disputants, as we do a pack of hounds, and to give them a logical education, that they may be fit for engagement at the stated times of the year. Thus a certain wealthy citizen by the name of Henochi in three years' time had made prodigious gains, even to the sum of 4000 *ricatu,* from one disputant, whom he maintained for that purpose. This disputant, with an amazing volubility of tongue, by ensnaring syllogisms and every artifice of logic, by distinctions, reservations, and exceptions, eluded every opponent, and silenced whom he would.

I was often present at these entertainments, and that with no small vexation. For it seemed to me a horrid and shameful thing that such noble exercises, which give lustre to our schools, should here be prostituted on the stage. And when I called to mind that I myself with the highest applause had disputed in public, and had obtained the laurel, I could scarce withhold my tears. And not only the dispute, but the method of disputing incensed me. For they hired certain stimulators, in their language *cabalci,* who, when they observed the ardour of the disputants to flag, just pricked their sides with lancets to rekindle it, and to rally their declining spirits. Other things through shame I omit, which in so polished a nation I could not but condemn. Besides these disputants, called in their tongue, by way of contempt, *masbaki,* that is strictly, wranglers, there were other trials of skill between beasts, both of the wild and tame kind, and also between birds of prey, which were exhibited to the spectators at a certain price.

I begged to know of my host how it was possible that so judicious a nation could think of leaving to the theatre those noble exercises whereby a faculty of speaking is acquired, truth is discovered, and the understanding sharpened? He replied that formerly these exercises were in high reputation among their barbarous ancestors; but since they had been convinced by experience that truth was rather stifled by disputes, that their youth were rendered petulant and forward thereby, that disturbances arose from them, and that the more generous studies were so much the more fettered, they turned over these exercises from the university to the playhouse; and the event has showed us that by reading, silence, and meditation the students now make far greater advances in learning. With this reply, though very specious, I was not however altogether satisfied.

In this city there was an academy or school where with the utmost decency and solidity the liberal arts were taught. My host introduced me into the auditory of this school on a particular day, when a *madic*, or Doctor of Philosophy, was to be created. The whole ceremony was this: the candidate made a learned and elegant dissertation upon a problem in natural philosophy, which being ended, the governors of the school inserted his name in the Register of Doctors, who from thence had authority to teach publicly. My host asking how I liked it? I answered that it appeared to me a mighty dry business in comparison of our promotions. Then I explained to him how Masters and Doctors were created among us, namely, by exhibiting certain specimens of their skill in disputation. At this, contracting his brows, he desired to know the nature of our disputations, and in what they differ from the Subterranean. I replied that they were usually upon curious and learned subjects, particularly such as relate to the manners, language, or dress of two ancient nations who formerly flourished in Europe, and that I for my part had written three dissertations upon the slippers of the ancients. With that he set up such a laugh as made the whole house ring. His wife, alarmed with the noise, flies to know the cause of it; but I was so much out of humour that I disdained to answer her, for I thought it a burning shame so grave and solid a matter should be treated with that ridicule and contempt. But understanding from her husband the truth of the case, she laughed as violently.

This thing, taking air, gave a handle to endless sneers; nay, the wife of a certain senator, of herself exceedingly prone to laugh, was so delighted that she had like to have burst herself. And she soon after dying accidentally of a fever, it was thought her death was occasioned by that immoderate laugh, which had inflamed her lungs. They were not indeed quite certain that such was the case; however, so it was whispered. She was otherwise a matron of a fine understanding, and a most useful lady, for she had seven branches, which is something rare in that sex. All the better sort of trees were much concerned at her death. She was buried at midnight without the city gates, and in the same garments she happened to have on when she died. For there is a provision by law that no body can be buried in the city, because they believe the air may be corrupted by the effluvia of the carcasses. It is also by law provided that the dead bodies shall be interred without any funeral pomp or rich dresses, inasmuch as all is shortly to be the food of worms. And these appeared to me to be very wise institutions.

Yet they had feasts in honour of the dead, and also funeral orations, which simply contained an exhortation to a virtuous life, and which placed before their eyes an image of mortality. At this the censors were present to observe whether the orators raised or depressed the character of the deceased beyond justice. And hence the Subterranean orators were extremely sparing of their encomiums, since to give immoderate praises was punishable by law. Not long after, when I was going to one of these funeral orations, I asked my host what was the state and condition of the departed hero? He replied, "He was an husbandman who died suddenly upon the road to this city."

Hereupon, in my turn, I burst into an excessive laughter, retorting thus their own weapons upon them. "And pray," says I, "why have not bulls and oxen, those companions of husbandmen, the honour of a funeral oration? They can equally supply matter, for they equally perform the same office."

But my host desired me to spare my jests, for that in these dominions husbandmen were held in the highest esteem on account of the great excellence of the duties they were employed in, and that no way of life was more honourable than that of agriculture. Thus every honest and industrious farmer was regarded by the citizens as their feeder and foster father. And hence rose the custom that when the farmers about autumn, or in the month of Palm Trees, repair to the city with a multitude of carriages laden with corn, the magistrates meet them without the gates and introduce them into the city with trumpets and other instruments in concert, after the manner of a triumph.

At this strange account I was struck dumb, especially recollecting the hard fate of our husbandmen, groaning under the deepest slavery, and whose employments are looked upon as low and illiberal, in comparison with those which are panders to our pleasures, such as cooks, poulterers, perfumers, and such like. And this I fairly owned to my host, at the same time enjoining him silence, fearing lest the Subterraneans should pass very unfavourable judgments upon mankind. Having promised secrecy, he carried me to the hall where the funeral oration was to be made.

I own I never heard anything executed more solidly, with greater veracity, or with so little an appearance of flattery as this;

and I judged it a proper pattern to which all funeral orations should conform. The orator first gave us a view of the virtues of the deceased, and then enumerated his vices and failings, with an admonition to his audience to avoid them.

As we returned from the hall, we met an offender in custody of three keepers. The same by decree in court had lately undergone the "punishment of the arm" (so they call the letting blood) and was now going to be consigned over to the public hospital or Bedlam. Upon inquiry into the reason of such sentence, I was informed that the criminal had disputed publicly about the qualities and essence of the Supreme Being, a thing here prohibited, where all these overcurious disquisitions are thought to be such exquisite folly and rashness that a creature of a sound understanding could not well fall into it. Therefore these subtle disputants after the venesection were, like madmen, condemned to confinement till they got out of this delirium. Ah! thought I to myself, what would become of our divines, whom we every day hear wrangling about the quality and attributes of the Deity, about the nature of spiritual beings, and other mysteries of that kind? What also would become of our metaphysicians, who by their transcendental jargon affect a degree of wisdom far above the vulgar, and even above human nature itself? Certainly, instead of hoods, caps, and other academical honours, which in our world are so liberally granted them, they would in this world be showed the way to the public hospital.

All this, and other things full as paradoxical, I remarked during the time of my probation in the seminary. At length the appointed time arrived when, by order of the Prince, I was to be conducted to court with a testimonial. I flattered myself that I should have the most honourable encomiums and approbations, depending partly upon my own accomplishments, since I had learned the Subterranean tongue sooner than could be expected, and partly upon the interest of my host, together with the renowned integrity of my judges. At last my testimonial was delivered me, which I opened with the utmost transport, impatient of reading my own praises, and of concluding from thence what my destiny was to be. But the perusal of it threw me into fits of rage and despair. The tenor of it was this:

> In obedience to the commands of Your Serene Highness, the animal lately arrived from another world, and calling himself a *man*, we herewith send, most carefully instructed in our seminary. Upon the nicest inquiry into his genius and manners, we have found him to be of competent docility, and extremely quick of apprehension, but of so weak and uneven a judgment that he hardly merits to be considered as a rational creature, much less to be admitted to any important office in the government. But since he excels everyone in swiftness of foot, we are humbly of opinion that he is extremely qualified for the post of King's Messenger. Given at our Seminary of Keba, in the month of Brambles, by Your Serene Highness's most humble servants,
> Nehec, Jochtan, Rapasi, Chilac.

Upon this I went to my host in a torrent of tears, and humbly implored that he would interpose his authority to procure a milder testimonial from the karatti, and that he would show them my university testimonial, in which I was complimented with epithets of "ingenious" and "honourable." He replied that that testimonial might have its weight in our world, where they regarded perhaps the shadow more than the substance, the outward bark more than the inward texture; but that it would be of no value with them, where they penetrate into the inmost nature of things; and exhorted me moreover to bear my fate as temperately as I could, especially as the testimonial could be neither revoked or altered; for that there was no greater crime than to ascribe undeserved virtues to anyone. But what comfort it was in the power of words to give, he gave.

As to the testimonial of the karatti, he added that they were the most incorrupt and upright judges, who could be bribed by no presents nor awed by no threats to recede a hair's breadth from truth; and that therefore there was no room for suspicion in this case. He also candidly acknowledged that the poverty of my judgment was a thing not unobserved by himself, and that he inferred from the readiness of my memory and the quickness of my apprehension that I was "not that sort of wood out of which mercury was to be made," and that I could not possibly meet with preferment upon account of that remarkable defect in my judgment; that he had gathered, from my discourses and description of Europe, that I was *born under a bad star in a country of fools.*[1]

And with these and a great many more professions of friendship, he desired me without delay to prepare for my journey. I followed the advice of this most sagacious person, especially as necessity required it, and as it would have been rashness to have opposed the order of the Prince.

We now began our journey in company with some other young trees which were dismissed from the seminary at the same time and sent to court for the same end. Our leader was one of the karatti, who upon account of his age and a weakness in his feet was carried by an ox; for it is an unusual thing here to have vehicles, these being indulged only to the decrepit and diseased; though the inhabitants of this planet are really more excusable for it than those of our world by reason of the slowness of their gait. I remember when I gave a description of our vehicles, that is, our coaches with horses into which we were stuffed like so much lumber and drawn through the city, the Subterraneans smiled at my account, especially when they heard that no neighbour envied another, unless he kept his coach and was drawn in it through the streets by a pair of mettlesome four-footed beasts. What with the slowness of the motion of these rational trees, we were three days upon this journey, though Keba is hardly four miles distant from the capital. Had I been alone, a day would have been sufficient. 'Twas a pleasure indeed that I excelled these Subterraneans in that advantage of foot, but it grieved me to the soul that for that very excellence I was condemned to a vile, ignominious office. "Would to God!" said I, "that I laboured under the same infirmity with them, since by this defect alone I might have escaped the low and ignoble drudgery I was destined to."

Our leader, overhearing me, replied thus: "If Nature had not made you amends for the defects of your mind by some one excellence of body, all would behold you as an unprofitable load upon the earth; for that very quickness of parts permits you only to see the surface of things, and not the substance; and since you have but two branches, you are inferior to the Subterraneans in everything that depends upon the hands."

Hearing this, I thanked God who had given me this swiftness of feet, since without this virtue I had no chance to be reckoned in the number of rational creatures.

During our journey, I was surprised to see all around me the natives so intent upon their labours that at the approach of passengers nobody left off work, or even threw their eyes round, though something extraordinary should even pass along. But at the close of day, their toils all ended, then they indulged in every amusement of the mind, the chief magistrate conniving and tolerating these diversions, as reliefs and strengtheners of the body and mind, and something full as necessary as meat and drink. This and other things made the journey highly grateful. The whole country is perfectly beautiful. Imagine it a spacious amphitheatre, and such an one as Nature alone could make. Where Nature was less profuse, all was supplied by the industry of the inhabitants, who were animated to these rural toils, and to the cultivating and improving of their land, by rewards from the magistrate; and whoever suffered his grounds to run to ruin, afterwards wrought for hire. We passed by many fair villages which, from the multitude of them, looked like one continued city and exhibited the same appearance all along. Yet we were something infested by the monkeys from the woods, which rambling up and down, and from an affinity in my shape imagining I was of their race, were continually teasing me with their approaches and touches. I could scarce suppress my rage when I perceived that this was a perfect comedy to some of the trees; for I was conducted to court (by express order of His Majesty) in the same dress in which I alighted upon the planet, namely, with my harpoon in my right hand, that His Majesty might behold what the dress of our world was, and particularly what was my own appearance upon my arrival. And very opportunely it was that I had my harpoon in my hand, that I might chase away those swarms of monkeys that gathered apace at last round me; though it was all in vain; for in the room of those that fled more came, so that I was forced to move every step like a man upon his guard.

[1]Holberg's Latin version:

"Stultorum in patria, pravoq; sub aere natum."

Juvenal, Satire X, line 50, in Juvenal and Persius (Cambridge, Mass.: Harvard University Press, 1957), p. 196:

"vervecum in patria crassoque sub aere nasci."

CHAPTER IV

The Court of the Potuan Empire

At length we came to the royal city of Potu, which for beauty and magnificence might vie with any. The buildings there are more numerous and extensive than at Keba, and the streets wider and more commodious. The Forum, which was the first place we were brought to, was filled with numbers of merchants and surrounded every way with shops of artists and tradesmen. But I saw with some astonishment in the middle of the Forum a certain criminal with a halter about his neck, and a large company of grave and elderly trees standing round him. Upon my asking what was the matter, and for what crime he deserved hanging, especially as I thought no crime here was capital, it was told me that this offender was a projector who had advised the abolition of a certain old custom; that those who stood round him were the senators and lawyers, who then and there examined the projector's scheme, so that if it should appear that it was a well-digested thing, and salutary to the commonwealth, the offender was not only absolved, but rewarded; but if injurious to the public, or if the projector by the repeal of this law appeared to have glanced at his own advantage, he was presently to be hanged as a disturber of the realm. And this is the reason why few are found to run this risk, or have courage enough to advise the abrogation of any law, unless the thing be so demonstrably evident and just that the success of it cannot be doubted of, so persuaded are the Subterraneans that the ancient laws and institutions of their ancestors are to be maintained and revered.

For they believe the government would be in danger if, for the wantonness of everybody, those laws were to be changed or disannulled. What, alas! said I to myself, would become of the projectors of our world, who, under a pretence of public emolument, are daily hatching and inventing new laws with an eye only to their private gains, instead of the common benefit?

At length we were introduced into a spacious house which was the usual place of reception for all who were sent from the seminaries throughout the empire. In the same place are brought up those who are to attend upon the Prince. Our captain, the karatti, bid us be in readiness while he went to acquaint His Highness with our arrival. He had scarce left us when we heard a noise like that of great rejoicings, and immediately the air echoed with the sound of trumpets and beat of drums. Alarmed at this noise, we went out and beheld a certain tree magnificently attended and crowned with a chaplet of flowers, and presently discovered that it was the same citizen whom we just now saw in the Forum with his neck in a halter. The reason of this triumph was the approbation of that law which, at the peril of his head, he had advised. But by what arguments he attacked the old law I could never reach to the knowledge, by reason of the great silence of the people; and hence it is that the least matter transacted in the senate in relation to the government never transpires or takes the least air. Far otherwise it is with us, where the actions of the senate and the whole of their debates are reported, weighed, and criticized upon in every tavern and street.

In the space of an hour the karatti returns and commands us all to follow him. We obeyed. As we went, we met certain young trees who offered to sale little printed books of curious and memorable things. Among the rest, I cast my eye upon a small book, the title of which was, "A Full and True Account of the Strange Flying Dragon That Appeared in the Element

Last Year." There did I behold myself, that is, my effigies engraved just as I appeared when I was whirling round this planet with my harpoon and my long rope. I could not help smiling at the figure, and said to myself, "*Oh, what a countenance! and what a fine engraving!*"[1] Having bought the book for three *kilacs,* which is equivalent to about two shillings of our money, I walked on gravely to the palace. Art and elegance seemed to preside here, rather than profusion and a vain magnificence. I observed the Prince had very few attendants, for such was his temperance that he had discarded whatever was superfluous. Nor is there indeed the same necessity for as many servants as our courts require. For as many branches as these trees had, so many arms; so that the common labours and business of the household could be done with at least thrice the expedition.

It was about dinnertime when we arrived at court, and since it was His Highness's pleasure to talk with me alone, I was introduced into the presence chamber. There is in this Prince a very remarkable mixture of mildness and gravity. Such was his steadiness that his countenance was never known to have the least cloud upon it. Seeing the Prince, I instantly fell upon my knees. The courtiers were astonished at this adoration, and when I told His Highness (who asked me) the reason why I bent my knee, he commanded me to rise, saying that such a sort of reverence was due to the Deity alone; adding that nothing could obtain the favour of the Prince but obedience and industry. When I rose, he asked me sundry questions, demanding to know my name, my country, and how and why I had come.

I answered, "*My name is Klim, and my country the greater world. I came neither on a ship over the waves, nor on foot over the land, but through the air.*"[2]

He then proceeded to inquire what I had met with in my journey and what were the customs and usages of our world. After which I proceeded to explain as sensibly as I could the wit, the virtues, the civilized manners of the men of our world, and everything that mankind pride themselves in. He received my account very coldly, and at some things which I thought would have raised his admiration, he perfectly yawned. Lord! said I to myself, how different are the tastes of mortals! that what gives one the most sensible pleasure, to another shall be quite nauseous! But what most offended His Highness was the relation I gave him of our law proceedings, of the eloquence of our lawyers, and the quick dispatch of the judges in pronouncing sentence. While I was endeavouring to make this still clearer to him, he interrupted me by turning the discourse to something else, and at length he proceeded to an inquiry into our religion and worship. I then explained to him in a concise manner the several articles of our faith; at the recital of which he somewhat softened his countenance, attesting that he could readily subscribe to them, and he could not choose but wonder how a race of people of such weak judgments should entertain such sound notions of God and His worship. But when he heard that the Christians were divided into sects without number, and that upon some differences in matters of faith people of the same blood and family would cruelly persecute one another, he answered thus: "Among us also there is a large variety of different sentiments concerning things pertaining to divine worship; but one man does not persecute another for that. All persecution for speculative matters or errors arising from the sole variety of our perceptions can spring from nothing but pride, one thinking himself wiser and more penetrating than the rest. But such pride must be highly displeasing in the eyes of the Supreme Being, who must be a lover of humility and meekness in mortals. We never tease an assembly of judges about anyone who shall happen to differ from the received opinions in points of speculation, provided he does it sincerely, and also conforms in practical matters to the public worship of the Deity. And in this we pursue the track chalked out to us by our ancestors, who always thought it inhuman to fetter the understanding and tyrannize over the conscience. In our politics we extremely recommend the observance of this rule, so that if my subjects should differ about the make of my body, the manner of my life, or about my economy or any such sort of thing, yet at the same time acknowledged me for their lawful sovereign to whom obedience is due, I think them all good subjects."

To this I replied: "May it please Your Most Serene Highness, such a conduct would in our world be called syncretism, and would be highly condemned by the learned." He did not give me room to say any more, and seeming to be a little displeased, walked away, and commanded me to stay till dinner was over.

His Highness sat down to table with his royal consort and their son, together with the High Chancellor, or *Kadoki*. This same Kadoki was in the first esteem among the Potuans for the politeness of his manners, as well as his prudence and wariness. For full twenty years he never once gave his sentiments in the Senate House but the rest immediately came into them, nor ever decreed anything with regard to the public but what stood firm and unshaken, so that his decrees were so many axioms. But then he was so slow of apprehension that for the least of them he used to require the space of fourteen days; and therefore in our world he would hardly be thought fit for business of great moment, where all delay passes for sloth and laziness. But since whatever he once apprehended he understood through and through, and since he executed nothing but upon the severest examination, hence he might be said to do more in reality than ten others who mighty readily set about business, and are frequently styled great geniuses, but whose decrees must afterwards be mended, altered, and licked into shape; insomuch that at the expiration of their office it is discovered that they have attempted everything and brought nothing to perfection. Among the maxims

41

therefore of the Potuan court this is one: That they who are so forward at business are like those who walk to and fro and tread a great deal of ground, but gain none.

When the family were seated, a virgin entered with eight branches and as many dishes, so that in a moment the whole table was covered. Presently another tree entered with eight vessels of different kinds of wine. This latter had nine branches, and so was judged extremely qualified for the domestic business of the court. And thus by two servants only this whole affair was commodiously performed, which in terrestrial courts is not to be done without a perfect army of servants. With the same dexterity the dishes were removed, as they had been at first placed. It was a frugal but not inelegant meal. Of the whole number of dishes, the Sovereign confined himself to one. Not so the great ones of our globe, who never think a supper grand, unless one course of dishes give way to a finer and more exquisite succession. During the repast, the conversation ran upon morality or politics, so that even these sensual pleasures had a seasoning of learning. Mention also was made of me, whom from the quickness of my apprehension they took to be "not the wood out of which mercury was to be made."

The repast being ended, I was ordered to produce my testimonial, which being perused, the Prince, directing his eyes down to my feet, said that the karatti had judged right and that so it ought to be. Quite thunderstruck with this answer, and overwhelmed in tears, I implored a revisal of the testimonial, since upon a more intimate scrutiny into the virtues of my mind, and the endowments of my understanding, I might reasonably expect a milder judgment to be made. His Highness being a merciful and equitable prince, not at all incensed at this forward and unusual request, enjoined the karatti then present to examine me anew, and as accurately as possible. During this trial, the Prince stepped aside to read some other testimonials.

The Prince having withdrawn himself, the karatti proposed a new set of questions to be solved by me. I answered them with my usual readiness; upon which he spoke thus to me: "You take a thing presently, but not entirely; for your solutions show that the question is readily perceived, but not intimately understood."

The examination being finished, the Prince went into the council chamber and soon returned with a final sentence to this purpose: That I had acted imprudently in calling in question the judgment of the karatti, and that therefore I had incurred the penalty which the third lesser space of the fourth greater space inflicts upon slanderers (by the greater and lesser spaces, or *skibal* and *kibal*, they mean books and chapters) and that I deserved to undergo the venesection in both my branches, and also to be imprisoned. The words of the law, *lib. 4. cap. 3.*, concerning defamation are these: *Spik. antri. Flak. Skak. mak. Tabu Mihalatti Silac.* But though the sense of the words was very clear and evident, and the law too sacred to be evaded, yet His Most Serene Highness, by a stretch of his prerogative, thought fit to pardon this offense of mine, occasioned through an immaturity of judgment, as well as ignorance of the law, which could hardly be said to be infringed by this indulgence to me, inasmuch as I was a stranger and a foreigner. And to give me a more ample testimony of his most gracious favour, he appointed me one of his Messengers in Ordinary, an honour I ought to hold myself highly satisfied with.

Immediately the *Kiva,* or Secretary, was sent for, who enrolled my name in the Book of Promotions, together with the names of several other candidates. This Secretary was a most extraordinary person, for he had eleven pair of branches and could consequently write eleven letters all at the same time, and with the same ease and expedition that we can one. Yet he had a very indifferent judgment, upon which account he never could expect any farther promotion, and so he grew old in the same post which he had filled for thirty years. I contracted a close friendship with him, and indeed I could not help cultivating an affection for him, because all the edicts and letters of state which he wrote I, as Messenger in Ordinary, dispersed over the province. I was often astonished to see him execute business with so much dexterity, for it was a common thing with him to write eleven letters at once, and afterward seal them all in the same instant. Among the blessings therefore of a family, a large number of branches is reckoned one. And hence the women in childbed, immediately after the birth of the infant, are wont to signify to the neighbours how many branches it has brought into the world with it. It was reported that the father of our Secretary was born with twelve, and that his family had long been famous for a plurality of branches.

The diploma which constituted me in my office being ordered to be drawn out, I now retired to my repose. But though my limbs were excessively tired, yet was I not able to compose myself to sleep. That ignoble employment to which I was condemned ran continually in my head, and I thought it the greatest debasement imaginable for one who was a candidate for holy orders and a Bachelor of Arts in the Upper World, to be changed into a vile Subterranean court messenger. With these mortifying thoughts did I waste a great part of the night, and during this agitation I several times perused my university testimonial, which I had brought with me (for as I observed above, the night is almost as light as the day). At length quite jaded with thinking, I sank into the arms of sleep. But what a variety of scenes presented themselves to my disturbed imagination! I thought I was returned to my own country, and relating aloud to vast numbers of people all that had befallen me in my subterranean tour; presently I was sailing in the air again, and engaged with the griffin once more, who gave me so warm a reception as that it waked me out of my sleep. But how was I shocked when I beheld by my bedside a monkey of the largest size, which, by reason of the doors being left open, had got into my chamber. This unlooked-for spectacle chilled all my blood, and made me alarm the house with my cries for assistance. Some trees which lay in the adjacent chambers immediately entering disengaged me from the struggle and drove the beastly creature away. I understood afterwards that this accident afforded the Prince plentiful matter for laughter. But that I might run no such risk for the future, he gave command that I should be habited after the Subterranean fashion and adorned with artificial branches. As for my European garments, they were taken from me, and for their novelty hung up in the Prince's wardrobe with this inscription: "The dress of a superterranean animal." Bless me! said I to myself, if Master Andreas, the tailor at Bergen who made this suit, should know that his workmanship was preserved among the curiosities of a subterranean prince, without doubt he would grow vain and think himself as great a man as any in the city.

After this misfortune sleep quite forsook me. In the morning my diploma was brought me, which gave me the full powers to execute my office. A multiplicity of business poured in upon me soon, and carrying the royal edicts and letters to every city of his dominions, I was perpetual motion itself. In these expeditions I explored the genius of the country, and in many places discovered an uncommon measure of politeness and understanding. Only the inhabitants of the city of Mabolki, which were all brambles, seemed to me something rude and uncultivated. Every province has its peculiar trees, or natives of the place, particularly the province of husbandmen, though in the great cities, and especially in the capital, there is a mixture of all sorts. The high sentiments I had entertained of the wisdom of this people increased as fast as I had fresh opportunities of inspecting into them. Those very laws and customs which I had disapproved, upon mature reflection, extorted all my admiration. I could

45

easily bring a cloud of instances of certain manners and usages which upon a transient view appeared absurd, but which to the curious inquirer would be full of solidity and wisdom. Out of a thousand I shall produce but this one, which gives you a perfect idea of this people. A certain student in the Humanities stood candidate for the vacant mastership of a school. His pretensions were strengthened in this manner, to wit, the inhabitants of the city of Nahami certified that the candidate had lived very quietly for four years together with a wanton and unfaithful wife, and wore his horns very patiently. The certificate was couched in the following style:

> Whereas the learned and venerable Jocthan Hu has required of his neighbours a testimonial of his life and morals, we, the citizens living in that street or portion of the city called Posko, do testify that the said Jocthan Hu has lived in wedlock for full four years with a disloyal wife, and that without the least noise or disturbance; that he has worn his horns with a laudable patience, and with such meekness has borne this misfortune that we judge him highly worthy to succeed to the vacant mastership, if his learning be but equal to his morals. Given under our hands this 10th day of the month Palm, in the 3000ndth year after the Great Deluge.

To this recommendation was annexed a testimonial from the seminary of the karatti of his learning and studies, which seemed to be more to the purpose. For what great merit cuckoldom had to bear the bell from all other doctors, I could not readily apprehend. But here lay the sense and meaning of this strange testimonial, viz., among the virtues that principally recommend a teacher, moderation is one. For with all his pomp of learning, unless he has an invincible patience, he must be but indifferently qualified for the scholastic employment, which should be exercised without severity or passion, lest by untimely corrections the minds of the youths should be hardened. And since a greater instance of moderation could hardly be given than this of the

46

candidate, therefore his neighbours insisted chiefly on this argument, as everything was to be hoped for from a teacher so renowned for this necessary virtue. It is said His Majesty laughed immoderately at so unusual a recommendation, but since it was far from being absurd, he conferred the vacant mastership upon the petitioner. And in effect he understood and discharged his duty with such address, and so engaged his pupils by his mildness and clemency, that they regarded him rather as a parent than a tutor, and such was their passion for learning under such soft and gentle government that through the whole dominions there were few schools that annually sent out such eminent, learned, and civilized trees.

As during the several years of my employment I had frequent opportunities of inspecting into the nature of the soil, into the genius and manners of the people, into their policy, religion, laws, and studies, I hope it will not be unacceptable to the reader if I collect into one view what he will meet with separately throughout the whole book.

[1] Holberg's Latin version:
> "Hei! qualis facies! & quali digna tabella!"
Juvenal, *Satire X,* line 157, in *Juvenal and Persius,* p. 204:
> "o qualis facies et quali digna tabella"

[2]Holberg's Latin version:
> "Qua veniam, causamq; viae, nomenq; rogatus,
> Et patriam: Patria est, respondeo, grandior Orbis.
> Klimius est Nomen; veni nec puppe per undas,
> Nec pede per terras; patuit mihi pervius Æther."
Book V, lines 651-654, in Ovid, *Metamorphoses,* vol. 1, p. 282:
> "qua veniat, causamque viae nomenque rogatus
> et patriam, 'patria est clarae mihi' dixit 'Athenae;
> Triptolemus nomen, veni nec puppe per undas,
> nec pede per terras: patuit mihi pervius aether.' "

CHAPTER V

Of the Nature of the Country and the Manners of the People

The Potuan Empire is of no very great extent. The whole globe is called Nazar, and is about two hundred German miles in circumference. A traveller may easily go round it without a guide, for the same language obtains everywhere, though the Potuans differ greatly in their customs and manners from the other states and principalities. And as in our world the Europeans excel the rest of mankind, so the Potuans are distinguished by their superior virtue and wisdom from the rest of the globe. The highroads at proper distances are adorned with stones that mark the miles, and abound with directing posts which show the ways and turnings to every city and village. It is indeed a very memorable circumstance, and worthy of admiration, that the same language is spoken everywhere, although the several kingdoms differ so widely in other respects, namely, in their manners, understanding, customs, and condition, that we see here all that variety which nature delights in, and which does not only simply move or affect the traveller, but even throws him into an ecstasy of wonder.

There are also seas and rivers which bear vessels whose oars seem to be moved by a kind of magic impulse, for they are not worked by the labour of the arm, but by machines like our clockwork. The nature of this device I cannot explain, as being not well versed in mechanics; and besides, these trees contrive everything with such subtlety that no mortal without the eyes of Argus or the power of divination can arrive at the secret. This globe, like ours, has a triple motion, so that the seasons here, namely, those of day and night, winter and summer, spring and autumn, are distinguished like ours; also towards the poles it grows colder. As to light, there is little difference between day and night, for the reasons before assigned. Nay, the night may be thought more grateful than the day, for nothing can be conceived more bright and splendid than that light which the solid firmament receives from the sun and reflects back upon the planet, insomuch that it looks (if I may be allowed the expression) like one universal moon. The inhabitants consist of various species of trees, as oaks, limes, poplars, palms, brambles, etc., from whence the sixteen months, into which the Subterranean year is divided, have their names. For every sixteenth month the planet Nazar returns to its first station, yet not upon the same day, on account of the inequality of its motion; for just like our moon, by its manifold phases it perplexes the literati of the firmament. Their dates or eras of time are various; these they fix from some memorable circumstance, and particularly from the great comet which appeared three thousand years ago and is said to have caused an universal deluge in which the whole race of trees and other animals perished, except a few which on the tops of mountains escaped the general wreck, and from whom the present inhabitants are descended.

The soil abounds with corn, herbs, and pulse, and produces all the fruits of Europe except oats, of which there is no want, since there are no horses. The seas and lakes afford delicious fish, and the shores and banks are adorned with the most entertaining variety of villages, some contiguous and some divided. The liquor they drink is extracted from certain herbs which flourish all the year. The vendors of this liquor are called *minhalpi,* that is, herb-brewers, who in every city are restrained to a certain number and who alone have the privilege of preparing it. Those who enjoy this advantage are commanded to abstain from all other business or lucrative employment. In particular it is provided that those who already are in any public offices, or who have salaries from the government, shall never concern themselves in this branch of trade, because these by their power and authority in the city might monopolize the business, and be able to undersell the rest from the revenues they already enjoy. An artifice often practiced by the courtiers and great men of our world, who in the shape of merchants or jobbers become immensely rich.

Their populousness is mightily promoted by a certain salutary law concerning procreation; for according to the number of children, their privileges and immunities are increased or diminished. He who is the father of six children is exempted from all taxes, ordinary and extraordinary. Hence a numerous issue is deemed as advantageous there as it is hurtful and inconvenient in our world, where often a tax is imposed in the way of capitation.

No one here fills two posts at once, because they are of opinion that the least employment requires the whole activity of the soul. And therefore, with the leave of my fellow creatures I must say that business is better done with them than with us. So sacred is the observance of this law that a physician does not direct his studies to the whole circle of physic, but bends all his application to the nature and cure of only one disorder. A musician plays upon only one instrument; quite otherwise than it is upon our earth where, by the variety of our pretensions, humanity is trampled on, bitternesses increase, and our duty is neglected; and where, by aiming at everything, we do nothing to good purpose. Thus a physician, while he affects to rectify the disorders of the state as well as those of the body, performs neither well. Thus, if another will be both a senator and a musician, we can expect nothing but discord. We are apt to admire such daring spirits as fly at all things, who mix officiously in matters of the highest concern and think there is nothing they are unfit for. But it is all rashness, presumption, and a total want of sense of their own strength that we thus blindly admire. Did they but thoroughly know the weight of public office and the shortness of their own abilities, they would reject the offered honours and tremble at the sound. No one here undertakes the least employment *invita Minerva* [contrary to one's abilities]. I remember to have heard an illustrious philosopher, by name Rakbasi, descanting upon this subject and thus expressing himself: "Every one of us should be acquainted with his own abilities, and be the strictest judge of his own virtues and vices; otherwise stage-players will appear to have more wisdom than we, for they do not choose the finest parts, but those that are the fittest for them. And shall a player see that on a stage which a wise man cannot see in life?"

The natives of this empire are not divided into nobles and commons. Formerly indeed this distinction obtained. But when the sovereigns observed that the seeds of discord spring from hence, they wisely removed all such privileges as were derived from birth, so that virtue alone is now the test of honour; and this will appear plainer hereafter. The sole pre-eminence of birth consists in a plurality of branches. The offspring is accounted noble or ignoble for this reason, because the greater plenty they have, the fitter they are for all manual operations.

Enough has been said in the foregoing part of this work concerning the genius and manners of this people; and therefore referring the reader to those passages, I conclude this chapter and proceed to some other particulars.

CHAPTER VI

Of the Religion of the Potuan Nation

The Potuan system of religion lies in a narrow compass and contains a confession of faith something longer than our Apostles' Creed. It is prohibited here, under pain of banishment to the Firmament, to comment upon the sacred books. And if any presume to dispute about the essence and attributes of God, or about the nature of spirits and souls, he is condemned to the venesection and then confined in the public Bedlam. For they think it the height of folly to offer to describe or define those things to which the human mind is as blind as the eyes of an owl to the light of the sun. They are all unanimous in adoring one Supreme Being by whose almighty power all things were created and by whose providence they subsist. Let but this principle be uncontroverted, and they never molest anyone for entertaining different sentiments concerning a method of worship. Those alone who openly attack this religion, as by law established, are regarded as disturbers of the public tranquillity. Hence I had the free exercise of my own religion, nor suffered the least affront upon that account.

The Potuans pray but seldom, but then it is with great ardency, insomuch that they seem to be in an ecstasy. And when I related that we pray and sing psalms very often while employed about the common affairs of life, the Potuans thought it a vicious custom, replying that an earthly sovereign would take it extremely ill to see anyone humbly approaching him with a petition, and at the same time brushing his clothes or curling his hair. Nor had they a much greater relish for our hymns and anthems, as holding it ridiculous to express grief and penitence in musical measures, since the displeasure of the Deity is to be appeased by sighs and tears of real sorrow, not by the artifice of tunes and instruments. This and more I heard, but not without some indignation, especially as my own father of blessed memory, who was once chanter of a cathedral, had composed several anthems in vogue to this day, and as I myself intended once to have stood for a vacant chantership. But I stifled my resentment, for the Subterraneans so strenuously defend their opinions and so speciously set everything out to view that it is no easy matter to refute even the plainest of their errors. There were also several other opinions upon religious subjects which they maintained with the same art and appearance of truth. Thus, when I had often observed to some acquaintance that they could hope for no salvation after death, as living in utter darkness, they replied that those who were so free of dealing damnation to others run the greatest risk of it themselves; that the source of all that is arrogance, which God must hate and disallow; and that to condemn the judgment of others and to use force to convince them were the same as to assume the whole light of reason, which is just the conduct of fools who think that they alone are wise. Moreover, when I was proving a certain opinion and had opposed to my adversary's reasonings the dictates of my own conscience, he extolled my argument and desired me still to persist in following those dictates of conscience, as he himself would always do, for then everyone following the testimony of his conscience, all contention would cease, and much matter of controversy be cut off.

Among other religious mistakes maintained by the people of this globe were these: They did not deny that good actions were rewarded and bad ones punished by God; but then they thought that branch of justice consisting in the distribution of

53

rewards and punishments took place only in a future state. I brought various examples of such as for their impieties had been punished in this life, but they alleged as many opposite examples of very wicked trees who yet were as fortunate as they were wicked to the end of their lives. In a dispute, said they, we are too apt to borrow only those weapons and attend to only those instances which make for our purpose and strengthen our cause, overlooking and disregarding such as might injure it. With that I instanced in myself, by showing that many who had injured me came to a miserable end. In answer they urged that all this proceeded from self-love, from my overweening opinon that in the eyes of the Supreme Being I was of more consequence than many others who, like me, had suffered the severest injuries undeservedly, and yet had beheld their persecutors blessed and prosperous to the last day of their lives.

Again, when accidentally I was commending the practice of daily prayer, they replied that indeed they did not deny the necessity of prayer, but that they were thoroughly persuaded that the truest piety consisted in a practical observance of the divine law. To prove this they borrowed an argument from a prince, or lawgiver. This prince has two sorts of subjects; some are continually offending and transgressing his laws through infirmity or contumacy, and yet these shall be found continually haunting the court to procure pardon for faults to be repeated as soon as pardoned. Others approach the court very rarely but, remaining peaceable at home, are habitual observers of their sovereign's laws. Who can doubt but that he must think this latter sort more worthy of his favour, and regard the first as bad subjects and troublesome creatures?

In these and the like controversies was I often engaged, though without success, for I was able to bring nobody over to my way of thinking. And therefore omitting all other religious disputes, I shall only give you their general and most observable doctrines, leaving it to the intelligent reader to applaud or censure them as he shall judge best.

The Potuans believe in one God, Omnipotent, Creator and Preserver of all things, whose omnipotence and unity they demonstrate from this ample and harmonious creation. And since they are admirably skilled in the study of nature, they have such magnificent and exalted sentiments of the nature and attributes of the Deity that they look upon it as a defect in the understanding to attempt to define what transcends their capacities. The year is distinguished by five festival days, the first of which is celebrated with the utmost devotion in such obscure places as that no rays of light can pierce them, indicating by this, that the Being they adore is incomprehensible. There the worshipers remain almost immovable from the rising to the setting of the sun, as though they were in an ecstasy. This high day is called "The Day of the Incomprehensible God," and it falls on the first day of the month of Oaks. The other festivals are celebrated at four other seasons of the year, and were instituted to return thanks to God for the blessings of His providence. The absentees, unless they are able to give very just reasons for their absence, are deemed bad subjects and live totally disregarded. The public forms of prayer are so devised as not to regard the people who pray but the welfare of the prince or the state. None prays in public for himself. The design of which institution is that the Potuans may believe that the happiness of individuals is so closely connected with that of the public that they cannot be separated. None are compelled by force or by fines to attend the public worship, for as they are of opinion that piety consists chiefly in love, and as experience teaches them that love is damped and not inflamed by force, therefore it must be an unprofitable and a wicked thing to use compulsion in the case of religion. This point they thus illustrate. Should a husband desire a reciprocal affection from his consort, and should he hope to conquer her

55

coldness and indifference by blows, he would be so far from kindling up her love by this method that her indifference would increase and end in abhorrence and detestation.

[The Potuans, in former times, sought to appease the wrath of the Godhead with offerings, splendid processions, and other ceremonies. This external worship of the Deity endured till the renowned philosopher Cimali, about eight hundred years ago, stood forward as the reformer of the religion, and published a book called *Sebolac Tacsi*, or, *The True Remarks of a Religious Tree*. This book I read very sedulously to the end, and considered it a work of which I should never be weary. It contains theological dogmas and moral maxims which the Potuans learn by heart. The Subterranean reformer abolishes the offerings and such like customs upon the following grounds: "Those virtues," says he, "are only real virtues, whereof the practice is troublesome and difficult to the corrupt heart. To make offerings, to sing psalms, to keep every other day sacred in honour of the ashes of the dead, and to walk in procession with the effigies of saints, partake much more of the nature of devout idleness than of spiritual business, if such may be called spiritual business which every vicious-minded person can readily exercise without its costing him the least self-denial. But he who endeavours with all his means to relieve the indigent, to govern his temper, and to subdue his revengefulness; who combats manfully against all concupiscence and lust and strives with all his might to curb his darling passions, exhibits alone the true sign of virtue and the fear of God. A splendid uniform and glittering arms are marks which distinguish the warrior from the man in trade, but the hero is always known by his bravery and valour, and by his patient suffering, unreluctant toils, and sacrifice of life and limbs for his beloved fatherland."

With such like examples Cimali has endeavoured to strengthen his precepts; and as the Potuans observe them very strictly, the converters, or the so-called missionaries of the Romish Church, who enjoin so much the observance of ceremonies and promise paradise to all who worship relics and images, or who during forty days glut and satiate themselves with the dainties and delicacies of the fields, vineyards, seas, oceans, and rivers, would lose both their time and labour among a people like this.][1]

These are some of the principal doctrines of the Potuan divinity, which to some must appear like mere natural religion; and so indeed it did at first to me. But they assert that all was divinely revealed to them and that some ages ago they received a book which contained their system of faith and practice. Formerly, say they, our ancestors lived contented with the religion of nature only; but experience taught them that the sole light of nature was insufficient, since all those noble principles through the sloth and carelessness of some were forgot, and through an airy philosophy of others (nothing being able to check their licentious career) were utterly depraved and corrupted. Hereupon God gave them a written law. Hence it appears how great is their error who obstinately deny the necessity of a revelation. For my part, I freely own that many points of this theology seemed to me, if not praiseworthy, yet by no means to be despised. To some I could not assent. But one thing there is deserving all our admiration, namely, that in times of war the conquerors, returning from the field, instead of that joy and triumph with which we celebrate victories and sing Te Deum, pass some days in deep silence, as if they were ashamed of having been obliged to shed blood. Therefore there is very little mention of military affairs in the Subterranean annals, which are chiefly records of civil matters, such as their laws, institutions, and foundations.

[1] Lewis Holberg, *Journey to the World Under Ground; Being the Subterraneous Travels of Niels Klim* (London: Thomas North, 1828), pp. 97-99.

CHAPTER VII

Of Their Policy

In the Potuan Empire an hereditary, and indeed lineal, succession has flourished for a full thousand years, and the same is at this day religiously observed. Their annals indeed discover that in one instance they departed from this order of succession. For since right reason seemed to require that rulers should excel their subjects in wisdom and all the endowments of the mind, hence it was thought necessary that virtue should be more regarded than birth and that he should be elected for their sovereign who should be thought the most excellent and worthy among the subjects. Upon this, the ancient succession being laid aside, the supreme power by the general voice was conferred upon a philosopher named Rabaku. At first he governed with such prudence and with such mildness that he seemed a pattern for succeeding princes. But these happy times were but of short duration, and the Potuans were too late convinced of the falsehood of that maxim which holds that the kingdom is happy where a philosopher is at the helm. For since the new sovereign was raised from the meanest fortune to the height of power, his virtues and all his arts of government could not procure or maintain that veneration, that respect, that majesty, which is the great support of a monarch's power. Those who but lately had been his equals or superiors could hardly be brought to bow to an equal or inferior, or to pay the new prince that measure of obedience due from subjects to their rulers; and therefore when any strict or troublesome commands were laid upon them, they murmured loud and never regarded what the prince then was, but what he was before his exaltation. Hence he was forced to have recourse to submissive flatteries; and even this availed not; for after these submissions, being obliged to issue out his commands and edicts, they were still received with frowns and with reluctance. Rabaku then perceiving that other means were necessary to keep the subjects to their duty, from a mild and popular behaviour he now changed his measures and treated his people with severity. But alas! by this extreme, those sparks which lay concealed under the ashes now broke into an open flame; the subjects rose in arms against their prince, and one rebellion not thoroughly subdued and laid asleep was the beginning of another. The monarch, finding at length that the government could no longer subsist but under a sovereign of illustrious descent whose high birth might extort a veneration from the people, made a voluntary abdication of the empire in favour of the prince who in right of birth should have succeeded. The ancient family being thus restored, peace was restored with it, and all those storms which had shattered the vessel of the commonwealth at once subsided. From that time it was made capital to attempt any innovation in the order of succession.

The empire therefore is now hereditary, and probably will remain so till time shall be no more, unless the most urgent and extreme necessity oblige them to deviate from this rule. Mention is made in the Potuan annals of a philosopher who devised an expedient to break through this law; his counsel was not to set aside the royal family, but to make choice of that son of the deceased sovereign, be it elder or younger, whose virtues were more eminent and who should be deemed most equal to the weight. This philosopher, having proposed this law, submitted himself (according to the custom of his country) to the usual test, namely, to have his neck in a halter, while they were debating about the utility of the proposed law. The Senate being assembled and the votes cast up, the proposal was condemned as a thing detrimental to the commonwealth. They believed it would be the source of perpetual troubles and would sow the seeds of discord between the royal progeny; that therefore it was more advisable for the old law to take place, and that the right of dominion should still devolve upon the first-born, although the younger issue might excel in the endowments of the mind. The law therefore not passing, the projector was strangled. And these are the only species of criminals that are punished with death. For the Potuans are persuaded that every change or reformation, however well-digested, gives occasion to disturbance and commotion, and puts the whole state into a fluctuating and unsettled condition; but if it be a rash and ill-digested alteration, it is followed with inevitable ruin.

The power of the Potuan monarchs, although subject to no laws, is yet rather a paternal than a regal power. For being naturally lovers of justice, power, and liberty, things totally incompatible elsewhere do here go hand in hand.

Among the laws of this kingdom, the most salutary is that by which the princes endeavour to preserve an equality between the subjects, that is, as far as the nature of government will admit. You see here no different ranks and titles of honour. Inferiors obey their superiors, and the younger the elder, and this is all.

The Subterranean memoirs show that some ages ago such classes of dignities were in use and that they were established by law, but it appeared that they were the source of infinite disorders. It was an intolerable evil for an elder brother to give place to his younger, or a parent to his child; so that at length each shunning the other's company, it put a stop to all conversation and good fellowship. But these were not the only grievances. For in process of time it came to that pass that the more noble and worthy trees, whom nature had blessed with the strongest capacities and with the greatest number of branches, were seated in the lowest places at feasts and assemblies. For no tree of real virtue and intrinsic worth could bring himself to sue for a title or mark of pre-eminence, which from his soul he despised. And on the contrary, the more profligate and worthless sort of trees would incessantly tease their royal master with petitions till they had even extorted a title that might in a manner hide the poverty of their nature and be a screen for their vices. Hence it came to pass that titles were at last looked upon as certain indications of the vilest trees. Their festivals and solemn meetings were, to strangers, a spectacle the most absurd that can be imagined. There might they behold brambles and bushes in the most honourable seats, while the lofty cedar and the noble oak, each of whom Nature had adorned with ten or twelve tier of branches, took the remotest and most obscure seats. Even the ladies had titles; they were counsellors of the houehold, counsellors of state, counsellors of court. And this blew up the coals of discord more in that weaker sex than in the other. To such an excess this vain ambition rose that they to whom Nature had been so unkind as to afford them no more than two or three pair of branches, even they absurdly affected the title of "trees of Ten or Twelve Branches." This vanity is just as ridiculous as if the most deformed monster in nature should affect to pass for a beauty, or a man of the meanest original give himself the airs of a man of quality. When this evil had arrived to its highest pitch, and the whole kingdom upon the brink of being ruined, every mortal grasping at empty names and dishonourable titles, a certain native of Keba had the hardiness to propose a law for the abolishing of this custom. This same person was, according to the usual custom, brought into the Forum with a halter about his neck. The Senate being met and proceeding to vote, the proposal passed without any open opposition and was judged useful to the commonwealth. Upon this he was crowned with a garland of flowers and led into the city in triumph amidst the shouts and acclamations of the populace. And when in process of time it was discovered how advantageous the repeal of these laws was, the projector was advanced to the honour of Kadoki, or High Chancellor.

Ever since this time the law for preserving this equality among the subjects has been inviolably observed. Yet the repeal did not put a stop to all emulation, for everyone now endeavoured to shine by true virtue and real merit. It appears from the annals of this empire that from that time to this there has been but one projector who twice attempted to revive the distincion of dignities; but for his first effort he was condemned to the venesection, and since he persisted in his attempt, he was banished to the Firmament. Now therefore no ranks or titles of honour obtain here, only the supreme magistrate declares some professions to be nobler than others, by which declaration, notwithstanding, nobody has a right of assuming the chief seats in public assemblies. This small difference we find in the edicts and letters mandatory of the sovereign, which generally end with these words: "We command and enjoin all husbandmen, inventors of machines for the manufactures, merchants, tradesmen, philosophers, officers of the court, etc."

I was informed that in the archives of the prince this Catalogue of Honour was preserved.

1. Those who had assisted the government with their wealth and fortunes in its greatest straits.
2. Officers who serve gratis and without salary or pension.
3. Husbandmen of eight branches and upwards.
4. Husbandmen of seven branches and under.
5. Inventors or erectors of machines for manufactures.
6. Operators who exercise the more necessary callings and employments.
7. Philosophers and graduate doctors of both sexes.
8. Artisans.
9. Merchants.

10. Officers of the court, with a salary of 500 *rupats*.
11. Officers of the court, with a salary of 1000 *rupats*.

This series of honours seemed very ridiculous to me, as it must to everyone of our globe. I guessed indeed at some of the reasons for this inverted order, what foundation it was grounded on, and by what arguments the Subterraneans would defend it. But I confess upon the whole it was a paradox I could not comprehend.

Among other things worthy of observation, I remarked the following: The more benefit anyone received from the government, with a proportional modesty and humility he carried himself. Thus I frequently saw Bospolak, the richest man in the Potuan dominions, receive all he met with such condescension that he lowered all his branches, and by inclining his head testified to every common tree his grateful sense of the public favours. Upon my asking the reason, I was told that thus it ought to be, since upon no subject more benefits were conferred, and that therefore he was the greatest debtor to the commonwealth. Not that he was obliged by any law to this condescension; but as the Potuans in general act wisely and judiciously, so they make a voluntary virtue of it, holding themselves bound to use such a behaviour as gratitude would dictate. Far otherwise it is with us, where those whom their country has loaded with wealth and titles receive their inferiors with a lofty and contemptuous air.

But the most deserving subjects of all, and who receive the most universal honour and respect, are the parents of a numerous offspring. These are the heroes of the Subterranean world, and their memory is held sacred with posterity. They are also the only persons upon whom the name of Great is conferred. Not so with us, where the destroyers of mankind are complimented with that title. One may easily guess what sentiments they would entertain here of Alexander the Great and Julius Caesar, each of whom, having slain their millions, died without offspring. I remember to have seen at Keba this epitaph of a husbandman: "Here lies Jochtan the Great, father of thirty children, the hero of his time." It must be observed that in order to acquire this glory the mere procreation of children is not alone sufficient, unless they be also liberally and virtuously educated.

In the enacting of laws, they proceed with a deliberation equal to that of the old Romans. The proposal of a new law is fixed upon all the courts and places of resort throughout the city. The citizens are free to examine it and send their sentiments and advices upon it to the College of Wise Men, instituted for this very purpose. Here everything is weighed that concerns the enacting, the disannulling, approving, correcting, limiting, or extending of this law. And when it has thus gone through all this trial and examination, it is offered to the prince for his consent and authority. This delay may seem absurd to some, but the consequence of this caution is that their laws are immortal, and I have been informed that not one of their laws for these five hundred years past has suffered the least alteration.

In the custody of the sovereign there is a list of the most worthy and valuable trees, together with certificates of their learning from the karatti and of their life and morals from their neighbours. Hence the republic is never in want of proper persons to fill the vacant offices. It is particularly worth remarking that no one has a right or freedom to live in any city or village without a certificate from the place they came from and security for their future behaviour.

A law once enacted by public authority, all future canvassing and criticising upon it is prohibited upon pain of death, so that in their politics their liberty seems to be more restrained than in their religion. The reason they assign is this: "If anyone err in matters of faith and speculation, at his own peril he errs; but if anyone call in question the established laws or endeavour to pervert the sense of them by some new gloss or interpretation, he is an enemy to society."

Something has already been said of the state and economy of the court. It has been observed that the Kadoki, or High Chancellor, is the supreme officer. Next to him is the *Smirian*, or High Treasurer. This post was in my time discharged by a widow of seven branches, called Rahagna, who for her eminent integrity and other great endowments was advanced to an office of that weight and trust. Long had she presided at the head of the treasury, even many years before the death of her husband, who, though extremely well-versed in the state of the finances, yet was entirely ruled by the counsels and authority of his wife and never ventured to act upon his own judgment; hence he was more her official or deputy than her husband. The edicts and ordinances indeed were issued out in his name as often as she was hindered by lyings-in or any other malady, yet nothing was esteemed firm and authentic till her subscription or seal was affixed to it. Rahagna had two brothers, one of which was butler and the other butcher to the court; nor, though they had a sister in the highest exaltation, did they dare to aim at anything greater by reason of the poverty and slenderness of their abilities: with so much equity are preferments here distributed.

This lady, though engaged in the most arduous affairs of the kingdom, yet at the same time suckled an infant she was delivered of soon after the death of her husband. This I thought was too troublesome and too mean an employment for so great a matron. And upon my giving my opinion, they replied in this manner: "Can you imagine that nature has given breasts to women only as a softer ornament, and not rather for the nourishment of their offspring? The quality of the milk and the temper of the nurse go farther than we imagine in forming the disposition of the infant. And mothers who disdain to nourish their

own issue dissolve one of the finest and strongest ties of nature."
And hence there is hardly a lady throughout all these dominions
but suckles her own children.

The heir apparent of the crown was a youth of six years
in whom 'twas easy to discover the seeds of many great and shin-
ing virtues. Nature had been so liberal as to adorn him with
six pair of branches, an uncommon circumstance in that tender
age. His preceptor, the wisest tree in all the empire, instructed
him in the knowledge of the Creator, in history, in mathematics,
and in moral philosophy. I obtained a sight of that moral system
or political compendium which he composed for the use of his
pupil. The title of it was *Mahalda Libab Helil,* which in the
Subterranean language signifies *A Key to Government.* It consists of a collection of precepts and maxims, the most solid and
advantageous; some of which I yet perfectly remember and
shall here set them down.

1. Aspersions or encomiums are not hastily to be credited;
but the judgment is to be suspended till an indubitable
knowledge can be procured.
2. When anyone is accused and convicted of a crime, it
should be examined what good the delinquent has ever done;
thus his good actions being compared with his bad, let reason
interpose and pronounce sentence.
3. Those counsellors who are given to contradiction and
contest the sovereign may safely confide in as the heartiest
subjects, for no one will expose themselves to danger but
those to whom the welfare of their country is dearer than
their private safety.
4. Let none but large-estated men compose the Senate.
Their advantage is united with the public advantage, whereas
those who possess but a movable estate look upon the kingdom not as their country, but as an inn, and themselves as
travellers.
5. The prince may make use of the ministry or agency of
bad men, if they should happen to be fit for a particular business, but never load them with uncommon favours; for if a

wicked or an obnoxious man be received into favour, the worst of subjects will rise under his patronage and work themselves into office.

6. Let him most of all suspect those who perpetually haunt the court: such either have committed, or are prepared to commit, the most daring things.

7. Let him be very backward to reward those who are most impatient of honours. For as no one begs an alms till oppressed with poverty and hunger, so none insatiably hunt after dignities but who despair to rise by real merit and virtue.

8. The eighth precept is indeed a very useful one, but what I could not be pleased with upon account of the odious example with which it was illustrated. The precept is this: No subject is to be considered as altogether useless; none are so dull but may be made subservient to some good purpose, nay, even may be made to excel in some point. For instance, one excels in judgment, another in ingenuity; one's excellence shall be in the mind, another's in the body; this shall make a good judge, that a better advocate. One shall have a vast power of invention, another shall labour at the execution of a thing; insomuch that there are few entirely unprofitable. That some creatures indeed seem so is not the fault of the Creator, but of those who will not perceive or inquire where their chief strength lies, and follow that clue. This position he thus illustrated. We have seen, says he, in this our age, one of the superterranean animals, who by the unanimous suffrage of all was deemed as an unprofitable load upon the earth, by reason of that quickness and forwardness of his judgment; but yet we see his great swiftness of foot is of no small service to us. Upon reading this paragraph I could not help saying, "This is a very honest preface, but a scandalous conclusion."

9. It is of no small importance to a prince who would know the arts of governing to be very nice and cautious in the choice of a preceptor to the heir of his dominions. Let him therefore choose one of remarkable piety and eminent learning, since from the institution of the future successor the welfare of the state must be determined. What we learn in the tender age of life passes into nature. Hence it is necessary that the young prince's tutor should be a lover of his

country, that he may instill into his prince a love for his subjects, the first and principal mark that all his precepts should be aimed at.

10. 'Tis necessary the prince should study the genius of his government and conform to it; and if he would correct the disorders of his subjects, let him do it rather from his own example than the laws.

11. Let none be suffered to be idle, since such are a dead weight upon their country. By constant industry and toil, the republic rises into strength and power; nor is there any room left for pernicious counsels and contrivances against the state. And therefore it is safer for the state to allow the subjects their insignificant diverisons than to indulge them in a laziness, which would be a source of conspiracies.

12. Let the prince preserve peace among his subjects; however, it would not be amiss to encourage an emulation among his counsellors, as it leads to the discovery of truth. A skillful judge will often extract the truth from the passions of the advocates.

13. He would act wisely, if in affairs of the last moment he heard the sentiments of every member of the Senate, and that rather apart than when convened. For in a full Senate, where opinions are openly given, it often falls out that the most fluent speaker bears all before him with a torrent of eloquence, and so the sovereign hears but one opinion.

14. Punishments are not less necessary than rewards; the first puts a stop to evil as the latter encourages good. Hence it may not be wrong even to reward a bad subject for a good action, if it were only that others may thereby be whetted up and incited to do their duty vigorously.

15. In promotions to honours and public posts, let regard be had principally to the person's dexterity and adroitness for that particular employment. Though piety and integrity are of themselves most commendable virtues, yet 'tis possible we may be deceived by their appearance. Everyone would affect a sanctity of behaviour if he knew that this show of virtue was the road to honours, and would in words profess the utmost probity and uprightness with the same view. Besides, it is no easy matter to form a judgment of a person's virtues till he is admitted to employment, in which, as upon a stage.

he is to exhibit specimens of his virtues. But nothing is easier than to make experiment of anyone's aptness for business beforehand. It is infinitely harder for the stupid and the ignorant to conceal their stupidity and ignorance than for a hypocrite to cover his impiety, or a knave his roguery. Besides, great abilities and much virtue are not so very opposite but they may be often found united in the same character. And if a person of large abilities be at the same time honest and virtuous, nothing more can be wanting. An ignorant is either good or bad; if bad, who knows what monsters ignorance and wickedness in conjunction produce? If good, his very dullness must indubitably hinder the exercise of his virtues. And if he of himself neither can nor dare attempt the commission of some atrocious crime, yet the servant, whose assistance he must make use of, in all likelihood may. A foolish landlord has commonly a roguish bailiff, and a dull justice a knavish clerk, who fearlessly commits frauds and errors under the protection of his master. In promotions, therefore, let dexterity be the principal thing regarded.

16. Let none be hastily censured as ambitious for aiming at an employment he is in reality unfit for, or for that reason excluded from all hopes of preferment. For if, in the distribution of public honours, the prince should happen to adhere to this rule too closely, the most ambitious will soon put on the mask of humility as a safer road and a shorter cut to preferment. And thus the sovereign would, contrary to his inclination, prefer the most forward worshipers of fortune as being to all appearance the most humble; that is, he would prefer those who about the time of any vacancy pretend to fly from court and retire into the shade, giving out by their friends that they are averse to grandeur. To illustrate this point, he inserted an example of one who, during the vacancy of a considerable employment he was all on fire to obtain, wrote to the prince to this effect: "That it was reported that His Serene Highness designed the vacant dignity for him though solicited for it by numbers; that he for his part must beg leave to decline an office to which he professed himself unequal; that he entreated His Majesty to confer it upon some more proper person, and that being perfectly contented with his present station, he aspired to nothing greater." The

69

monarch, moved with so strong an attestation of humility, preferred this humble hypocrite to the said dignity. But he soon learned that he was abused, for no minister ever behaved with such pride or acted with such weakness.

17. To set a poor insolvent at the head of the treasury is the same thing as to put a hungry man in your pantry. Nor is a covetous rich man a better choice. The former has nothing, and the other thinks nothing enough.

18. Let there be no foundations or establishments for the maintenance of slothful trees. Accordingly, throughout this empire the monasteries and colleges admit only the industrious and the diligent: those who either by some useful manufacture help to advance the interest of the republic, or who by their studies and learning can be an ornament to the society they are members of. A few monasteries indeed are to be excepted, which maintain the aged and the helpless, such by the privilege of age being exempted from all labour.

19. When the disorders of the state call loud for reformation, it will be right to proceed slowly in it. For to endeavour to extirpate inveterate evils at a blow is as absurd as to prescribe purging, bleeding, and vomiting all at once to a patient.

20. Those who boldly attempt everything and undertake a multitude of affairs together are either fools who have not duly compared their own strength with the weight of the things, or else they are wicked and unnatural members of their society who consult their own interest alone instead of that of the commonwealth. A prudent man will try his arms before he takes his burden up; and an honest subject who loves his country will not transact the affairs of its superficially.

CHAPTER VIII

Of the Academy

In this empire there are three great schools or universities, one at Potu, another at Keba, and a third at Nahami. The studies pursued there are history, economy, mathematics, and law. As to their divinity, since it is so short and concise as that the whole is contained in the compass of a couple of pages importing that we ought to love and adore Almighty God, the Creator and Governor of things, Who in some state of existence hereafter will reward virtue and punish vice, as this, I say, is the main of their divinity, so it is no academical study, nor indeed can it be, since it is prohibited by law to have any controversy about the essence or attributes of God. Physic, in like manner, is not reckoned among the studies of the university; for since these trees live all sober lives, internal diseases are almost wholly unknown. I say nothing of metaphysics and such transcendental learning, since it has been observed above that to dispute about the essence of the Divine Being, about the qualities of angels, or the nature of spirits incurred the "punishment of the arm" and confinement in their Bedlam.

The academical exercises are these: The young students, during the time of their probation, are obliged to give solutions of certain difficult and curious questions which are proposed at stated times, with a reward to those who give the most ingenious and elegant expositions. By these means, the true genius of the students is discovered, what the utmost reach of their capacity is, and in what branch of knowledge they are most likely to shine.

Everyone employs himself in only one science. A universal scholar is a chimaera, and the affectation of such a character is a mark of a loose and unsettled genius. Hence it is that the sciences, confined within such narrow bounds, are soon brought to perfection. The several doctors likewise exhibit yearly specimens of their learning. The moral philosopher clears some abstruse speculative point. The historian compiles a history, or some part of history. The mathematician throws fresh light upon his science by some new and ingenious hypothesis. The lawyers are obliged to make some eloquent harangues; and these alone study rhetoric or oratory, because it is to these alone such a study will be advantageous when they come to be advocates. When I told them that all our academical specimens of all sorts were in the laboured and oratorical style, they freely condemned such an institution, replying that if every artisan were obliged to make a shoe and exhibit specimens of such their work, 'tis certain that shoemakers alone would bear away the prize. I purposely omitted to speak of our scholastic disputations, because such exercises were there but in equal estimation with dramatical performances. Their doctors and public teachers never deliver their instructions in a harsh, pedantic, and imperious manner, as the philosophers of our world, but forming some agreeable and delightful fiction, they dress up and inculcate a salutary truth with all the charms of fancy and imagination.

'Tis surprising to behold with what solemnity the academical promotions are made. For they take the extremest care not to furnish the least matter for ridicule or to be guilty of any theatrical levities, rightly judging that a plain and grave simplicity should distinguish the exercises of a university from the diversions of a stage, lest otherwise the liberal arts should run into disesteem. Upon this, I would not venture to mention the least syllable of our academical degrees and promotions since what happened to me at Keba, when I gave a description of this kind of honours, was ample reason for my eternal silence upon this head.

Besides these academies, the great cities have their several seminaries or colleges, where the nicest examination is made into the talents of every scholar, what his particular capacity is, and in what kind of learning he gives the most promising hopes of excelling. During the time of my probation in the seminary at Keba, there were four sons of the High Priest who were all educated in the art of war; four others of senatorian quality were instructed in trade; and two young virgins learned navigation. For here the genius alone is regarded without any respect to sex or condition. The examination being made, the governors of the seminaries give testimonials to the examinants with a veracity I have elsewhere spoken of. These testimonials are perfectly just and impartial, though I myself thought otherwise, since that which I obtained from them appeared to me absurd, ridiculous, and unjust.

None is here suffered to be an author till after thirty years of age, and till he shall be deemed by his judges ripe and fit for such an undertaking; consequently, few books are here published, but then they are well-digested and full of meaning. Hence, though I had written five or six dissertations while under age, I never discovered it to any creature for fear of drawing down their ridicule. Enough has now been said of the religion, policy, and literature of this people. But there are, besides, several things peculiar to them which are worthy of our observation and remembrance.

If one tree challenges another, the challenger is forever forbidden the use of arms. He is condemned, like a minor, to live under guardianship, as not knowing how to rule his affections. With us the case is different, where appeals to the sword are marks of an heroic soul, especially in the North, which must have given birth to this abominable custom, since challenges and duels were entirely unknown among the Greeks, Romans, and other ancienter nations.

I observed one strange custom in their manner of administering justice. The names of the contesting parties are concealed from the judges; and the differences are not decided in the place where they arose, but the case is sent to the more remote provinces to be determined. The reason of this strange custom is this. Experience taught them that judges were often corrupted by presents or swayed by partiality. These temptations they think they effectually remove if the parties are concealed, if the names of the plaintiff and defendant, together with the names of the lands or estates litigated, be all unknown. The reasons and arguments alone are sent, at the discretion of the prince, to whatever court of justice he thinks fit, with certain marks and characters; for example, "Whether A, who is in possession, ought to restore the thing possessed at the suit and motion of B." I should rejoice to find such a custom introduced among us, since we often experience the fatal force of corruption and partiality in the minds of our judges.

Justice in general is freely administered without respect of persons. Against the prince only no action can lie during his life, but upon his death the public accusers, or (if one may so call them) the Council for the kingdom cite him to judgment. There in full Senate the actions of the departed monarch are strictly examined, and at length sentence is pronounced, which, according to the merit of the deceased, is distinguished by different words and characters such as these: *Laudably; Not illaudably; Well; Not ill; Tolerably; Indifferently;* which words are proclaimed aloud to the people and afterwards engraved on the monument of the deceased. The Potuans give this account of that custom: That the prince while living cannot be proceeded against without great commotions and disturbances; for that during his life a perfect obedience and inviolable veneration should still be paid him, which indeed is the very basis of government. But when that obligation is dissolved by death, the subjects then have liberty to call his actions to a strict account. Thus by this salutary though very paradoxical law, the security of the sovereign is provided for, his authority not at all invaded, and the welfare of the people at the same time promoted. For these characters, though given to the dead, are to the living so many spurs to virtue. The Potuan histories for four hundred years afford only two instances of princes who bore the last-mentioned character, that is, that of *Indifferent*. All the others obtained either the *Laudable* or the *Not illaudable* character, as appears from the inscriptions upon their sepulchral monuments, which have escaped the injuries of time. The character of *Indifferent*, which in the Potuan language is called *Rip-fac-si*, causes such grief in the royal family that the successor of the deceased prince and all his kindred mourn for six whole months. And so far are the heirs from resenting the odious character given by the judges that it becomes a new incentive to them to signalize themselves by noble and worthy actions and to efface the infamy of the family by a conduct full of virtue, prudence, justice, and moderation.

The cause why one of the two princes above-mentioned had the title of *Indifferent* given him was this: The Potuans are a brave and warlike people; they never declare war themselves, but if war be declared against them they push it with all imaginable vigour. By these means they are the umpires between contending nations, and the several kingdoms of this globe submit to their mild and pacific sway. But a prince, by name Mikleta, seized with the ambition of extending his dominions, made war upon a neighbouring kingdom and subdued it. But as much as the victorious Potuans gained by the conquest, so much they lost of their ancient renown; the love of the bordering nations was now changed into dread and jealousy; and that high idea of their justice, by which the state grew into reputation, was now vanished. The Potuans finding this, to regain the lost affections of their angry neighbours, branded the memory of the deceased prince with this mark of infamy. What the crime of the other *Indifferent* prince was, is not altogether so clear.

Their public doctors or teachers are such as have attained to the third age. To explain this it must be observed that here life is divided into three ages. The first is that in which they are instructed in public affairs. In the second they publicly pursue and exercise what they have learned. And in the third, being honourably dismissed from their employments, they then take upon them the instruction of the juniors. Hence, none have a right to teach in public but such as are grown old in the administration of public affairs, since none are so capable of laying down solid rules as those who have drawn their knowledge from long experience.

If anyone already infamous for the immorality of his life should however give wholesome advice to the state, the name of the person is suppressed, lest it should lose its effect from the character of its author, and the decree pursuant to such advice is sheltered under the name of some more honourable person. Thus the good opinion is known, and the bad author concealed.

I was informed that with respect to religion it was prohibited to dispute about the prime articles of faith, particularly about the essence and attributes of the Deity. But as to all other points, it is free for everyone to propose their opinions and engage in controversies. For, say they, the inconveniences which arise from such contentions may be compared to storms which indeed throw down houses but at the same time cleanse the air and prevent that putrefaction which would arise from a stagnant atmosphere. The reason of their having few holidays is lest a spirit of idleness should creep upon them, for the Potuans believe that good people as duly worship God when employed in useful labours as they do by vows and prayers.

The study of poetry meets with but cold encouragement; yet they are not altogether destitute of poets. But the Subterranean poetry differs from prose only in the sublimity of style; and they received what I told them concerning our rhyme and measure with the utmost derision.

Among the Potuan doctors some are called Professors of Taste. It is their province to see that the minds of the youth are not employed in senseless controversies and things of no use, to take care that no trivial and vulgar writings get abroad to poison and debauch the taste, and to suppress or blot out from every book whatever is written in defiance of common sense. And to this end alone certain persons are appointed to revise and censure books; far otherwise than it is in our world where the licensers of books shall suppress the very best, only perhaps because they deviate something from the reigning opinions, from the received manner of expression, or because they lash the vices of the age with too strong a sincerity and too fine a vivacity. By this means, great geniuses are in a manner suffocated and stifled, and writings of a good stamp are forever buried. But yet, as the Potuans have a free commerce with the neighbour nations, among other commodities some books of a poor and trivial turn will creep abroad. Upon which account censors are appointed by the State, who from time to time visit the booksellers' shops. These are called *syla-macati,* that is, "purgers of booksellers' shops." For as among us there is a certain sort of men who brush and cleanse our chimneys once a year, so those censors, who pry and examine into the books that are put to sale, cleanse away all the dregs, that is, such books, or parts of books, as would deprave the taste, and convey them to the jakes. Bless me! said I to myself, what havoc would be made among our books, if such an institution were to take place among us!

77

But what cannot be enough commended is the care they take in sounding the genius of their youth, in order to know what course of life they will be fittest for. For as in music a judicious ear distinguishes every little sound, in the same manner these piercing judges of the virtues and vices of the mind form their sentiments from some seemingly inconsiderable hints, from perhaps a cast of the eye, from a frown, from dejection, mirth, laughter, speech, and even silence. 'Tis by these things they easily know everyone's propensity, and also what is contrary to his constitution.

But to return to what concerns myself. I passed my time, it may be well imagined, not in the most agreeable manner with these paradoxical trees, who treated me with disdain upon account of that too forward and unsettled judgment which they imputed to me. I grew impatient under those scoffs they were ever flinging out; for they even went so far as to give me the nickname of *Skabba,* which in their language signifies "overhasty." But what chagrined me most was that my very laundress, though of the dregs of the populace and one of the most miserable and indigent trees herself, did not even scruple to call me by that name of reproach.

CHAPTER IX

The Author's Journey round the Planet Nazar

Having continued in the unpleasing employment of King's Messenger for two whole years, and carried the royal mandates and letters patent to every province of the empire, I at last grew tired of so troublesome and so unworthy an office. Accordingly I again and again petitioned His Serene Highness to grant me an honourable dismissal, and at the same time solicited a more reputable employment. But I met with nothing but repulses from His Highness, whose constant reply was that a more important office was above my strength and capacity. He alleged also that the laws and customs of the country were death to my hopes, in that they admitted only fit and proper persons to the most eminent and arduous posts of government; that therefore I must make a virtue of necessity, and rest myself contented till I had done something to merit better fortune. He concluded his advice in terms like those of the poet, *"The maxim 'Know thyself' comes down to us from the skies; it should be imprinted in the heart, and stored in the memory."*[1]

These repeated refusals were enough to throw me upon the most daring and desperate designs. From that day forward my invention was upon the rack to produce something that should demonstrate the excellence of my genius and wipe away my present infamy. Accordingly, for a whole year I studied the laws and customs of the country with an invincible application, resolved to discover whether there were in them any defects that required a reformation. I opened my design to a certain bush with whom I had contracted a close intimacy and with whom I used to converse very freely upon all subjects, whether grave or gay. He thought my design not altogether absurd, but extremely questioned whether it would be of any service to the state. He added that it should be the care of a reformer to be a thorough master of the nature and genius of the country he intends to reform, because the same thing might, in different countries, produce different effects, as the same medicine may be good for some bodies, and pernicious to others. He likewise informed me of the danger I exposed myself to in this experiment, that no less than my life depended on it, which must be a forfeit to the state should my project have the misfortune to be condemned by the judges. He therefore ardently entreated me to bestow a little more reflection on this affair; though he did not plainly dissuade me from my attempt, since he thought it not impossible that a sagacity like mine might at length discover something useful, as well to myself as to the state.

I took the advice of my friend, and for a time laid aside my scheme, and with a laudable patience continued to discharge my duty by visiting the various cities and provinces of the kingdom after the usual manner. These repeated expeditions furnished me with an opportunity of making inquiries into the state of the kingdom as well as that of the bordering nations; and lest what I had observed in my travels should escape my memory, I penned it all down, and making a little volume of it, humbly presented it to the Prince. How much His Serene Highness was taken with this work appeared afterward, by his doing me the honour to commend my labours in full Senate; and having again attentively perused my book, he was pleased to make use of my services in a farther discovery of the whole planet Nazar. I expected a different recompense for my labours, but was forced to say with the poet, *"Virtue is praised and left to shiver."*[2] But since I was fond of novelty and had hopes that so bountiful a prince would never leave me unrewarded after my return, I set about the work with a good degree of pleasure.

The whole globe of the planet Nazar, although scarce six hundred miles in circumference, yet to the inhabitants appears of an immense extent by reason of the slowness of their motion. And hence to this day a great many countries, and particularly the more remote ones, are utterly unknown to the natives. A Potuan would hardly be able to travel over this globe on foot in two years. But what embarrassed me most was the fear I had that a variety of languages would put me to great difficulties. But I was soon undeceived and revived to hear that the inhabitants of the whole planet, though wonderfully different in their manners, yet all spoke the same tongue; and besides this, that the whole race of trees were in the main harmless, sociable, and beneficent beings, so that I might without the least danger make the tour of the whole globe. This redoubled my ardour, and in the month of Poplars I began my journey.

What follows is so marvelous that it looks more like a poetic fiction, or the chimaeras of ungoverned fancy, than reality and truth; especially since those varieties, both of body and mind, which in this journey I met with, are such as one would never expect to find between the most distant nations. It must be observed that many kingdoms here are separated from each other by seas and straits, not unlike the Archipelago in Europe. These straits are seldom crossed, but for the benefit of travellers there are certain ferrymen that keep their stations on the banks in readiness to transport the passengers. It is very rare that the natives ever venture beyond the limits of their own country; and if compelled by necessity to make a voyage, they soon return, as if impatient of a foreign soil. Hence, as many nations as there are, you see so many new worlds, in a manner. The principal cause of this vast dissimilitude is the different nature of the lands, as appears from the various colours on the surface and from the surprising difference between the plants, herbs, and fruits. It is the less wonder, therefore, if with that diversity of the soil, and the products of it, there should also be found a no less surprising variety of inhabitants, and even opposite natures and tempers. In our world, indeed, even nations the most remote differ very little from each other in genius, manners, learning, shape, and colour. For since the nature of the earth is almost everywhere the same except that one part is more fruitful than another, and since the nature of our plants, herbs, and water is nearly the same everywhere, hence nothing heterogeneous or uncommon is produced, as in this subterranean planet where every tract of land has its own peculiar property. Strangers are allowed to trade and travel, but not to settle out of their own country; nor, indeed, could such a liberty be well granted considering the great diversity and opposition of natures between each other. Hence all foreigners that you meet with are either merchants or travellers.

The countries which border upon the Potuan dominions are nearly of the same nature with them. Their inhabitants were formerly often at war with the Potuans; but at this day they are either in alliance with them, or having been subdued, they now rest contented in their subjection to so mild a power. But if you once cross the great sea which divides their whole globe, new scenes present themselves, together with new and strange creatures unknown to the Potuans. Only one thing they have in common, and that is that all the creatures of this globe are rational trees and all use the same dialect. This makes travelling very pleasant, especially as the merchants and foreigners perpetually passing through every province give people an opportunity of seeing creatures extremely strange and unlike themselves. Thus much I thought proper to premise, lest tender ears should be offended with the subsequent narration, and the author reproached with want of veracity.

It would be a tiresome and an unprofitable task to recount everything singly and in exact historical order that I met with in my travels. Let it suffice that I give an account of those particular people only whose character, description, and manners have something so unusual and marvelous in them that upon their account this planet of Nazar may be reckoned one of the principal prodigies of the universe. I must here call to mind an observation I have before made, that this whole race and country of rational trees differ very little in sense and judgment from the Potuans; but in their rites and customs, in their make and temper, there is so much diversity that every province you would swear to be a new world.

In the province of Quamso, which is the first beyond the sea, the inhabitants are subject to no infirmities or diseases of body, but each enjoys a perfect health from youth to latest age. I could not help thinking them the most happy of mortals. But upon a slight acquaintance with them, I found myself infinitely mistaken. For as, upon one hand, I saw nobody sad or sorrowful, so upon the other, I saw nobody pleased and joyful. For as we never highly relish the serenity of the heavens and the weather unless we have been sensible of the hardships of a different temperature of the air, so these trees taste no felicity because it is perpetual and uninterrupted, and never know the pleasure of health for want of knowing the misery of diseases. Their life is one eternal indolence. Their enjoyments are never exquisite, as those alone can taste the sweets of life who have their pleasures seasoned with a little pain. I protest that I never found in any country upon the face of the earth such lifeless creatures or such cold and insipid conversations. The people are harmless, but deserve neither your love nor hatred. You fear no affront, and you expect no favour. In a word, here is nothing either to please or displease. Besides, as that continual health never brings the image of death before their eyes nor ever moves their concern towards the afflicted and diseased, so they pass their days in dull security, and never know the generous warmths of pity and compassion; nor do the least footsteps of love or any such tender affection appear there. In truth, diseases remind us of our mortality, excite us to die well, and keep the soul as it were equipped for its journey to that world from whence none return; and as they afflict us with pain, so they inspire a sympathy towards others when afflicted. This leads one easily to discern how much diseases and the danger of dying contribute to charity, love, and all the social affections, and that those people unjustly complain of their Creator for appointing these afflictions, which are so full of real advantage. It must be observed that these trees, as often as they remove into other places, are exposed to the same evils and casualties of life that others are. This is a proof to me that they are indebted to the climate for this peculiar advantage, if indeed it can be called an advantage.

The province of Lalac, surnamed Mascatta, or "the Blessed," seems to correspond with its name, for there the earth produces all things spontaneously. But this extraordinary circumstance does not render the natives one jot happier. For as there is no need of labour to procure their daily sustenance, they spend their days in softness, sloth, and luxury, and so lay the foundation of innumerable diseases and untimely deaths. The nature of this country affords ample matter for our serious reflection; in particular it appears from the condition of the people that husbandmen, servants, and labourers are far happier than those who, free from the fatigue of providing for themselves, are devoted to idleness and pleasure. Hence follows a train of vicious actions, desperate resolutions, and violent deaths, which are here observed to be very common. For the perpetual affluence in which they live, in length of time quite wears away all taste and sense of pleasure, and almost infallibly introduces a downright loathing of life. Thus this region, which appeared at first like the Abode of the Blessed, was in reality the seat of sorrow, and more an object of my compassion than my envy.

The next province is that of Mardak; they are cypresses, all of the same form and height, and differ only from each other by the different make of their eyes. Some have oval eyes, some square eyes; some have small ones, others have eyes so large as to take up the whole space of the forehead. Some are born with two, others with three, and some with four eyes. There are also those who have only one eye; and these might be reputed the offspring of Polyphemus, but that their one eye is seated in the hinder part of the head. And hence, according to the different shape of their eyes, they are divided into so many tribes, the names of which are as follows:

1. Nagiri, or those who have oval eyes, and to whom consequently every object appears oval.

2. Naquiri, those who have square eyes.

3. Talampi, the small eyes.

4. Jaraku, those who have two eyes, one of which is more oblique than the other.

5. Mehanki, three eyes.

6. Tarrasuki, four eyes.

7. Harramba, those whose eyes occupy the space of the whole forehead.

8. Skadolki, those who have only one eye in the hinder part of the head.

The most numerous, and of course the most powerful tribe, is that of the Nagiri, or those who have oval eyes, and to whom consequently all objects appear oval. From this tribe are taken the senators, the priests, and all such as bear office in the state. These sit at the helm, nor do they admit anyone from another tribe to a post in the government unless he shall first confess, and confirm his confession with an oath, that a certain tablet dedicated to the sun and placed in the most conspicuous part of the temple appears to him to be oval. This sacred tablet of the sun is the principal object of the Mardakanian worship. Hence the honester part of the citizens, who start at perjury, are excluded from all public honours, and what is worse, are exposed to a thousand sneers, railleries, and even persecutions; and though they over and over protest that they cannot disbelieve their eyes, they are still complained of, and what is only a fault of nature is imputed to their obstinacy and malice.

The form of the oath, which all who are admitted to public employments and honours are forced to subscribe to, is this:

Kaki manasca quihompu miriac Jacku mesimbrii Caphani Crukkia Manaskar Quebriac Krusundora. That is: I, A. B., do swear that the sacred tablet of the sun appears to me to be oval, and I promise that I will persist in this opinion to my last breath.

After this oath, they are declared fit for the service of the state and are incorporated into the tribe of the Nagiri.

The day after my arrival, as I was sauntering in the market place, I beheld an old man whom they were hurrying away to be scourged. A large crowd of cypresses followed him with scoffs and revilings. Upon my inquiring the cause, I was informed that he was a heretic who openly taught that the tablet of the sun seemed to him to be square; and in that diabolical opinion he had obstinately persisted after repeated admonitions.

This roused my curiosity to go to the temple and try whether I had orthodox eyes or no. I examined the aforesaid tablet with all the eyes I had, and really it appeared square to me. This I ingenuously told my host, who at that time had the post of edile. With that he fetched a deep sigh and confessed to me that it appeared square to him too, but that he dare not say so publicly, for fear of being dispossessed of his employment by the governing tribe.

All pale and trembling, I left this execrable city, fearing

86

lest my back must expiate the crime of my eyes, or left branded with the title of heretic, I should be sent with ignominy out of their dominions. In truth, no institution ever appeared more horrid, barbarous, and unjust than this, where hypocrisies and perjuries alone are the avenues to preferment. And when I returned to the Potuans, I took every opportunity to express my indignation against that detestable race of people. But while I was in one of my angry moods and venting my spleen according to custom, a certain juniper tree, with whom I had lived in a good degree of intimacy, made me this answer: "It is true," says he, "that the conduct of the Nagiri will always appear absurd and iniquitous to the Potuans; but to you it should not seem at all strange that this diversity of eyes should cause such cruelties, because you have formerly assured me that in most of the European dominions there are governing tribes which fall upon the rest with fire and sword upon account of some defect, not of their eyes indeed, but of their reason; and you yourself extolled such a proceeding as a pious act, and of advantage to the government."

I presently understood the drift of this observation and blushed for shame. I left him soon, and was ever after a staunch advocate for toleration, and entertained milder sentiments of people under error.

Kimal, the next principality, is accounted the most potent by reason of its immense wealth. For besides the silver mines, which are there in great abundance, vast quantities of gold are gathered from among the sands of their rivers. Their seas too afford the most costly pearls. And yet upon a due examination of this country, I could discover that happiness did not consist in wealth alone. For as many inhabitants, so many divers and diggers there were, who, bent upon gain, seemed condemned to perpetual slavery, and such a slavery as one would think was fit only for criminals. Those who are rich enough to be exempted from these toils are obliged to keep constant watch. The whole country is so infested with thieves and robbers that it is not safe to go without a guard.

Hence this nation, beheld with envious eyes by their neighbours, drew pity from me more than envy. Fear, jealousy, suspicion, and distrust reign in every mind, and each looks upon his neighbour as a designing enemy. So that endless solicitude, wasting cares, and pallid complexions are the fruits of the boasted felicity of this province. It was not without anxiety I travelled over this region; for in every road, and upon every frontier, I was obliged to give an account of my business, name, and country to the guards and examiners, and I found myself exposed to all those vexations which travellers experience in countries that are jealous of strangers. There is a volcano, or burning mountain, in this province from whence ascend perpetual whirlwinds of fire.

After having run over this principality, and that with more trouble than I experienced throughout my whole journey, I pursued my course full east. I everywhere found the inhabitants sociable and well-behaved, but extremely paradoxical. The natives of the little kingdom of Quamboia surprised me most. There the order of nature is inverted. The more the natives advance in years, the more wanton and voluptuous they grow; and age produces such fantastic vices and such lascivious freaks as youth alone in every other place is guilty of. Here none are entrusted with the cares of state unless they are under forty years of age. When they exceed this term, they are too giddy for business, like children.

I saw here the aged frisking and gamboling in the streets like boys, and spending their time in puerile diversions, while on the other hand the youths took the liberty to reprove them, and sometimes drive them home before them with a whip. I saw an old decrepit male tree whipping a top in the market place, and was informed he was some years ago a person of very great consequence, no less than President of the Grand Council.

This inverted order obtained also in the weaker sex. Hence, when a certain youth was to be married to an old lady, all were of opinion he must undergo the fate of Acteon; which is diametrically opposite to what happens among us, where if an old man has a mind for a young bride, he has ample reason to fear an injury of that sort. Once I remember I met two old baldheads engaged in a duel. Amazed to find such vigour at such an age, I inquired the cause of this duel, and was told that the quarrel arose about a mistress they had met with at one of their haunts, and who had equally pleased them both. They who told me this added that if the governors of these two old sinners were to know of their difference, their backs would be sure to smart for it. The same evening a report flew about that a certain venerable matron had hanged herself for despair, because she had met with a repulse from a young beech she was enamoured of.

This inverted order of nature demands of course an inversion of the laws. Hence, in that chapter of the law which treats of guardianship, it is enacted that the administration of goods shall not be granted to anyone unless he be under forty years of age. Moreover, contracts are deemed ineffectual if entered into by persons above forty unless such contracts are signed by their tutors or children. In the chapter concerning subordination, there is this injunction: "Let the aged of both sexes be obedient to their children." Every person in office is always dismissed before he arrives to the age of forty, [as they are then declared minors by the Council, and are delivered over to the superintendence and management of their young kinsfolk.][3]

I did not think it convenient to continue longer in this place, where if I had happened to have stayed but ten years, I must have been obliged by law to become a child again.

[When I had finished my journey, I compared this people's

condition with the way of life and the regulations which we have here above, where numbers, in their manhood, think and write like philosophers, but who, in their old age, hunt eagerly after riches, empty titles, and other illusive fooleries. This comparison reconciled me, in some degree, again with the Quambojians, and taught me not to have so contemptible an opinion of them, as I in the beginning had entertained.]⁴

In the province of Cocklecu there is a very perverse custom, and such as would be highly condemned among us. The order of things is indeed inverted, but the fault is not owing to nature but solely to the laws. The natives are all junipers of both sexes, but the males alone perform the drudgery of the kitchen, and every such ignoble labour. In time of war indeed they serve their country, but rarely rise above the rank of common soldiers. Some few get to be ensigns, which is the very highest military honour the males ever arrive to. The females, on the other hand, are in possession of all honours and employments sacred, civil, or military. I had lately derided the Potuans for observing no difference of sex in the distribution of public offices, but that was nothing to the frenzy of this people. I could not conceive the meaning of so much indolence in the males, who, though of far superior strength of body, could yet so tamely submit to such a yoke, and for ages together digest such an ignominy. For it would have been very easy, at any time, to have freed themselves from so shameful a tyranny. But long and ancient custom had so blinded them that none ever thought of attempting to remove such a disgrace, but quietly believed it was Nature's appointment that the government should be lodged in female hands, and that it was the business of the other sex to spin, to weave, to clean the house, and upon occasion take a beating from their wives.

The arguments by which the ladies justified this custom were these: That as Nature had furnished the males with greater strength of body, her intention in that could only be to destine them to the more laborious and servile duties of life. Strangers are amazed when going into a house they see the mistress of the family in the countinghouse, with a pen in her hand and her books before her, and at the same time find her husband in the kitchen scouring the dishes. And indeed, whatever house I went to, if I inquired for the master of the family, I was still conducted into the kitchen.

Horrible were the effects of this unnatural custom. For as in other countries there are abandoned women who prostitute themselves for hire, so here the young men sell their favours, and to that end hire some house of pleasure, which shall be easily known either by a writing over it or some other infallible sign. And when the men drive this wicked trade with too great effrontery, and in too barefaced a manner, they are had to prison, and whipped like our street-walkers. On the other hand, the matrons and virgins here, without the least reproach, can prowl up and down, gaze at the young fellows, nod, whistle, tip the wink, pluck them by the sleeve, importune them, write love verses upon their doors, boast of their conquests, and reckon up their gallantries with as much satisfaction as the fine gentlemen of our world entertain you with their amours. Moreover, it is no crime for the ladies here to make amorous poems and send presents to the youths, who, on the contrary, counterfeit coyness and modesty, as knowing it indecent to surrender to a lady upon the first summons.

There was at the time I was there a mighty disturbance about a noble youth, the son of a senator, who had been ravished by a young woman. I heard that it was whispered among the friends of the injured youth that a suit would be commenced against the ravisher, and that at the next consistory court she would be sentenced to repair the dishonour by marriage, since it could be indubitably proved that he was a person of an innocent life and conversation.

[O happy Europe! exclaimed I on this occasion, and O, in particular, thrice happy France, and thrice happy England! where the weaker sex are in complete accordance with their name, and where the women obey so implicitly the commands of their husbands, that they appear much more like machines or automatons than beings endowed with a free will!][5]

During my stay here I had not the courage openly to condemn this depraved custom. But upon my leaving the city, I told several that these junipers acted in downright contradiction to nature, since from the universal voice and consent of nations it was evident that the males alone were formed for all the arduous and important affairs of life. To this they replied that I confounded custom with nature, since the weakness we impute to the female sex is derived solely from education. This is clear from the form of government established at Cocklecu, where in that sex you find all the virtues and large endowments of mind which the masculine sex in other places arrogate to themselves. For the Cocklecuanian women are grave, prudent, constant, and secret. The men, on the contrary, are light, empty, frothy creatures. Hence when anything absurd is related, the common saying is: "That's a manly trifle." Again, when anything is done rashly and unthinkingly, the proverb is: "We must make allowances for manly weakness." Notwithstanding this, I could not acquiesce in these arguments, being thoroughly convinced of the impropriety and deformity of this custom. The indignation I conceived against so much female pride and insolence gave birth to an unfortunate design, which I put in execution soon after my travels, as in its proper place shall be related.

Among the sumptuous edifices of this city, the most admirable was the Royal Seraglio, the residence of three hundred youths of exquisite beauty. They were all maintained at the expense of the Queen, and kept for her private pleasures. As I happened to hear that my person was much commended, I was afraid of being clapped up in the Seraglio and hurried away with all imaginable haste.

From this place I proceeded to the Philosophical Region, so styled from the inhabitants who are continually buried in the profound speculations of philosophy. I was all on fire to see this country, which I fancied must be the center of sciences and the true seat of the Muses. Instead of vulgar fields and meadows, I expected to find one continued lovely garden; and in this imagination I hastened my pace, and counted the hours and minutes as they flew. However, the ways through which I passed were very stony, with every now and then a ditch or cavern, insomuch that sometimes I was forced to go through a length of craggy way and sometimes through miry bogs where for want of bridges I was obliged to wade through, and drag my weary limbs after me, quite dirtied to the waist; yet I fortified myself against these accidents with all the consoling arguments I could think of.

While for a full hour I had been labouring under these difficulties, I met a peasant, of whom I inquired how far I had to Mascattia, or the Philosophical Province. He replied I ought rather to ask him how much there was left of the journey, since I was in the very heart of the place.

Amazed at this answer, "How is it possible," said I, "that a land inhabited only by philosophers should appear rather like the haunts of savage beasts than like a cultivated country?"

He returned that in a little time things would have a better face, as soon as ever the natives could get time to think upon such trifles. "At this present," says he, "we are all solely intent upon an extraordinary discovery, no less than that of a passage to the sun; that therefore it was very excusable to leave the soil to itself, it being impossible to do two things at once."

I presently understood the drift of this cunning countryman's discourse and pursuing my journey, I at last arrived at the metropolitan city Caska. In and about the gates instead of guards and sentinels I saw only a few tame fowl, and upon the walls heaps of birds' nests and cobwebs. Philosophers and swine indifferently walked the streets, nor was the one distinguished from the other but by shape, being otherwise perfectly alike in dirt and nastiness. The philosophers had all cloaks of the same form, but what the colour was I could not discern for the dust upon them.

There was one quite buried in thought coming directly towards me; and meeting him, "Pray, sir," says I, "what may be the name of this city?"

At this he paused, and for a time continued as immovable as if he had no life in him; at last, says he, turning his eyes upwards, " 'Tis almost noon."

An answer so foreign to the purpose was a demonstration of great absence of mind, and convinced me that it was better to study sparingly than to run mad with too much learning.

I proceeded directly to the center of the city to see if beside philosophers I could have the good luck to meet with a reasonable creature. The Forum of the city, which was very spacious, was adorned with statues and columns. I was endeavouring to read the inscription upon one of them, and being thus employed, suddenly I felt my back grow warm and moist. Turning my head to see from whence this warm shower proceeded, I saw a philosopher making water against me. For being buried in profound thought, he had taken me for one of the statues there that are used for necessities of this kind.

Stung to the soul with such an affront, especially as the philosopher instead of apologizing for the mistake only laughed in my face, I gave him a smart box on the ear. Enraged at this, he fell upon me, seized me by the hair, and dragged me round the Forum. But when I found there was no prospect of appeasing his wrath, I endeavoured to make reprisals upon him with all my might and vigour; and I believe, with regard to our blows, the receipts and disbursements might be pretty equal on both sides. At length, after a long contest, we both fell upon the ground. At this spectacle, a crowd of philosophers flocked from all parts and with inexpressible fury fell upon me with their fists and sticks, and then once more dragged me by the hair all round the market; insomuch that I was just upon the point of giving up the ghost.

At last, rather tired than satiated, they left off beating me and brought me to a spacious house, where when I struggled against the door with both my feet and vowed I would not enter, Messieurs the philosophers threw a rope round my neck, and tugging me in like a squealing pig, they felled me flat upon the floor. The house and all things in it were in the utmost confusion, and not unlike the disorder people are in at Lady Day or Michaelmas, when they are moving house. I then humbly entreated these wise men to put an end to their resentment and suffer themselves to be moved to pity and compassion, representing to them how little for the honour of philosophy it was to abandon themselves to a blind rage, and give a loose to those very passions they are the forwardest to declaim against. But I preached to the winds. For that very philosopher who had so plentifully watered my back forthwith renewed the fight and redoubled his blows upon me, like a smith upon an anvil, as if nothing but my death could stop his fury. This plainly taught me that no anger equals a philosophical anger and that they who can talk so well upon the beauty of virtue care to practice it as little as any.

At length there came in four philosophers, the form of whose robes spoke them of a singular order. They presently appeased the uproar and seemed to commiserate my fate, and after they had conferred apart, they removed me to another house. Glad was I that I had escaped these barbarians, and at last fallen into honest hands. They inquired the cause of all this tumult, and I told them every tittle. They smiled at so pleasant an accident, telling me that it was a common thing for the philosophers to make water against the statues, and that probably my antagonist, wholly absorbed in meditation, had mistaken me for a statue. They informed me likewise that that person was an astronomer of great eminence, and that my other persecutors were professors of moral philosophy. I could now hear all this with pleasure, believing myself entirely out of danger.

Yet one thing alarmed me mightily, and that was the great attention with which they surveyed my form. Besides, their reiterated questions concerning my manner of life, my country, and the cause of my journey, together with the whispers that ensued, gave me a violent jealousy. But good God! what horror invaded my soul when they conducted me into an antomy chamber, where there was a frightful heap of bones and carcasses upon the floor that gave a stench enough to poison me. I thought I was fallen into a den of thieves and murderers but the anatomical instruments which hung upon the walls took away that fear and convinced me that my host must be a physician or a surgeon.

Half an hour was I left alone in this place, when a matron enters with my dinner. She seemed very humane, and eyeing me attentively, she would every now and then fetch a deep sigh. Upon my inquiring the cause of her grief, she replied that my impending fate drew those sighs from her; that I was indeed fallen into very honest hands, "for my husband," continues she, "who inhabits this house, is public physician of the city and Professor of Medicine; and the others you saw are his colleagues. But astonished at the extraordinary make of your body, they have determined to examine the inward machinery of it, and to make a dissection of you, in order to add some new light to anatomy."

96

This account threw me into a most violent palpitation, and setting up a horrible cry, "Oh! how! madam," said I, "can you call them honest men who make no scruple to rip up the bowels of an innocent person?"

To which she answered: "I say again you are fallen into the hands of honest men, who will do nothing with a bad design, and have resolved upon this operation for the sole illustration of the science of anatomy."

"Alas!" said I, "I had rather fall into the hands of thieves and murderers, from whom I might possibly make my escape, than be dissected by such very honest gentlemen." And immediately throwing myself at her feet, shedding at the same time a flood of tears, I implored her to intercede for my life.

She told me her intercession would avail very little against the resolution of the Faculty, which was irrevocable; but however, that she would deliver me from death by some other means.

With these words she took me by the hand, and leading me through a back door, brought me as far as to the gate of the city. Being now ready to take my leave of my preserver, I endeavoured to express my gratitude in the best language I was master of; but she presently interrupted me, and telling me she would not leave me till she saw me out of all danger, she continued to accompany me. As we walked together, we entered into various conversations concerning the state of the country, and I heard her with the utmost avidity. But at length she made a digression to a circumstance not very agreeable to my ears, and I conjectured that for her services she required some things of me which were morally impossible. For she told me with the greatest concern that in this country the fate of married ladies was extremely hard, for that their philosophic husbands, immersed in learning, neglected conjugal duties.

"For my part, I protest," says she, with an oath, "we should all be very wretched, if now and then a good-natured, compassionate stranger did not administer comfort to us in our misfortunes, and occasionally apply a remedy to them."

I pretended not to understand this harangue, and mended my pace. But this coldness served only to enflame her. Whereupon *she became violently enraged, and stretching out her hands, with streaming hair and mad with passion,*[6] she reproached me with ingratitude. I nevertheless continued my pace till at last she laid hands upon my clothes and endeavoured to stop me. With that I forcibly started from her, and having vastly the advantage of her in swiftness, I quickly got out of her sight. One may judge of the extremity of the rage she was in by the words I could hear her pronounce, namely, *kaki spalaki*, that is, "ungrateful dog." I digested this affront with a Spartan nobleness of mind, and was glad at my heart that I could any way escape from this land of philosophers, the bare remembrance of which fills me with horror.

The next province I arrived at was that of Nakir, the capital of which is a fine, large city of the same name. I cannot say much of this place, because I passed with the utmost haste through the countries adjoining to that I lately left, and longed to be among people less philosophically, and especially less anatomically given. For such a terror had seized me that I could not help asking everyone I met whether he were a philosopher; and even in my dreams, the carcasses and instruments of dissection still swam before me.

The natives of Nakir were very courteous, for everyone I met offered me his service unasked, with long attestations of his honour and honesty. I thought this very ridiculous, since I suspected none of them, nor called their integrity in question. I expressed my wonder at these compliments, and observed that I could not conceive to what purpose they were made; at which they only renewed their protestations of service with a thousand oaths.

Leaving this place, I overtook a traveller bending beneath the weight of his burden. Seeing me, he stopped and inquired whence I came. When I told him I had passed through the province of Nakir, he congratulated me upon my escape, assuring me that the inhabitants were a people famous for their skill in tricking, and hardly a traveller passed, but was their prey. I answered if their actions at all corresponded with their words, they must be people of the greatest honour, of which every one boasted extremely, and assured me of it with a multitude of execrations. The stranger smiling at these words, "Take care," says he, "of those who trumpet their own virtues, and especially of those who readily send themselves to the devil to convince you." That piece of advice I buried deep in my mind, and I have since experienced that my adviser had reason.

I now arrived at a lake, the waters of which were of a yellowish colour. On the bank there was a vessel of three ranks of oars, in which passengers, for a small consideration, were ferried over into the Land of Reason. Having agreed for my passage, I went aboard, and with the highest pleasure imaginable began my voyage, inasmuch as I presently observed that these Subterranean vessels are impelled by secret springs and machines which cleave the waters with an astonishing rapidity, and all without the agency of rowers. Being landed on the other side of the lake, I hired one of the guides which ply in the several ports, and under his conduct I travelled on. In the meantime my guide told me everything that related to the government of the city and the manners of the people. I understood from him that they were all logicians to a man, and that this city was the true seat of reason, from whence it had its name. And upon my arrival I found all he had told me was true. Every citizen, from his great penetration and the composedness of his manners, had the appearance of a judge. I could not forbear lifting my hands to heaven and crying out, "Oh! infinitely happy country, where every member is a Cato."

But when I had more accurately examined the condition of the city, I observed that business went but dully on, and that the republic in a manner languished for want of fools. For as their good sense weighs everything in the justest balance, and as not a soul can be cajoled by specious promises and studied words, it follows that all those prudent means and methods by which the minds of subjects are excited to the best and noblest actions, and that too at the cheapest and easiest rate, must here lose all their efficacy. In short, the bad effects of such an exact knowledge of things were explained to me and pathetically lamented by the Superintendent of the Treasury.

"One tree," says he, "is here distinguished from another by nothing else but his name and the make of his body. No emulation among the subjects, since marks of distinction are thought not worth acquiring, and nobody is wise because everybody is so. Folly, I confess, is a defect, but to have it wholly banished may not be so desirable. Let every state, indeed, have a competent number of wise men for the public employments. Some must govern, and some must submit to be governed. What other states effect by the most trifling inducements, our magistrates can procure only by solid rewards, which often drain the treasury. Wise men require the kernel if they serve their country, but fools are put off with the shell. Thus, for instance, the distribution of honours and titles, with which fools are taken as with a hook and spirited up to the most hazardous enterprises, can be of little force among a people who know that solid fame and honour are to be acquired only by inward worth and virtue. A people of this stamp are not to be deceived with specious sounds. Your soldiers, I think I have heard you say, are animated to undergo the utmost severities from the hope of an immortal name in history. This is what our people cannot conceive. They think that this mode of speech, for instance, 'Dying in earnest, and living in a history,' is the veriest jargon in the world, and that it is mere dotage to proclaim aloud the praises of one who can not hear nor understand them. I pass over numberless inconveniences which flow only from our exquisite knowledge and which prove to demonstrate that at least half the members of every civil establishment ought to be fools. Folly is to society what fermentation is to the stomach; too much, or none at all, are alike injurious."

I heard all this with the greatest amazement. But when in the name of the Senate he offered me the freedom of the city, and repeated his entreaties that I would fix my abode here, I could not forbear blushing from a suspicion that his request proceeded from a preconceived opinion of my foolishness, and that he took me for such a sort of ferment as might be of use to a state labouring under the misfortune of too much wisdom. I was confirmed in this suspicion when I heard the Senate had decreed to send a colony abroad, and in their places to take in an equal number of fools from the neighbouring nations. And so with a sort of resentment, I left this race of reasoners. Yet for a long time I could not help reflecting upon that Subterranean axiom of theirs, unknown to the politicians of our world, namely, that in a well-constituted society, it is necessary that at least half the members should be fools. I wondered so salutary a maxim should remain undiscovered by the worthy spirits of our age. But possibly it might be known to some who were however unwilling to have it inserted in the class of political truths, since with us there are great plenty of fools, nor is there (Envy apart!) a village or city with us but what is handsomely stored with this goodly ferment.

Having rested some time, I renewed my travels and visited several countries which I pass over in silence as having nothing remarkable in them. I supposed I had now seen all the marvelous things in the planet Nazar. But arriving at the province of Cabac, fresh wonders offer themselves, and even such as exceed the bounds of credibility. Among the natives of this region, some are born without heads. They speak by a mouth placed in the middle of the breast. Upon account of this great defect in nature they are exempted from all such difficult employments as require the least headpiece. The only posts they are admitted to are chiefly those about the court. Thus the Chamberlain, the Master of the Ceremonies, the President of the Seraglio, and the like are all taken from the class of people that are without heads [From the same class are also elected beadles, sacristans, grave diggers, and others whose business can easily be performed without the assistance of many brains.][7]

Nevertheless some that have no heads are, by the special indulgence of the government, received into the Senate for some merit of their ancestors and that without much detriment to the republic. For experience tells us that the whole authority of the Senate is lodged in the hands of a few leading members, and that the rest only help to fill up the number and to assent and subscribe to the resolutions of others. And in my time there were in the Senate two that were born without heads who nevertheless enjoyed the senatorial stipends. For though they were destitute of sense by reason of that defect of nature, yet surely they might give their vote with others, happier in one thing than their colleagues, namely, that nobody was angry with those who had no heads, but vented all their rage against the others. And hence it is evident that it is safer sometimes to be born without a head. This city may vie with any in magnificence and splendour. It has a court, a university, and several noble temples.

Cambara and Spelek are the two next provinces. The natives are all limes. But in this they differ, that the former seldom live beyond the age of four years, whereas the others seldom fall short of four hundred. Here you might see fathers, grandfathers, great-grandfathers, and so on; they would tell you old stories and adventures of their own that happened ages ago, and by their lively representations make you think you were almost present at them. As much as I pitied the first, I envied the last. But after I had more inly examined the state of both, I found my error.

In Cambara everyone within a few months after their nativity arrived to their full maturity of body and mind. One year was enough to form and perfect them; in the rest they prepared for death. Not Plato's self could have imagined a more charming republic; here all the virtues flourished to perfection. Being hourly convinced of the shortness of life, they are always ready for death and regard this life only as a passage to a better. We may imagine every one of them a philosopher who, with a happy indifference to his present state, aims only at securing that solid and durable pleasure which is the reward of virtue and piety. In a word, this seemed to be the abode of angels, the kingdom of saints, and the truest school of wisdom and virtue. Hence one may judge how unjust their murmurs are who complain of the brevity of life, making it the foundation of a quarrel at their Maker. Our life is short because we lose the greatest part in sloth and pleasure; it would be long enough if our time were better employed.

But in the other region, where life is lengthened to four hundred years, I discovered all the vices under heaven. The present state of things they look upon as eternal and immortal, [and as if it would never decline; and therefore uprightness, integrity, honesty, chastity, and decency are fled, and have given place to falsehood, deceit, extravagance, luxury, and immorality.][8] There was also another inconvenience resulting from long life. Those who had unhappily lost their estate or fortunes, those who were maimed in their limbs or were fallen into incurable diseases made the most piercing complaints, and knowing no end to their miseries, often laid violent hands on themselves. The shortness of life, therefore, is to the wretched the best of remedies. Both these countries afforded me matter of much admiration, and upon my departure filled me with very philosophical reflections.

I pursued my journey through certain desert and rocky places which lead to Spalank, or the Country of Innocence. This place is so called from the innocence and peaceful humour of the natives. These are all beeches, and esteemed the happiest of the whole creation. They are subject to no passions and affections, and consequently free from all vices.

Upon my arrival I found all I had heard was true, and that actually they were governed not by laws, but by their own innate virtue and disposition. Envy, anger, hatred, pride, vainglory, discord, and all which among mankind bears the name of vice is here proscribed and banished. But with the vices there were also many things wanting which adorn the human species and seem to distinguish them from brutes. Except divinity, natural philosophy, and astronomy, all the arts and sciences were wholly unknown. They had not the least idea of law, politics, history, ethics, and eloquence, the very names of which were never heard of. As there was not the least spark of envy, so there was no emulation to excite and animate the soul to worthy deeds. There were no splendid edifices, no palace, no Senate House, no Forum, no magistrate, no riches, and consequently no desire of them or contention about them. In two words, if they had no vices, they had no politeness, art, or elegance, nor any of those things which, though in reality no virtues, are yet extremely like virtues and render men civilized and social. To say the truth, I seemed here to be rather in a forest of real trees than in a rational society. I stood a long time in doubt what judgment to form of these people, and whether such a state were in reality desirable. At length reflecting that an uncultivated creature was however better than a vicious creature and that, though they had no arts, they had also no thefts, murders, and other atrocious crimes which destroy both body and soul, I could not help pronouncing them happy.

Walking carelessly along one day while I was among them, I struck my left leg against a stone. It swelled violently and gave me excessive pain. An honest countryman, seeing this accident, presently ran to me and with a certain herb he held in his hand and applied to the wound, the anguish forthwith abated and the swelling decreased. These people, thought I, must have extraordinary skill in the art of healing. Nor was my conjecture wrong. For since their studies were confined within so narrow a compass, they were not contented with the outward rind of knowledge like our modern connoisseurs, but went to the bottom of things.

When I thanked my benefactor for his services and told him that God would be his reward, he answered me in so solid, so learned, and so devout a manner, though in terms perfectly simple and rural, that I had really some apprehensions it was an angel in the shape of a tree. It appears hence with what little reason we dislike that calm philosophy of some men who neither wish nor grieve, are neither angry nor pleased, who divest themselves of all the impetuous passions of the soul, and whom we therefore accuse of leading a life of indolence and softness. It appears also how much mistaken they are who are advocates for the necessity of vices among men, who style anger the whetstone of courage, emulation the spur of industry, and distrust the parent of discretion. For who does not know that from ill eggs ill birds are hatched, and that many virtues which mortals pride themselves in, and which are celebrated in verse, are rather the disgrace than ornament of humanity if beheld with a philosophical eye.

I left this place and arrived at Kiliac, where the inhabitants are born with certain marks impressed upon their forehead signifying the exact number of years they have to live. These surely

I thought must be the most fortunate people under the sun, since an unexpected death could surprise none of them in a sinful action. But then, as their last day of life was known to everyone, they deferred their repentance to the last; insomuch that if you found one among them sincerely devout and honest, it was one whom the marks upon his forehead directed to think of his quietus. Some I observed who walked with their heads hanging down; they had almost lived out their time and were counting the remainder of their days and hours upon their fingers, expecting with horror their last approaching moment. This gave me to see the general wisdom of the Creator in concealing from mortals the time of their death.

Having travelled over this country, I came to a strait, the water of which was black; and being ferried over, I landed upon the province of Askarac. Here new monsters met my eyes. As Cabac produces animals without a head, some among these people are born with seven heads. To these, as being possessed of an amazing knowledge, the citizens formerly paid almost divine honours; and out of their tribes alone commanders, consuls, senators, and other great officers were elected. But, alas! as many heads as they had, so many different geniuses they had. They confidently and readily undertook to discharge various employments at one and the same time, and left nothing unattempted while they held the reins of power. But from that multiplicity of business and from their various ideas interfering and jostling with each other, they made wretched work of it; and in process of time so great was the confusion that it required the labour of an age to recover from the disorder these omniscient magistrates had thrown things into. Hence a law was enacted to exclude forever these seven-headed trees from all public offices of importance, and that the government should hereafter be entrusted to "simple heads," that is to say, those who have only one head. Ever since those very people who had been revered as gods have been sinking into the same contempt as the headless inhabitants of Cabac. For as they who had no head at all could do nothing, so these with many heads did everything perversely. But though they are forever removed from all state trusts, yet they serve as an ornament to the kingdom. They are carried about like public spectacles to show the world how liberal nature has been in their formation. Though to say the truth had she been less lavish of her favours she had been in reality much kinder. Of all this race there were only three in my time in employment, to which, however, they not admitted till they had consented to an amputation of six of their heads. After this, the confused ideas they laboured under vanished, and they were brought to common sense. Thus men prune trees of their superfluous branches to derive more health and vigour to the rest. Very few undergo this operation upon account of the extreme pain and danger. From hence I drew this useful maxim, that all excess is hurtful and that simplicity is true wisdom.

From hence I passed to the principality of Bostanki, a people as to their outward make little different from the Potuans; but as to the inward they have this singularity, that their heart is situated in their thigh, so that it may be truly said of them that they carry their hearts in their breeches. Hence, among all the inhabitants of this globe these are accounted the most fearful and pusillanimous.

Upon my arrival, I entered into an inn near the gate, and as the fatigue of travelling had made me something weary and fretful, I rattled my host for being slow in his attendance. But he, falling on his knees, implored for mercy, and extending his thigh for me to feel the great palpitation of heart he was in, from storming I fell to laughing, and bid him dry his tears, and cast away all fear. He rose, and in a transport kissed my hand, and set about supper immediately. In a minute or two the whole kitchen resounded with cries and lamentations. I ran thither, and to my vast astonishment there did I behold my very fearful host beating and whipping his wife and the maids about. Seeing me, he took to his heels and ran away. I turned to the weeping family and begged to know what crime they had committed to provoke so meek a man to so great rage. They on the other hand stood mute with their eyes fastened to the ground, not daring to tell the cause of their affliction. But upon my persisting to inquire, and adding threats to my entreaty, the mistress spoke to me in this manner: "You seem, sir, to be a great stranger to the manners of the world. The natives of this principality can't bear the sight of an armed enemy, and out of their own houses tremble at the least noise; yet they all domineer in the kitchen, they exert their bravery on their defenseless family, and are only then valiant when no resistance can be made. On this account they are the jest as well as the prey of the neighbouring states. But in the bordering kingdom, to which we are tributaries, the case is otherwise. There they never fight but against an armed enemy. There the males command abroad, and serve at home."

I admired the wisdom of the hostess, whom I looked upon as worthy of a better condition. And, indeed, upon a closer inspection into the nature and disposition of people, this matron, it must be owned, was extremely in the right, since from innumerable examples it is clear that Hercules is not the only one who has yielded to a distaff, but that it is the common fate of brave and warlike men to submit, with all due patience, to the female yoke; and that on the other hand the veriest cowards in all nature, who like the Bostankians carry their hearts in their breeches, are yet heroes in the kitchen. This people live under the protection of a neighbouring kingdom to whom they pay tribute for it.

From hence I passed by water to Mikolac. Coming out of the boat, I missed my cloak-bag. I presently charged the boatman with the theft, who stiffly denied it. Upon this I went and complained to the magistrate, telling him that if I had not the liberty of bringing an action against the boatman for breach of trust or theft, I hoped he would at least compel him to make simple restitution. But my adversary not only persisted in denying the fact, but threatened me with an action of slander. In a case so doubtful the court called for witnesses. But as I could bring none, I desired my antagonist might purge himself by oath. At this the judge smiled, and spoke as follows. "My friend," says he, "in this province we are bound by no religion, nor have we any other gods beside the laws of our country. Accusations here must be made good by legal methods, such as proving the delivery, estimating the value, exhibiting receipts, and producing witnesses. Whoever is destitute of these not only loses his cause, but is liable to be sued for calumny. Make the case plain by proper evidence, and what you have lost shall be restored to you."

Thus losing my cause for want of witnesses, I not only lamented my own misfortune but that of the republic itself. For from hence it appeared, what a weak unsettled society that must be which depends for its security upon human laws alone, and how frail are all political edifices unless cemented together by religion. I stayed three days here in continual fears. For though the laws of the country are in reality very good and though crimes are punished with the utmost severity, yet no safety can be reasonably expected in a country too atheistical to have the least sense of religious obligation and where they scruple the commission of no crimes, provided they can but conceal them.

From this land of atheists, I travelled on over a steep mountain to the city of Bracmat, which was situated in the plain at the foot of the mountain. The inhabitants are junipers. The first person I met came directly rushing at me and threw me backwards. I did not well understand this, and asking the reason of it, the juniper begged my pardon a thousand times. Presently after, another with a staff he had in his hand gave me a blow upon the reins that almost took away my senses. But in the same moment he made a long harangue to me in excuse of his imprudence. Suspecting, therefore, this people to be either totally blind or very weak-sighted, I took care to avoid everyone I met. In fact, all this arose from the exquisite sense of sight which some are here endowed with. They can clearly discern remote objects, which are impenetrable to vulgar eyes, but then they do not see what is nearer and almost at hand. These are called Makkatti, and they devote themselves principally to the studies of metaphysics and astronomy. They are of very little service in the world by reason of their too delicate vision. They make very pretty "minute philosophers," but in solid matters and things of daily use, they commit innumerable blunders. However, the government makes some use of them, and sends them to the mines for the discovery of metals. For though they see scarce anything upon the surface of the earth, their sight exerts itself upon anything beneath it. I concluded from hence that there are some who are blind from too great a delicacy in the organs of vision and that they would see better if their eyes were worse.

Having gained the top of another very steep and rocky mountain, I now entered the province of Mutak, the capital of which looked like a grove of willows, the inhabitants being all of that species. Proceeding to the market, I there found a robust, healthy young man, sitting in a place of ease (of which there are many round the market place), and imploring the mercy of the Senate. I inquired the meaning of this and was informed that the said person was a criminal to whom they were going to give the fifteenth dose. Surprised at the answer, I stepped aside and desired my host to explain this riddle. He replied thus: "Most nations punish crimes by whipping, branding, hanging, and the like; but nothing of that kind obtains in this country. For we study not so much to punish crimes as to mend the criminal. The culprit upon the seat is a wretched author who, for his violent itch of writing, which neither law nor advice could restrain, has been condemned by the Senate to the public punishment. This is left to the Censors of the city, who are all doctors of physic and who are now going to macerate and bring him low by frequent purgings till they have conquered and extinguished the lust of scribbling."

He ended his discourse with desiring me to go to the shop of a public apothecary. I went with him accordingly, and to my vast amazement beheld phials and gallipots all properly arranged, with such inscriptions as these: "Powder of Avarice." "Pills for Lust." "Tincture against Cruelty." "Lenitive of Ambition." "Cortex against Pleasure," etc. Words cannot express the strange confusion of mind this odd spectacle threw me into. But a perfect ecstasy of surprise ensued when I observed a parcel of manuscripts with these titles: "Sermons of Master Pisagus, a Morning's Perusal of Which Gives Six Stools." "Meditations of Dr. Jukes, a Specific in the Coma Vigil, or Want of Sleep," etc. I thought the people out of their senses, and to examine more accurately the virtue of their medicines, I opened the first of these books. It was such insipid stuff, that at the first chapter I began to make faces; and reading on I found my bowels rumble, and soon after had a tenesmus. But as I knew I had no occasion for purging I threw the book down and ran away.

I then observed that nothing in the whole world was without its use and that the most pitiful performances were serviceable for something. I found also that this people were no fools, however absurd I at first took them to be. My host averred to me that he was cured of lying awake from only perusing Doctor Jukes's book, the virtue of which was so profound and potent that Vigilance itself must snore at it. These things occasioned in me a tumultuous variety of thought. And lest they should break in upon that chain of philosophical reflections I had heretofore made, I resolved soon to leave the country. And happily

111

enough the strange things I soon saw in other provinces jostled out almost all thoughts of this place. But notwithstanding, after I had finished my tour round this globe and was reflecting upon the Mutakian philosophy, their manner of curing disorders was not altogether so absurd. For I am convinced that in our Europe there are some books that would purge the most costive, or give sleep to the most wakeful. As to the disorders of the mind, I own I could not subscribe to the Mutakian principles in this point, though it must be confessed there are some infirmities of body which we confound with the disorders of the mind.

I departed from Mutak, and crossing over a lake of a yellow hue I arrived at Mikrok, and proceeding to the capital city I found the gate shut. I was obliged to wait till the drowsy sentinel was pleased to open it, which was some considerable time, it being secured with a multitude of locks, bolts, and bars. Entering, I observed a deep silence reign throughout the whole city, except that my ears were now and then assaulted by a noise as of people snoring. I could not help fancying I was got into the region of sleep, as the poets talk. Would to God, says I to myself, that several of the magistrates, senators, and a few other honest countrymen of mine who are dear lovers of peace had had the luck to be born in this blessed city! How sweetly and quietly would they live! And yet from the signs in the streets, and inscriptions on the houses, it was evident that arts and sciences were not unknown here and that laws were exercised.

Led by these signs I found out an inn. No entrance to be had. The doors were all fast. And though it was noon with the rest of the world, it should seem it was night to the inhabitants of this city. At last, after having knocked and bounced a long while, I was let in. Time is here divided into twenty-three hours; nineteen of them are sacred to sleep, the other four to business. Suspecting, therefore, these people to be monstrously negligent both in their public and private affairs, I desired something to be brought me to eat which they had ready in the house, fearing if I had ordered anything to be dressed the cook should fall asleep while it was about. But all things are here done in the concisest and most compendious manner; everything superfluous is omitted; and therefore this diminutive day of theirs is long enough for all sorts of business.

After dinner, which was brought upon table with a surprising expedition, my host waited on me round the city. We went into a temple where we heard a discourse, short indeed with respect to the time, but long enough considering its importance. The preacher went directly to his subject. He used no flourishes, no tautologies, nor said one superfluous thing. So that when I compare this discourse with the long nauseous ones of Master Peter, the former is in reality more copious than the latter. With the same brevity proceedings in law are dispatched. The advocates say all in few words, and then produce their witnesses. I remember to have seen a copy of a treaty of alliance between this and a neighbouring kingdom. It was couched in these terms: "Let there be perpetual friendship between the Mikrokians and Splendikanians. Let the limits of the two kingdoms be the River Klimac, and the top of Mount Zabor. Signed," etc. Thus in three lines they express what with us would require a volume. Hence I am persuaded one may come to the point with less noise and less loss of time if superfluities were to be retrenched; as a traveller would find his journey half as short again were he always to go directly straight. The natives here are cypresses, and are distinguished from other trees by wens in their forehead, which wens have a stated increase and decrease. When they increase, a certain humour distills from them, which falling upon the eyes brings on a drowsiness and is an indication of the approaching night.

From hence to Makrok is one day's journey. Here the inhabitants never sleep. Entering into the city, I stopped a person, though he seemed to be in haste, and begged he would be pleased to direct me to a good inn. He replied he was very busy, and made the best of his way forward. So great was the general hurry of this place that they seemed not to walk through the streets, but to run or fly as if they were afraid of being too late. The least I could think was that some part of the city was on fire or that some other sudden and unlooked-for disaster had frightened the citizens out of their senses. At last I cast my eyes upon a sign before a house which signified it was an inn. Here some were entering, others departing, others stumbling for haste, insomuch that I was a quarter of an hour bustling in the yard before I could gain admittance.

In a moment I was asked a multitude of impertinent questions. One said, "Where do you come from? Where are you going to? How long do you stay here?" Another said, "Will you dine alone, or with company? If the latter, what room will you dine in, the red, the green, the white, or the black room? Or will you dine above stairs, or below?" with a thousand impertinences of this kind. My host, who was a clerk of one of the inferior courts of justice here, went away to dinner but soon returned, and then gave me a long tedious account of a lawsuit that had been depending these ten years, the hearing of which was now coming on before the fourteenth court. He told me he hoped it would be ended within two years, since there were but two courts remaining, beyond which there was no appeal. He left me in great astonishment, and convinced me that this nation was extremely busy in doing nothing.

When my landlord was gone, I walked about the house, and by chance dropped upon a library. It was large and well-stocked with respect to the number of books, but a very indifferent one with respect to the contents. Among those books which to appearance were in best condition, I observed the following:

1. Description of the Cathedral   24 vols.

2. Relation of the Siege of Pehunc   36 vols.
3. Of the Use of the Herb Slac   13 vols.
4. Funeral Oration upon the
    Death of Senator Jaksi   18 vols.

My landlord at his return to me entertained me with a description of the state of the city; and from what he said I concluded that more business was transacted by the sleepy Mikrokians than by the waking Makrokians; that these played with the shell while the others ate the kernel. The people here too are all cypresses, and as to the outward make of their bodies differ very little from the Mikrokians excepting the wens upon their foreheads. They have not the same blood or juice in their bodies which other trees of this globe have, but instead of blood they have a thicker juice in their veins which is of a mercurial quality and appearance. Nay, some think it is quicksilver itself, inasmuch as in a barometer it is found to have the same effect.

At the distance of about two days' journey from hence lies the republic of Siklok, which is divided into two societies in alliance with each other but governed by different and opposite laws. The first is called Miho, founded by Mihac, a famous lawgiver of old, and the Lycurgus of the Subterraneans. In order to render his republic stronger and more lasting, he made sumptuary laws which forbid all luxury on the severest penalties. And accordingly this society for its great continence and parsimony may be justly called another Sparta. One thing I wondered at, and that was that in a government so well-constituted and which piqued itself upon the excellence of its laws there should be so many beggars. For wherever I turned my eyes, there was a tree begging an alms, which is a very troublesome thing to travellers. Upon a nice inspection into the state of the republic, I was convinced that these miseries flowed from the too great economy of the people. For all luxury being proscribed, and the rich baulking their genius and giving into no indulgences, the common

115

people of course must lead an indolent, idle, and beggarly life for want of matter to make a proper gain of. I concluded from hence that rigid parsimony in a state produces the same inconveniences as an obstruction of the blood in a human body.

In the other province, that of Liho, they live splendidly and jovially, and spare no expense. Here arts and professions flourish; the people are encouraged to industry, and every citizen has an opportunity to raise a fortune. Whoever is poor among them may fairly impute it to his own negligence. Thus the profusion of the rich gives life to the body politic, as the circulation of the blood in the human body gives strength and vigour to the limbs.

The territory of Lama borders upon this. Here is the celebrated school of physicians. With so much ardour is the study of physic here pursued that none are looked upon as genuine doctors unless they come from the illustrious school of Lama. And hence this city is crowded with so many doctors that you see more of them than of all other sorts of people put together. Whole streets are filled with shops of apothecaries and anatomical instrument-makers. Loitering about the city, I met a tree offering to sale the bills of mortality for the year last past. I bought one of them, and to my great surprise found the births and burials stand thus: born, one hundred and fifty; buried, six hundred. I could not conceive that in a place where Apollo himself seemed to have fixed his residence there should be such a yearly havoc among the citizens. I asked the tree what unusual plague or pestilence had raged in the city the last year. He replied that two years ago the number of the deceased was greater, that this was the common proportion between the births and burials, and that the inhabitants of Lama were perpetually afflicted with distempers which hastened their deaths; insomuch that in a short time the city would be empty if it were not supplied and recruited from the neighbouring provinces. Upon this I hurried out of the city, not thinking it prudent to stay longer here,

especially as the name of a physician and the sight of the anatomical instruments after what I had suffered in the country of
philosophers could not be very agreeable.

Therefore leaving this place, I never stopped till I came to
a town four miles distant where the people live without physicians and without diseases. In the space of two days, I arrived
at the land of Liberty. The people here are accountable to no
authority. They consist of separate families without being subject to any laws or power whatsoever. Yet an appearance of
society is preserved, and in public matters they consult the
seniors, who perpetually exhort them to peace and unanimity
and admonish them never to depart from that primary precept
of Nature, of doing to others as you would be done by. On all
the gates of the cities and villages a statue of Liberty is erected
trampling upon chains and fetters, with this inscription over the
head: GOLDEN LIBERTY. In the first city I entered all was quiet
enough; yet I observed some of the citizens distinguished themselves by certain ribbands which they wore and which, as I afterward understood, were marks and symbols of two factions which
then divided the people. The avenues and courtyards of the
houses of the great were lined with armed soldiers who always
held themselves in readiness, because the truce being about two
days ago expired, the war was upon breaking out afresh. I fled
away trembling as fast as I could, nor thought myself free till I
had conveyed myself out of sight of this land of Liberty.

The next province is Jochtana, of which I had heard a short
description which very much alarmed me and led me to think
it must be the seat of disorder, confusion, and insecurity. For this
country was the sink and receptacle of all religions. All the
several principles and doctrines which prevail in any part of this
globe retire here as to their center, and are taught publicly. Recollecting, therefore, what troubles had been excited in Europe
by religious differences, I was almost afraid to approach the

117

capital city, the several streets and portions of which have all churches and temples for different and opposite sects.

But my fears soon vanished when I observed a profound agreement and concord reign in every part. With respect to their politics, there was the same face, the same sentiments, the same tranquillity, and the same care in all. For as the laws made it capital for one member of the state to disturb another in his way of worship or to molest him upon account of any religious difference, hence whatever dissensions they had were without the least appearance of hostility, their disputes were without bitterness or invectives, and they had no aversions, because they had no persecutions. There was a perpetual but very honest and worthy emulation among the several sects, every one of which endeavoured to demonstrate the excellence of their religion by the purity of their life and morals. Thus by the wisdom of the magistrate all these different sentiments excited no more troubles in the state than did the different shops of the artists and merchants in the Forum, where the buyers are invited by the sole goodness of the commodity and where they use neither fraud, force, nor disparagement. By these means the least seed of discord is stifled in the birth, and that sort of emulation only encouraged which is honourable in itself and advantageous to the state. This convinced me that the religious troubles which reign in many places arise not from the variety of religions, but from persecution alone.

A sensible and learned Jochtanian explained to me more at large the genius of this government and the causes of its tranquillity. I heard him with rapture, and his observations I shall keep engraved on the table of my heart. I did indeed for some time make replies and objections to him, but was at last forced to own myself vanquished since he irresistibly proved all his points by arguments drawn from experience. Ashamed, therefore, to contradict my senses and give the lie to positive matter of fact,

I was forced to own that liberty of belief was the true fountain of this tranquillity and concord.

However, once more I attacked my adversary with an argument different from all I had used. I told him it was the duty of a lawgiver in erecting a government to regard the future, rather than the present happiness of mortals, and that he should conform his scheme not so much to their palate as to the laws of God.

To this he replied in this manner: "My good friend," says he, "you are greatly deceived if you imagine that God, the fountain of truth, can be pleased with dissembled worship. In other nations where all are obliged by public authority to one certain rule of faith, what a door is opened for ignorance and hypocrisy! Few, or none, have the will or the courage to discover their true sentiments, and so they profess one thing and believe another. This makes the study of divinity a cold, lifeless thing, and begets a negligence in the discovery of truth. This also makes profane learning more cultivated, for the priests themselves, lest they should be branded with the title of heretics, relinquish the pursuit of sacred things and divert their studies to other subjects where their minds may range without danger and where their liberty is not fettered. The vulgar will still condemn all who depart from the reigning doctrines. But hypocrites and dissemblers must be hateful to God, to Whom a sincere though erroneous belief must be infinitely less displeasing than an orthodox but pretended faith."

Hearing this, I kept silence, unable to dispute the point any longer with so wise a people.

I had now been almost two months out upon my travels, when at last I arrived at Tumbac, a territory contiguous to the Potuan dominions. I thought myself now at home, my wearisome journey being almost finished. The inhabitants of this region are chiefly wild olives, extremely devout, and extremely censorious. In the

119

first inn I entered I waited two hours for my breakfast, knocking and calling for it almost all that time in vain. The reason of this delay was the unseasonable devotion of my host, who would not for the world put his hand to the least thing till he had finished his morning prayers. However, that breakfast was one of the dearest in all my travels, and I protest I never met with a landlord more devout or more unmerciful. Well! thought I to myself, this landlord had better have prayed less and been more honest. But I dissembled my resentment, well knowing how dangerous it is to provoke a saint.

The citizens here were all Catos, all censors of manners. They walked up and down the streets with pensive looks and folded arms, declaiming against the vanity of the times and condemning every innocent pleasure. Not a gesture, not a smile escaped their observation. And thus by their perpetual censures and envenomed zeal they passed for persons of eminent sanctity. For my part, as I was spent and exhausted with fatigues, I made no scruple of indulging in several innocent diversions. But I got a bad name by so doing, insomuch that every house I entered was like a court of justice where I was sure to be arraigned. Some, when they saw I was not at all moved by their rebukes and admonitions, shunned me like a plague or a contagion.

I forbear to say more upon the moroseness of this people; however, one circumstance I must not omit, because it gives you their exact character, and from this sample you may judge of the rest. A certain Tumbacian with whom I had been acquainted at Potu, being at an inn and seeing me go by, stepped out to me and pressed me to go in. I waited on him. As he had heard that I was far from being an enemy to pleasure, he gave me such a lecture and upbraided me with my life and morals in such terms that my hair stood on end and every joint of me shook. But while our Cato was discharging thus the artillery of his censures, the glass had passed very insensibly but very briskly from one to the other, till in short we both fell fairly fuddled on the floor and were carried off half dead. Having slept off this debauch and recovered my reason, I set myself to examine into the nature of these people's religion; and I made a fair discovery that their zeal flowed rather from some vicious humours, or a predominancy of the bilious juices, than from true piety. But I never communicated this to anyone, and left them without saying a word.

At last, after two complete months, I arrived at Potu, so extremely weary with such incessant exercise that my legs had scarce strength to support my body. It was on the tenth day of the month of Beeches that I entered this capital. I went forthwith to His Serene Highness and offered him my little historical collection, which he immediately ordered to be printed. (For it must be noted that the art of printing, of which the Europeans and Chinese boast themselves to be inventors, was of far greater antiquity among the Potuans.) The people in general were so pleased with this account of my travels that they were never weary of reading it. All day long they were running about the streets selling my journal, and crying as loud as they could, *A Journey Round the World,* by Skabba, the King's Messenger. Elated with this success, I gave a loose to my ambition and aspired to some employment of greater weight and dignity. But seeing my hopes not quickly answered, I preferred a new petition to the Prince, wherein extolling my late labours, I earnestly implored His Highness to vouchsafe me a proper recompense. The Prince, who was humanity in the abstract, was sensibly touched with my case, and graciously promised that he would have a due regard to me. He was as good as his word, but his whole favour terminated in the enlargement of my annual salary. I thought I had reason to expect a far better recompense, and therefore I could not rest contented with this.

But as I would not trouble His Highness any further, I opened my grief to the Chancellor. He heard me with his usual humanity and promised me all the good offices in his power, but at the same time admonished me to desist from so wild a petition and begged me to consider the measure of my abilities and the weakness of my judgment.

"Nature," says he, "has been but a stepmother to you, and has denied you those powers of the mind which are requisite for the more arduous offices of the State; and therefore you should not aim at what it is not possible for you to procure. Nay, the Prince himself, were he to comply with this weak request of yours, must suffer in his fame as a violator of the laws. Rest contented therefore with your condition and renounce a hope which Nature has made unreasonable." In conclusion, he owned I had some merit and particularly extolled my late performance. "But it is not," says he, "merit of this kind that paves the way to State preferment. 'Tis true you have drawn a very pretty picture of the world; but if for a performance of this kind we were to gratify you with the most honourable employments, why might not a painter for drawing a great likeness or a sculptor for exhibiting a statue in just proportion with as much reason expect to be made a senator? Merit should doubtless meet with a recompense, and rewards should be assigned to the deserving; but then they should be rewards of such a nature as that the commonwealth receive no detriment and suffer no ridicule."

These admonitions silenced me for a while. But as I could not bear to think of growing old in this vile employ, I resumed that desperate resolution which had lain dormant a long time of attempting a reformation in the State, by which project I might at one and the same time help forward the public good and my own too.

A little before I set out upon my late travels, I had closely studied the nature of this government to see if I could discover any defects, and at the same time what remedies were proper for them. Since that, in the province of Coklecu I had observed that the government there was in a tottering condition by reason of the admission of women to the management of public affairs, that sex, being naturally ambitious, still aiming to extend their power, nor ever resting till they have acquired a full and absolute authority. Hereupon I determined to bring in a bill to exclude that sex from the administration of public affairs. I flattered myself I should find multitudes to abet and espouse this point, since it was an easy matter to make it very clear and to show beyond contradiction the misfortunes that flow from this defect in the State, and the danger the male sex was in unless the wings of such an unnatural power were timely clipped. And if it should so happen that the abolition of this ancient custom should appear to some to be too hazardous an attempt, in such case I humbly offered that the female power should be at least restrained and abridged.

This scheme of mine had three ends in view. First, to remove an inconvenience the State laboured under. Secondly, by producing a specimen of my sagacity and judgment, I had hopes to mend my condition. And, thirdly, I thought by these means to revenge certain taunts and affronts I had received from many of the females of this country. I frankly confess that my own private interest and a desire of revenge were the *primum mobile* of this project. But then I artfully concealed these views, lest under a pretense of public good I should seem only to pursue my own, and so tread in the steps of other innovators whose schemes breathe nothing but the public good when it is evident to the dullest observer that their private interest is the spring that moves the whole machine.

And now, having dressed my project out to the best advantage and strengthened it by the most powerful reasons I could invent, I waited upon the Prince and humbly offered it to him. His Highness, who had always testified a great regard to me, was

123

thunderstruck at the boldness and folly of my undertaking, which he foreboded must end in my irreparable ruin. Wherefore he endeavoured to dissuade me from this mad attempt by the strongest entreaties. I, for my part, relying as well upon the utility of my project as upon the favour of the male sex (who I was in hopes would not desert the common cause), remained immovable to all His Highness said, nor could his repeated admonitions vanquish my obstinacy. In fine, according to the custom of the country I was brought to the Forum, and there, with my neck in a halter, I stood waiting the judgment of the Senate. That venerable body debated the matter and soon came to a resolution, which resolution was sent up to the Prince for his confirmation, and, being returned by him, was read aloud by a public officer. It ran thus:

> After due examination, we are of opinion as follows: That the project of Skabba, the King's Messenger, to exclude the female sex from public business, cannot take effect without the highest detriment to the commonwealth, since no less than half of the nation, which consists of the said sex, must look upon this innovation as a very great hardship, and their resentment may occasion infinite disorders. Moreover, we are of opinion that it is absurd and unjust entirely to exclude trees of the finest talents from public honours, especially as Nature, who does nothing in vain, can never be supposed to have given them all those noble advantages to no purpose. We are persuaded that, for the welfare of the State, regard ought to be had not to the name but the abilities of a person. And as a country may often labour under a want of able persons, we think it a great folly, by one act of Senate, to render one entire half of the nation incapable and unworthy of employment solely upon account of their birth. For these and divers other good reasons we are of opinion that the said Skabba, for this foolish and rash attempt, ought to be punished according to the custom of our ancestors.

The Prince was extremely concerned for my misfortune, but

as he never rescinded the decree of the Senate, he signed it with his own hand and affixed the royal seal to it, and commanded it to be made public, inserting however this mollifying clause, that as I was a foreigner, a native of a new and unknown world where forward geniuses are in great esteem, I should be exempted from capital punishment. But lest by a total remission of the sentence the laws should suffer an infringement, it was therefore thought fit to detain me in prison till the beginning of the month of Birches, and that then, with other violators of the law, I should be banished to the Firmament.

This sentence being published, I was clapped into prison. Some of my friends persuaded me to protest against this sentence, since among my judges there were so many matrons and virgins, all judges in their own cause. Some advised me, as the safer way, to make a fair acknowledgment of my crime and lay the blame upon my own native human weakness. But this last advice I rejected with great constancy, out of respect to mankind, upon whose character such a confession would leave an indelible blemish.

I heard soon after that His Highness had determined to give me an absolute pardon if I would but only prostrate myself at his feet, confess my fault, and implore his favour, although Rahagna the Treasurer opposed that motion with might and main. But, to speak the truth, I was not displeased with the sentence. For death was not half so terrible to me as that employment they picked out for me; and I was weary of conversing longer with these trees, who had so high an opinion of their wisdom. I hoped also to meet with better treatment in the Firmament, where I had heard that all strangers, without distinction, were kindly received.

¹ Holberg's Latin version:

> "*Metiri se quemque suo modulo ac pede fas est.*
> *E coelo magnum descendit Nosce teipsum,*
> *Figendum ac memori tractandum pectore.*"

Horace, Epistle I, 7, 98, in Ludovicus Holbergius, *Nicolai Klimii Iter Subterraneum*, p. 91:

> "*Metiri se quemque suo modulo ac pede verum est.*"

Juvenal, *Satire XI*, lines 27-28, in *Juvenal and Persius*, p. 222:

> "...*e caelo descendit* γνῶθι σεαυτόν
> *figendum et memori tractandum pectore,*..."

² Holberg's Latin version:

> "*Virtus laudatur & alget.*"

Juvenal, *Satire I*, line 74, in *Juvenal and Persius*, p. 8:

> "...*probitas laudatur et alget.*"

³ Lewis Holberg, *Journey to the World Under Ground* (1828), p. 160.

⁴ *Ibid.*, pp. 160-161.

⁵ *Ibid.*, p. 165.

⁶ English translation from Ovid, *Metamorphoses*, vol. 1, p. 413. Holberg's Latin version:

> "*Consumptis precibus, violentam transit ad iram*
> *Intendensque manus, passis furibunda capillis,*"

Book VIII, lines 106-107, in Ovid, *Metamorphoses*, vol. 1, p. 412:

> "*Consumptis precibus, violentam transit ad iram,*
> *intendensque manus passis furibunda capillis*"

⁷ Lewis Holberg, *Journey to the World Under Ground* (1828), p. 184.

⁸ *Ibid.*, p. 187.

CHAPTER X

The Author's Banishment to the Firmament

I have hitherto said nothing concerning the strange and very singular punishment the Potuans have, of banishing to the Firmament, wherefore I think myself obliged in this place to give some account of it.

Twice every year certain birds of an enormous magnitude appear upon this globe. They are called Cupac, that is to say, birds of post, and at stated seasons they come and go. It has long perplexed the Subterranean naturalists to account for this periodical visit. Some think they descend upon this planet in quest of certain insects, or large flies, of which there are prodigious numbers about this time of the year and of which these birds are exceedingly voracious. This opinion is strengthened by the circumstance that when these flies disappear the birds fly off towards the Firmament. An evident proof of this we have in other countries where birds by the same instinct of nature appear, and for the very same causes. Others think that these birds are trained up and instructed to this very end and purpose by the inhabitants of the Firmament, like our falcons and other birds of prey. This hypothesis receives some countenance from that tenderness, care, and dexterity which these birds use in bringing home their prey and laying it gently down before their masters. Other circumstances also show that these creatures are either thus instructed or else that they have a certain portion of reason to direct them; for at the approach of the season of departure they are so tractable and tame that they suffer certain nets, or small chains, to be thrown over them, under which they lie quiet for many days and are fed out of hand by the inhabitants with the aforesaid flies, of which they take care to provide a great quantity for this very purpose. For it is necessary to keep feeding them till all things are prepared and got ready for those who are to be banished. The apparatus for their departure is as follows: On those nets in which they are entangled a box or cage is fastened with cords. Every cage is capable of containing one person. The time now drawing near and the insects failing which supplied them with food, the birds mount upon wing, and cutting the air, return to the place from whence they came. Such was this wonderful passage by which I and several other exiles were to be translated to a new world.

There were also at this time two citizens of Potu who for different crimes were sentenced to banishment and were now preparing for their journey. One of these was a metaphysician who had incurred this punishment by disputing concerning the essence of God and the nature of spiritual substances. He had satisfied the law for his first offense of this kind by undergoing the "punishment of the arm;" but being a second time detected, he was condemned to be banished to the Firmament. The other was a fanatic who, having conceived some doubts concerning religion and concerning the civil rights of the state, attempted to subvert the foundations of each. He refused to obey the public laws under pretence that such obedience was contrary to the dictates of his conscience. His friends endeavoured by the most powerful arguments to cure him of this conceit by showing him how many delusions these impulses of conscience and imaginary inspirations were subject to; they told him that zeal and conscience were often confounded with melancholy and certain corrupt humours of the body; they demonstrated to him the egregious folly of thus appealing to the authority of conscience, and how unjust it was to contend that the impulses of his mind should be a rule to others, who might make use of the same argument and oppose conscience to conscience. At last they proved to him that whoever firmly held this principle, pretending conscience for his disobedience, ought to be excluded from the rights and benefits of the community, since every good subject should pay an implicit obedience to the laws; but that a fanatic neither could nor would pay such an obedience since his conscience was his sole rule of politics. But as these reasons had no effect upon the mind of our fanatic, he continued obstinate and incorrigible, and so was condemned to the Firmament. Thus at this time there were only three of us to undergo this punishment, a projector, a metaphysician, and a fanatic.

About the beginning of the month of Birches, we were all carried from prison to separate places. What became of the metaphysician and the fanatic I know not, as being too full of cares for myself to mind anything else. Being brought to the destined place of departure, I was forthwith thrust into the box or cage with as much provision as would serve me for two or three days. Soon after this, when the birds found no more flies brought them, as if they took the hint they left the place, and flew off with incredible celerity. The distance of the Firmament from the planet Nazar is reputed by the Subterraneans to be about a hundred miles. How long I was in passing from the one to the other I cannot say, but to me this ethereal voyage seemed to be no more than about four and twenty hours.

After a profound silence at last a confused noise seemed to reach my ears, from whence I conjectured I was not far from land. Then it was I perceived that these birds had been carefully exercised and instructed, for with great art and care they landed their burden so as not in the least to injure or hurt it. In a moment I was surrounded with a prodigious number of monkeys, the sight of which put me into a very great fright, remembering what I had suffered from these animals upon the planet Nazar. But my fright redoubled when I heard these monkeys articulately discourse with one another, and when I beheld them clad in diverse-coloured vestments. I then conjectured that they were the inhabitants of this country. But as after that heap of wonders I had been accustomed to, nothing now could well seem new or strange, I began to recover my courage, especially as I had observed that these creatures approached me with an air of civility and good nature, taking me gently out of my cage and receiving me with the humanity due to strangers. Even ambassadors in our world are hardly received with more ceremony than I was. They all came one after another and addressed me in these words: *Pul asser.* When they had repeated this salutation pretty often, I repeated the same words. Upon this they set up an immoderate laugh, and by a multitude of comic gestures signified they were highly delighted to hear me pronounce them. This made me conclude these people to be a light, babbling race of creatures, and vast admirers of novelty. When they spoke, you would think so many drums were beating, with so much volubility and so little out of breath they held on their chattering. In a word, as to dress, manners, speech, and form of body, they were the very reverse of the Potuans. At first they were all astonished at my figure, and the chief reason of that astonishment was that I wanted a tail. For as among the whole brute creation none so much resemble the human form as monkeys, so, had I had a tail, they would have taken me for one of their own species, especially as all those who had hitherto been transported from the planet Nazar to this place were of a form extremely unlike their own. About the time of my arrival here the sea ran very high by reason of the near approach of the planet Nazar; for as with us the tides of the ocean correspond with the course of the moon, so the ocean of this Firmament increases and decreases according to the vicinity or remoteness of the aforesaid planet.

Presently I was conducted to a very noble house, all beautifully set off with costly stone, marble, mirrors, vases, and tapestry. At the gate were sentinels posted, which gave me to understand that this could not be the dwelling of a vulgar monkey. And I was soon informed that it was the house of the consul or chief magistrate. He was very desirous of conversing with me, and therefore hired some masters to instruct me in their language. Near three months had been spent upon my instruction, at the expiration of which, as I could now speak the tongue pretty fluently, I hoped to gain the applause and admiration of all upon account of the forwardness of my genius and the strength of my memory. But my tutors thought me slower and duller than ordinary, insomuch that they lost all patience and threatened to leave me off. And as at Potu I was called in derision Skabba, or Quick-Parts, so here, by reason of my stupidity and dullness, they gave me the name of Kakidoran, which signifies a clown, or dunce. For those alone are here esteemed who are quick and nimble and cover their sense in a confused and rapid volley of words.

While I was learning the monkey language, my host took me round the city, which I beheld dissolved in every kind of luxury. What with the multitude of coaches, chaises, valets, and a crowd of people hurrying every way, we were obliged to use a sort of force to get on. Yet this was nothing if compared to that luxury which reigned in the metropolis, where, as in its center, you might see all that mortal vanity could invent. Being now taught the language, I was brought to this famous capital by my host, who hoped to purchase the favour of a senator by making him a present of so uncommon a curiosity as I was. For the form of government here is aristocratical, so that the sovereign authority resides in the Grand Senate, the members of which are all noble from first to last. None of plebeian family can ever hope to be more than a centurion or sheriff in the provinces or lesser cities. Sometimes, indeed, one of this class may arrive at the consulate, yet never without some very extraordinary merit. Thus it was my host obtained the consulship, for so fertile was his genius that in the space of one month he projected twenty-eight new laws. And though not half of them were calculated for the good of the public, yet they were specimens of a fruitful invention and procured him a great character. For throughout the whole Subterranean world, there is no place where projectors are in more esteem than in this.

The capital city is called Martinia; it gives name to the whole country and is famous for its fine situation, for the grandeur of its buildings, its commerce, and naval force. For extent of ground and number of inhabitants, I believe it may rival Paris. So crowded was every street that we were forced to beat our way through to go to that part of the city where the Syndic of the Senate lived. For he it was to whom the consul was to present me.

When we drew near to the Syndic's house, my friend the consul went into an inn to put himself in order and to compose his person and habit in a manner fit to appear before the Syndic. Immediately there appeared a little army of occasional valets or footmen, commonly called *maskatti,* whose assistance every one makes use of before they enter the palaces of the senators. These brush your clothes, take out the spots, and with the exactest care adjust whatever is discomposed, even to the smallest plait. One of these maskatti took the consul's sword and wiped it clean and bright, and then returned it him. Another dressed his tail with ribbands of various colours, for these monkeys have nothing more at heart than the ornaments of their tails. There were some senators, and especially some of the wives of the senators, whose tails on high occasions could scarcely be dressed out to the best advantage under two or three hundred pounds sterling. A third approached the consul with a geometrical instrument to take the dimensions of his clothes and to see if all hung in due proportion.

A fourth brought a bottle of paint and with it improved his visage. A fifth examined his feet, from which he pared the superfluities. A sixth brought him perfumed water to wash with. In short, one brought a towel, another a comb, another a looking glass, and all with an exactness not inferior to that of a geometrician measuring and adorning his map. Oh! thought I to myself, how much time and expense must the dress of the ladies here require, when there is so much fuss in tricking out one of our sex? And, indeed, the Martinian ladies exceed all bounds, and cover their defects with such a load of paint as makes their persons offensive. For when the sweat and paint are pretty well united, it exhales an odour like that of your great kitchens; what you smell you know not, but this you know, that it is something very disagreeable.

My host, thus painted, powdered, combed, and polished, went to the Syndic's palace, attended only with three valets. When he came to the courtyard he pulled off his shoes, lest he should afterwards disoblige the marble floor with dirt or dust. He was forced to stay a full hour before the Syndic was informed that he was there, nor was he introduced without a proper gratification to some of the guards and servants. The Syndic, seated on a gilt settee, as soon as he espied me entering with my host, burst out into an ungovernable laughter, and afterward asked me a thousand trifling, foolish questions. To every reply I made him, he redoubled his fits of laughter.

For my part, I was of opinion that to play the buffoon was reckoned among the virtues here, since the government had made this person Syndic, which is the second dignity in the Senate; and I observed as much to my friend. But he assured me he was a monkey of great abilities, as appeared from the multitude of business of various sorts which even in his greener years he went through. For such was his readiness of perception that even over a glass he would transact affairs of the utmost weight; nay, even at dinner, or at supper, between the courses, he would often draw up a new law. I inquired if such laws, conceived in so short a space of time, were of any considerable duration. To this he only replied that like other laws they continued in force till it pleased the Senate to abrogate or repeal them.

The Syndic having conversed with me about half an hour, and, with full as great a degree of loquacity as our European barbers, turned himself about to my friend and told him he would take me into the number of his servants, though upon account of my slow intellects he much doubted whether I could be good for anything.

"I have myself," replied my friend the consul, "observed a natural torpor or dullness in him, but give him time for reflection and you will find he has no contemptible judgment."

"That signifies little here," returned the Syndic, "since our multiplicity of business admits of no delay." With these words he fell to examining my limbs and my body, and after having surveyed them a short time, he commanded me to lift up a certain weight from the ground, which I did without much trouble. Upon this he told me that though Nature had been unkind to me with respect to my intellects, yet that she had in a manner compensated that defect by an extraordinary strength of body. I was then ordered to withdraw to another apartment where the domestics and attendants received me with a good deal of pleasure, though their excessive impertinence and gestures were troublesome enough. So many questions they asked me concerning our world I knew not how to answer them, and so gave them what came uppermost, some truth, some falsehood, just to allay their impatient curiosity.

At length my friend, returning, told me His Excellency did me the honour to retain me in his court. From the foregoing conversation of the Syndic I could guess that the employment designed for me was no very important one, probably his valet or his butler; and upon inquiring what it was, my friend said to me, "His Excellence has been graciously pleased to appoint you one of his body chairmen, with an annual salary of twenty-five *stercolates*. (A Martinian stercolate is equal to about seven shillings and sixpence sterling.) He has moreover engaged that you shall have the honour of carrying only himself or his lady.

I was thunderstruck with this answer, and remonstrated in the most pathetic manner how unworthy an office this was for one of my ingenious education and family. But some courtiers rushing in in heaps interrupted me from speaking more, and half killed me with their impertinence. For all the Martinians are light, frothy, talking creatures that have a smooth, fluent jargon of words without the least mixture of seriousness or gravity. At length I was conducted to an apartment where supper was ready; and having taken a moderate repast, I retired to my repose.

I threw myself upon my bed, but such was the disorder of my mind I could take no sleep. The disdain I was received with shocked me to the highest degree, and nothing less than a Spartan patience could digest so gross an indignity. I heartily deplored my fate, which seemed severer now than what I had experienced in the planet Nazar, and I could not help saying to myself, "What would here become of the Kadoki, or High Chancellor of Potu, a person of inestimable worth in his own country, but who required at least an entire month to form a new law? What would be the fate of Palmka in this place, where the senators make laws between the courses at meals?" After a serious consideration, I found myself translated from a land of sages to a country of fools. At last being tired with thinking, sleep overpowered me. I know not how long I slept, since there is here no difference between night and day. For it is never dark except at one stated time when the subterranean sun is in an eclipse by the interposition of the planet Nazar. This eclipse is very remarkable because the aforesaid planet, being not far from the firmament, overshadows the whole sun and so always makes the eclipse total. But as this happens but seldom, it makes no alteration of season, which is here invariably the same upon account of the constant presence of the sun. Hence the inhabitants are forced to have recourse to various inventions, as groves, baths, walks, and grottoes, to qualify the heat.

I was scarce awake when a monkey entered my chamber who told me he was my comrade in office, and with a light cord (being ordered so to do) he applied a fictitious tail to my posteriors to make me look more like a monkey. He then bid me get ready, because the Syndic within an hour was to be carried to the Academy, to which place he and his brother senators had received a formal invitation. It seems there was to be a promotion to a doctor's degree at ten o'clock that morning.

It must be noted here that though the days are not distinguished from the nights by reason of the perpetual presence of the sun, yet are they distinguished into hours, half hours, and quarters, and that by means of clocks or hourglasses so that day and night together take up about twenty-two hours. Hence, if all the clocks in the city were to stop at once, it would be impossible for the citizens to recover the true time till they had consulted some of the clocks in the next neighborhood. For there neither are, nor can be, any sundials, because there is never any shadow, the sun continually darting perpendicular rays upon the place. So that were you to dig a well here, it would be illuminated to the bottom. As to the year, that is regulated and governed by the course of the planet Nazar round the sun.

At ten o'clock we took up His Excellence and carried him to the Academy. Entering into the auditory, we beheld the doctors and masters seated in order, every one of which rose up as the Syndic passed by, and turning themselves about, paid him their compliments with their tails. This is their manner of doing reverence. And this accounts for their care in adorning their tails. For my own part, I confess these inverted salutations seemed extremely foolish and absurd. For to turn one's back upon anyone is among us a mark of indifference or contempt. But every nation has its particular taste.

The aforesaid doctors and masters were seated on each side of the auditory. In the lower part of it was placed a chair in which sat the candidate. Before the act of promotion, the following question was discussed in a solemn disputation, namely, "Whether the sound which flies and other insects make comes through the mouth or the posteriors?" The President undertook the defense of the former opinion, which was attacked by the opponents with so much ardour that I was afraid it would have terminated in a bloody battle. And most certainly they had come to blows, but that the Senate rose up and cooled the flame by their authority.

During the dispute a certain monkey played upon a pipe: this was the moderator, who by the management of his music, either in soft or in smart strains, would quicken the dispute when it flagged and languished, or bring it down when it was noisy and violent, though very often all his art had no effect, so very hard a matter it is to preserve the temper when the dispute is upon such interesting subjects. The same thing often happens in our world where, when the dispute turns upon some very dubious and almost inexplicable point, one may observe the combatants are often worked up to the most violent agitations of mind or body. However, this threatening quarrel which promised nothing but blood and slaughter ended all in compliments and praises. Something like this obtains in our European universities where, according to general custom, the President, when the dispute is closed, descends victorious and triumphant from the chair.

This preamble ended, they proceeded to the act of creation

with these ceremonies. The candidate was placed in the middle of the auditory; three of the university beadles walked gravely up to him and threw a whole pailfull of cold water upon his head; they then perfumed him with incense, and lastly gave him a vomit to take off. Having performed this with the utmost solemnity, they retired bowing and declared him aloud a true and legitimate doctor. Amazed at so many wonderful ceremonies, I asked a certain learned monkey who stood near me the meaning of all this. He told me (pitying at the same time my ignorance) that by the water, the incense, and the vomit it was understood that the candidate was to forsake his old vices and to assume a new set of manners to distinguish him from the vulgar. Hearing this, I deplored my own stupidity, and, full of admiration, forebore to ask any farther questions for fear I should be thought to have never conversed with anything above brutes.

At last all the musical instruments struck up at once, and the new doctor, clothed in a robe of green and girt with a sash of the same colour, was escorted home from the auditory with all Parnassus at his heels. But as he was of a plebeian family, he had not the honour of a coach, but was seated in a vehicle not unlike a wheelbarrow and drawn by hand, the university beadles marching before in their respective habits. The whole ended in a very handsome entertainment, where the guests drank so plentifully that many of them were carried home extremely intoxicated and were so ill for many days after that without the help of proper medicines they would hardly have recovered. So that from the beginning to the ending of this whole ceremony nothing was wanting to the due solemnity of it; and I protest I never, even in our world, saw a more truly academical promotion, or any candidate commence doctor more legitimately than this.

In the courts of justice causes are dispatched with a surprising dexterity, and I was charmed with that readiness of apprehension, that velocity of conceiving things, so peculiar to this nation.

Very often before the advocates have wound up their pleadings, the judges rise and give sentence with equal expedition and elegance. I often frequented these courts to inform myself thoroughly of their manner of proceeding. At first hearing their decrees seemed just and equitable enough; but upon a more careful examination they were in reality absurd, unjust, and full of contradictions, insomuch that I would sooner commit my cause to the chance of a die than to the judgment of the Martinian lawyers.

I forbear to say anything concerning the laws of this people by reason of the capricious changes they perpetually undergo. They are as fickle in these as in their fashions. Many are here punished for crimes which were not crimes at the time they were committed but commence such by virtue of an after-law to make them so. For which reason nothing is more common than appeals from the inferior to the superior courts, the plaintiff having hopes that while the suit is depending, the old law (which lost him his cause in the lower court) may be repealed. This is owing to the suddenness with which their laws are invented and promulgated. Such lovers of novelty are this people that they perfectly nauseate the most useful statutes solely upon account of their antiquity.

The advocates are in great reputation for their shrewdness in disputation. Nay, there are some among them who disdain to undertake a cause that is not unjust or at least very doubtful, for in so doing they might be deprived of an occasion of exerting their parts and giving specimens of their ability to turn black into white. The judges will often favour a bad cause in compliment to the counsel for defending it so well. "We perceive well enough," say the judges, "the injustice of this cause, but then it has been managed with such inimitable art that in justice to the advocate for his performance we ought to strain a point of law." The students in this profession are taught law at different prices; for instance, those who teach their pupils to manage a bad cause, or, according to the proverb, to make the best of a bad market, require twenty stercolates for their trouble; the art of managing a good one shall cost but ten. Their forms of law are so many they resemble a huge chaos without bottom and without shore. For the Martinians, having a sublime genius and a quick perception, detest everything that's plain and simple and think nothing worth their care that is not very knotty and intricate.

The same taste prevails in religion, which does not consist in practice but in idle speculations. Thus there are two hundred and thirty different opinions about the form or figure of the Supreme Being, and three hundred and ninety-six about the nature and quality of souls. The Martinians never resort to their temples or churches with the view of hearing anything useful or of improving themselves in the art of living and dying well, but only to observe with what art and dexterity the holy orators acquit themselves; for the more obscure their language is, the more they are admired, their audience having very little relish for what they understand. More pains are taken about the expression than about the matter, the preachers affecting the smooth, round period more than the strength of reason, and the audience expecting to be amused with a sounding pomp of words without a meaning. For this reason I did not dare say anything concerning the Christian religion, which, consisting of naked, simple truths, could never recommend itself to their *goût*.

Projectors are nowhere in so high reputation as here. The more odd and impracticable the scheme, the greater is the inventor's glory. When I had accidentally been explaining to a certain monkey the nature of our terraqueous globe, and had informed him that the surface of it was inhabited, he presently conceived a project of digging through the earth and opening a passage to the Superterraneans. This device met with universal applause, and a society was thereupon instituted and called the Superterranean Company, to which the inhabitants flocked in shoals, and, according to the language of those times, bought in stocks. However, as this affair introduced a great deal of confusion into the kingdom and ruined a multitude of families beyond redemption, they found the folly of the scheme and dropped it all at once. And though the nation smarted so severely by it, yet the projector not only escaped with impunity but with almost general praise, this people entertaining the highest idea of his great abilities.

Perceiving this turn of mind to prevail, I endeavoured by the same means to procure myself a reputation among the Martinians, and to mend my fortune by some new project of my own. After a due examination of the state of the public, I discovered several flaws in it. I saw the whole country was full of the more subtle sort of artists, but that it laboured under a want of useful traders and workmen. Upon this I proposed a law for the institution of certain manufacturers that might be of great service to the nation. But every proposal of this kind met with nothing but sneers and contempt from this vain people. I then accused my own stupidity in these terms: "What a sot have I been? and how richly do I deserve to end my days in the ignoble office of chairman?"

Yet I did not altogether despond, and being convinced I should never do them nor myself any good by salutary counsels, I resolved to try whether I could not get over the difficulty by some ridiculous invention or other. I opened my design to one of the gravest monkeys I knew, who encouraged me to it mightily. And when he proved to me that numbers there had made their fortunes by mere trifles and boyish gewgaws, and more especially by the invention of some new fashion, I then resolved to swim with the tide and among fools to play the fool myself. Upon this, I called to mind all the most ridiculous and extravagant

141

inventions of Europe, and being at liberty to pick and choose, I fixed upon those ornaments of the head which we call periwigs, and determined with myself to introduce this fashion. What contributed to bear me out in this attempt was the great number of goats in this kingdom, whose wool or hair would be very proper for my purpose. And as my good tutor (now at rest) long exercised the occupation of a periwig-maker, I was not altogether ignorant of the art. In short, I procured some goat's hair and made a periwig fitted to my own head, and thus adorned, I appeared before the Syndic. Startled at so new and unusual an appearance, he asked me what it was, and immediately snatching it from my head, he put it upon his own and ran to the glass to survey himself. But how shall I express his wonder and delight? He burst into an ecstasy of pleasure, crying, "O ye gods!" and forthwith sent for his lady to join with him in his joy. Her wonder was equal to his, and embracing the Syndic, she vowed she never saw anything so charming, and every soul in the family was of the same opinion. The Syndic then turning towards me, "My dear Kakidoran," says he, "if this invention of yours should take with the Senate as it does with me, you may promise yourself everything." I thanked His Excellence, and soon after put a petition into his hands addressed to the Senate, which I begged the favour of him to offer. It was conceived in these terms:

Most Excellent, most Generous, most Illustrious, most Noble, and most Wise Senators:

The natural propensity by which I am influenced to promote the public good has now moved me to contrive this new and hitherto unheard-of ornament for the head, which here I most humbly offer to Your Excellencies, and submit it to the examination of this august tribunal, not doubting but it will meet with a most gracious reception, especially as the invention must conduce to the glory, as well as ornament, of the nation, and make the admiring world confess that the Martinians excel the rest of mortals, not only in the virtues and endowments of the mind, but in those ornaments of the body which render the person grand and majestic. I solemnly vow to all Your Excellencies that in this I never consulted my own interest, and therefore I require no reward. It is enough for me in my slender capacity to have promoted the public welfare, and the kingdom's honour. But if the most illustrious Senate are pleased to decree me a suitable reward for my labours, I shall receive it with a grateful heart, that such their munificence may be known throughout the world, and others animated to the like or greater inventions. In this view I cannot oppose the liberality of the Senate and people of Martinia. As to the rest, I commend myself to the favour of Your Excellencies, and am,

May it please Your Excellencies,
Your most obedient

Martinia	And most humble servant,
7th day of Astral.	Kakidoran.

The Syndic produced the petition with the periwig in open Senate. I heard that all business was laid aside that day, so much did the examination of the periwig engage the general attention. Upon the close of all they praised the work, extolled the artist, accepted of his good will, and appointed him a reward. In the whole Senate there were but three who opposed this motion; but they got no credit by it and were looked upon as rude, unpolished creatures, totally unworthy of the senatorial function.

This decree being passed, I was commanded to appear before the Senate, where a senior monkey rising up thanked me in the name of the whole commonwealth and assured me they would reward me in a manner suitable to my great merit. He likewise asked me how much time it would require to make such another ornament?

I replied that as to the reward it was sufficient recompense to receive the applauses of so venerable a body; as to the other point, the making a second periwig, provided I might have the assistance of as many monkeys as I could instruct in the art, I could undertake in one month to furnish almost the whole city.

At these words, the Syndic rose and said, "Heaven forbid, Kakidoran, that such an ornament should be common to all the city and grow into disesteem by frequent use! No; let the nobility be by this distinguished from the vulgar."

This opinion was seconded by all the Senate, and the public censors were ordered to take due care that this decree should be inviolably observed, that the nobility receive no dishonour by the promiscuous use of periwigs, and that so bright an ornament should be reserved solely for their use.

But this edict had the same effect that all sumptuary laws have, and only excited a stronger desire in the commons to transgress it. And as this invention had the happiness to please everyone, the richer citizens, by friends or money, procured titles of honour to qualify them to wear periwigs, insomuch that in a short time a very great part of the city was ennobled. At length, when petitions arrived from the several provinces to be allowed to come into this fashion, the Senate took the matter under consideration and made a repeal of the law with a permission for the promiscuous use of periwigs; so that I had the pleasure to see the whole nation periwigged, if I may use the expression, before I left Martinia. And a most delightful sight it was! Such general satisfaction did this contrivance give that it gave birth to a new epoch, or date of time, which was called in the Martinian annals The Year of Periwigs.

To return to myself. Surrounded with applauses and clothed in a purple robe, I was carried back in a chair to the Syndic's house, and my comrade chairman now performed the office of a horse for me. From that hour I was admitted to the Syndic's table. After this lucky prelude of my fortune I pursued my design, and by the joint labours of those I instructed, I in a short time finished off periwigs enough to accommodate the whole

Senate; and about the end of the month the following diploma of nobility was brought me.

Whereas a certain person, by name Kakidoran, native of a city called Europe, has by a glorious and useful invention highly obliged the whole Martinian nation, it is our will and pleasure to associate him into the body of our nobility; and we do accordingly decree that he and his heirs henceforth be reputed as true and genuine nobles, and enjoy all such privileges, rights, and immunities as are claimed by the Martinian nobility. Moreover, we have decreed to honour him with a new name, so that instead of Kakidoran he shall now be styled Kikidorian. And lastly, it is our will and pleasure to settle an annual stipend upon him of two hundred *patari*, to enable him to support his new dignity.

    Given at our Court of Senate
        in Martinia, the 4th day
        of Merian, under our Great
        Seal, etc.

Thus from a poor chairman was I transformed to a nobleman, and for some time I lived in the highest repute and with the utmost felicity. And as the Martinians saw I was in high favour with the Syndic, every creature made his court to me. The flattery of the preferment-hunters went so far as to strive which should write the most fulsome panegyrics upon me, in which they kindly gave me a great many virtues I never had. Some, though they knew I was a native of an unknown world, yet reckoned up for me a long list of ancestors, and drew out genealogies in a direct line from heroes of the earliest ages. These computations could not be very agreeable to me, nor was it possible for me to think it an honour to be descended from monkeys. Moreover, as it is usual with the Martinians to celebrate the tails of the quality, as our poets sing the beauties of their mistresses, accordingly some of the Martinian poets celebrated my tail in verse, though I never had any. In short, to such a height did their flattery rise that a certain person of no mean extraction, whose name I spare upon account of his family, actually offered me the enjoyment of his wife if in return I would use all my interest for him with the Syndic. This vile propensity to flattery, to which all the Martinians are extremely subject, makes it not worth one's while to read their histories, which are little more than a heap of extravagant encomiums, though the language of them is everywhere polite and elegant. Hence this country produces better poets than historians, which is owing to the fine imagination of the Martinians.

I enjoyed a tolerable good share of health while I was in this country, though the heat, occasioned by the continual presence of the sun, was not a little troublesome. Once I was seized with a diarrhea attended with a high fever, but it was of no great continuance; but during my illness the physician I made use of was ten times more troublesome than my disorder by reason of his impertinence and loquacity, which are so peculiar to this people. Having occasion for a physician in that ill state of health, a doctor of physic came *à volontier*, and offered me his assistance. I could not forbear laughing at the sight of him, because who should this be but my very barber? I questioned him how it happened that from a barber he was so soon metamorphosed into a doctor? He replied he exercised both professions. Upon this I was a little dubious whether I ought to trust the care of my health to such a general trader, and frankly told him that I had rather have a physician who professed the art of physic alone; but he vowed and protested to me that there was not one such throughout the whole city. I was therefore obliged to venture myself with him.

The haste the doctor was in increased my wonder, for having prescribed for me a potion, he abruptly took his leave, declaring he could not possibly stay longer because he was obliged to attend upon some other affairs in which he was engaged at that very time. And when I asked him what those affairs could be which required such violent haste, he told me he was under a necessity of being at a market town in the neighbourhood by such an hour to act as a notary public, which was another of his employments. This multiplicity of business is in great vogue here, and everybody is very ready to undertake any of the most opposite and contradictory offices. This confidence is occasioned by that wonderful liveliness of genius which dispatches business in a trice. Yet from the various mistakes and blunders they daily commit, I concluded that these geniuses which are so full of fire are rather an ornament to the commonwealth than of any real use to it.

After I had spent two years in this territory, partly as a chairman and partly as a nobleman, I fell into an adventure which had like to have been fatal to me. In His Excellency's palace I had met with the highest civilities; I had also the honour to be extremely in the good graces of his lady, insomuch that I seemed to have the first place in her friendship. She often favoured me with tête à tête conversations, and though she seemed highly pleased with my company, yet all she said was with so much modesty and delicacy that it was impossible to put a sinister interpretation upon her conduct in this respect, nor could I with all my penetration guess that the source of all this wondrous goodness was an impure passion, more especially as she was a lady of quality and as eminent for her virtue as for her birth and family. But, in process of time, from some equivocal speeches of hers I could not but entertain a few suspicions which were considerably increased by several evident symptoms,

> The wan complexion, and the dying eye,
> The steadfast gaze, th' involuntary sigh.[1]

At length the mystery was cleared up, a young virgin, her confidante, bringing me the following billet.

Lovely Kikidorian,
My birth and the natural modesty of my sex have till now

concealed those sparks of love which lurked within my bosom, and withheld them from bursting into an open flame. But now, sinking under the oppression, I can no longer resist the violence of my wishes.

Let this soft secret all thy pity move,
Extorted from my soul by raging love.[2]
I am yours,
Ptarnusa.

Words cannot utter the confusion this passionate declaration threw me into. But as I thought it better to be exposed to the vengeance of disappointed love than to disturb the laws of nature by mixing my blood with a creature not of the human species, I returned the following answer.

Madam,
The repeated favours I have received from His Excellency the Syndic, the benefits he has heaped upon an undeserving stranger, the moral impossibility of complying with your request, together with innumerable other reasons which I forbear to recount, all this, Madam, determines me to hazard Your Ladyship's resentment rather than consent to an action which would render me of all two-footed creatures the most vile and abominable. Not death itself is half so terrible. The crime too would bring an indelible stain upon a most illustrious family, and she who commands it must be the greatest sufferer. Let me conjure you, therefore, to pardon this refusal and be satisfied that in every other respect I shall always pay the profoundest obedience to Your Ladyship's commands. I am,
Madam,
Your most humble
And most obedient servant,
Kikidorian.

This answer I sealed up and gave it to the bearer to deliver to her mistress. It had the effect I suspected. Her love was changed into the strongest aversion. However, she deferred her revenge till she had recovered that letter she sent to me. She then suborned false witnesses, who swore that I attempted to violate the Syndic's bed. This story was cooked up with so much art and such an air of probability that the Syndic, not making the least doubt about it, threw me into prison. In this extremity there was but one thing to be done, and that was to make confession of the crime and implore His Excellency's mercy. By these means I hoped to divert or soften his anger and procure a mitigation of my punishment. For it was ridiculous to think of contesting the matter with a powerful family, especially in a country where not the merits of the cause but the sole quality of the person is regarded. Therefore, omitting all sort of defense, I had recourse to the most abject supplications and tears, imploring, not a total remission of my punishment, but only to have it moderated.

Thus by the confession of a crime I never dreamed of, I changed the punishment of death for a perpetual captivity. My diploma of nobility was taken from me and torn in pieces by the hands of the common hangman, and I myself was condemned to be a galley slave all my days. The galley or vessel I was sent to work in belonged to the government and lay in readiness for its voyage to the Mezendores, or Land of Wonders. This voyage is undertaken at a stated time of the year, namely, in the month Radir. They sail to these parts in quest of such commodities as are not to be had in their own country, so that the Mezendores are a kind of Indies to the Martinians. A body of merchants, as well nobles as citizens, are erected into a society called the Mezendorian Company, among whom the merchandise of the returning vessel is divided according to their several subscriptions and shares. The vessel moves both by sails and oars, and to every oar two slaves or captives are assigned; and to this drudgery was I condemned during this voyage. With what reluctance I entered upon it, it is easy to guess, especially as I had done nothing to deserve being thus exposed to servile labour and to the lash among wretches and slaves.

Various were the sentiments of the Martinians concerning my misfortune. Some were of opinion I was culpable and therefore deserved the punishment, but then the sight of me in that miserable condition drew compassion from them. Others thought some regard ought to have been had to my former services, and that therefore my punishment need not have been so severe. But some of the honester monkeys muttered among themselves that I was accused falsely, though no one dared openly undertake my defense through fear of my powerful accusers.

I determined, however, to bear my calamity with patience. My greatest comfort was the approaching voyage, for as I had always a strong passion for novelty, I was in hopes of meeting with something new and wonderful, though I could not give credit to all the sailors told me, nor bring myself to think that there were such prodigies in nature as I afterwards met with. There were several interpreters in our vessel whose assistance the Mezendorian Company made use of in these expeditions, for all contracts as to buying and selling were made by them.

[1]Book IX, lines 536-537, in Ovid, *Metamorphoses*, vol. 2, p. 40:
"et color et macies et vultus et umida saepe
lumina nec causa suspiria mota patenti"
[2]Book IX, lines 561-562, in Ovid, *Metamorphoses*, vol. 2, p. 42:
". . . miserere fatentis amores,
et non fassurae, nisi cogeret ultimus ardor,"

CHAPTER XI

The Author's Voyage to the Land of Wonders

Before I proceed to the description of this voyage, I must caution the rigid and censorious critic not to be too much out of humour at the relation of some things which perhaps may appear not to deserve any credit, as being contrary to the usual course of nature. I shall here recount things very incredible, but very true, and of which I myself was an eyewitness. The vulgar and illiterate who never have set a foot beyond the limits of their own native country are apt to look upon all such things as fabulous to which they have not been accustomed from their infancy. But the learned, and especially such of them as are conversant in physical inquiries, who know how fertile Nature is in her productions, will look with a more favourable eye upon the wonderful parts of this narration.

It is now well known that there were a people formerly in Scythia called Arimaspians, who had only a single eye apiece in the middle of their foreheads; and others in the same parts of the world whose feet were set on the contrary way to ours. We read of people in Albania who were grey-headed from their childhood. The Sauromatians used to make a meal but once in three days and to fast the intermediate ones. Mention is made of certain families in Africa who had the art of fascinating or bewitching people with the sound of their voices. The inhabitants of Illyria were remarkable for having two pupils in each eye, and used, when they were provoked, to stare their enemies to death. In the mountains of India, there are some men with dogs' heads, and who have been heard to bark like those animals; others with eyes in their shoulders. And in the farthest parts of the same country there have been found animals resembling men, with hairy bodies and wings like birds, who never eat but live upon the scent of flowers, which they draw through their nostrils. Now I may ask, who would have given credit to these and the like things if Pliny, a very grave historian, had not solemnly affirmed, not that he had heard or read of such things, but that he himself had seen them? In like manner, who would ever have thought that the earth was hollow and that another sun and other planets were contained within its bowels, had not my own experience cleared up that mystery? Or how could an account of a world inhabited by trees endowed with reason and a power of local motion have ever gained belief, had not my discoveries proved the existence of it beyond a possibility of doubt? I am not inclined, however, to quarrel with any man for his incredulity, since I must confess that before I undertook this voyage I was a little in doubt myself whether the relations of travellers in general were anything better than pompous fables and insignificant amusements.

It was in the beginning of the month Radir that we set sail. We had a fair wind for some days, and our vessel sailing right before it, we had no occasion to handle our oars and were therefore at liberty to divert ourselves. But on the fourth day the wind sank and we were forced to take to our oars. The captain, perceiving I was unaccustomed to such hard labour and unfit to bear it, would often give me leave to rest a while, and at length he entirely freed me from this servile office. Whether he thought me innocent and therefore showed me so much kindness, or whether he judged me worthy of better treatment on account of the curious invention of periwigs which I had the honour of, as I have before related, I cannot take upon me to determine.

I must, however, observe that he carried three wigs along with him this voyage, the combing and curling of which were committed to my charge. So that I was on a sudden advanced from being a galley slave to the dignity of the captain's wig-dresser. This civility of the captain's to me was the reason that as often as we arrived at any port, I was always one of the number who were appointed to go on shore. This was extremely agreeable to me, as it gave me an opportunity of fully satisfying my curiosity.

We kept on our course for some time without meeting with anything remarkable, but after we had lost sight of land we fell among the sirens, who as often as the wind abated and the sea grew calm would swim to the ship and beg our charity. The language they spoke resembled the Martinese, so that some of our ship's crew were able to talk with them without the help of an interpreter. One of the number, after I had given her a piece of meat, fixing her eyes steadfastly upon me, cried out, "Hero! proceed, and rule a conquered world!" I only smiled at the prophecy, as thinking it an empty piece of flattery, though our sailors assured me very seriously that these sirens were seldom or never out in their predictions.

We had been under sail about eight days when we discovered land, which the mariners called Picardania. As we were entering the harbour, we saw a jackdaw hovering about us, who upon inquiry I found to be a person of great dignity and at that time inspector-general of the customs. I could scarce refrain from laughing when I heard that an office of so great trust was committed to a jackdaw, and from the appearance of their chief I conjectured that wasps and hornets must be the tide-waiters and customhouse officers.

After this bird had flown two or three times round the ship, he made for the shore again, and presently after returned with three other daws and alighted upon the forecastle. I was ready to burst with laughing when I saw one of our interpreters approach these birds with a profound respect, and immediately enter into a long conversation with them. The reason of their coming was to inspect what merchandise we had on board, it being their business to inquire whether we had any contraband goods and particularly any of the herb commonly called *slac*. It is very common for these creatures to search every corner of the ship, and to unpack every bale of goods, to see if they can discover any of this herb, the importation of which is prohibited by the magistrate under a very severe penalty. The inhabitants barter several sorts of commodities which are very useful and necessary towards the support of life in exchange for this herb, from whence it happens that the plants which grow in Picardania, though every whit as good as this, are held in no esteem. The Picardanians in this resemble the Europeans, who are often fond of things for no other reason but because they are fetched from remote countries and grow in foreign soils.

The inspector, after he had had a long conference with our interpreters, went down into the hold with the rest of his companions, and returning soon after, with an angry countenance declared that he forbade us trading with the Picardanians because we had acted contrary to the faith of treaties in importing prohibited goods. But the captain, who knew by experience how to mitigate the officer's anger, presented him immediately with a few pounds of slac, upon which his anger subsided and he gave us leave to unload our cargo. As soon as this was over a vast flock of daws came fluttering about us. These were all merchants who came to traffic.

The captain, intending to go ashore, ordered me and some others to accompany him. Accordingly four in number of us left the ship, namely, the captain, myself, and two other monkeys, to wit, our supercargo and interpreter. We were invited to dinner by the inspector-general. The inhabitants have no tables, as not making any use of chairs, for which reason the cloth was laid in the middle of the floor. A most delicate and magnificent repast was presently served up, but in very small dishes; and as the kitchen was at the top of the house, each dish was brought in supported by two pair of jackdaws, as if it descended from the clouds.

After dinner the officer took us along with him to show us his library. There was a vast collection of books, but of a mighty small size, the largest folios being scarce so big as one of our primers. I had much ado to withhold laughing when I saw the librarian fly up to the top shelves to fetch down some of the octavos and duodecimos.

The houses of the Picardanians are very little different from ours as to the building and the disposition of the apartments, but the bed chambers are suspended just beneath the roof, after the manner of birds' nests. It may be asked, perhaps, how it is possible for daws (who are reckoned amongst the smaller kinds of birds) to build houses of such a magnitude. But it was evident from a house which was then building from the ground that the thing was very possible, for several thousand labourers were employed about it at the same time so that what was wanting in strength was supplied by numbers and by the agility with which they flew about their work. For this reason they will finish a house almost as quickly as our bricklayers can.

The inspector's lady did not appear at table by reason of her lying-in; for at such times the mother never stirs out as long as her little ones are callow, but as soon as ever they begin to be fledged her husband gives her leave to go abroad.

We did not stay long in this country, for which reason I can say nothing as to the government thereof, or the manners and customs of the inhabitants. Everything was in great confusion at that time on account of a war which was just then broken out between the daws and their neighbours the thrushes, especially as news was brought the day after our arrival that a great

155

battle had been fought in the air in which the daws were entirely routed. The general was afterwards tried by a court-martial and sentenced to have his wings clipped, which is looked upon as a very heavy punishment in this country, and very little different from what is inflicted for capital offenses. After we had disposed of the cargo, we set sail from thence. At a little distance from the shore we saw great quantities of feathers floating about upon the water, and from thence conjectured that it was the spot where the late battle had been fought.

After a prosperous voyage which lasted only three days, we arrived upon the coast of Crotchet Island. We immediately came to an anchor and went on shore, preceded by an interpreter who carried that sort of musical instrument along with him which is generally called a bass. This ceremony appeared very ridiculous to me, as I could not comprehend for what reason he should load himself with such a useless burden. As the coasts seemed to be deserted and there was no appearance of any living creature, the captain ordered our interpreter to play a march to give notice of our coming. Upon this about thirty musical instruments, or basses, with one leg came hopping towards us. I thought at first that what I saw was all enchantment, as I never in all my travels met with anything so wonderful.

The make of these basses, whom I afterwards found to be the inhabitants of the country, was as follows: their necks were pretty long with little heads upon them; their bodies were slender and covered with a smooth kind of bark or rind in such a manner as that a pretty large vacuity was left between the rind and the body itself. A little above the navel Nature had placed a sort of bridge with four strings. The whole machine rested upon one foot, so that their motion was like that of hopping, which they performed with wonderful agility. In short, one would have taken them for real basses from their similitude to that instrument, had it not been for their hands and arms, which were in every respect like our own. One of these hands was employed in holding the bow, as the other was in stopping the strings.

Our interpreter began the conference by taking up the instrument he had brought with him and playing a slow strain. An answer was presently returned him in the same strain, and thus they went on warbling their thoughts to one another for a considerable time. Their conversation began with an adagio which I cannot but say had a good deal of harmony in it, but it soon slid into discords which were very grating to the ear. The conference ended with a harmonious and delightful presto. Upon hearing this last our men were exceedingly pleased, since it was a token, as they told me, that the price of their cargo was agreed upon. I was afterward informed that the slow music in the beginning was only a prelude to the discourse and was employed in mutual compliments on both sides; but that when we heard the discords, they were disputing about the price of our commodities, and that the presto in the conclusion signified that the business was happily determined.

Accordingly, a little while after we unloaded the ship. The commodity for which there is the greatest demand in this country is rosin, with which the inhabitants rub their bows, which are their instruments of speech. Such as are convicted of any great crime in this country are generally sentenced by the judge to be deprived of their bows, and a perpetual privation of the bow is equal to capital punishment amongst us. As I understood there was to be a final hearing of a lawsuit in a neighbouring court of justice while I stayed there, my curiosity prompted me to hear some of their musical law proceedings.

The counsel instead of making a speech moved their bows, and played each of them a kind of tune. So long as the pleadings lasted, I could distinguish nothing but dissonant and jarring sounds, for all the eloquence of the bar consists in the loudness of their notes and the quick motion of their hands. After the hearing was over, the judge, rising slowly from the bench and taking up his bow, gave the court an adagio, which is the same thing as pronouncing sentence. For as soon as he had made an end, the executioners advanced directly to the criminal to take away his bow.

The boys in this country resemble that kind of instrument which in our parts of the world we call a kit. They are never suffered to handle a bow till they are three years old. Upon their entrance into their fourth year they are sent to school to learn their gamut from masters appointed for that purpose, as children in Europe are to learn their alphabet. They are kept under the discipline of the ferule till they are able to play thoroughly in tune and to give their instruments a clear and distinct expression.

We were very much molested by these boys during our stay there, as they were perpetually teasing us with their scraping. Our interpreter, who had a very good hand himself and perfectly understood the language, told us that the only meaning of this music was to beg a little rosin of us. They begged in a whining tone of the adagio kind, but as soon as ever they had got what they wanted they ran into the allegro, or jig time, which was their method of returning thanks. However, a repulse would at any time spoil all their music.

Having dispatched our affairs to our satisfaction, we left this place about the month Cusan, and after a voyage of a few days came in sight of another coast. Our crew guessed it to be Pyglossia, from the fetid smell which came from thence. The inhabitants of this country are not unlike human creatures except in one particular, which is the want of mouths. This lays them under a necessity of speaking *a posteriori,* if I may be allowed the phrase. The first person who came aboard our ship was a wealthy merchant. He very civilly saluted us from behind, according to the custom of the country, and then began to talk with us about the price of our goods. The barber belonging to our ship to my great misfortune was at that time sick, for which reason I was obliged to make use of a Pyglossian barber. The people of this profession are more talkative, if possible, in this country than they are in Europe, so that while he was shaving me, he left such a horrid stench behind him in the cabin that we were obliged to burn great quantities of incense to sweeten it again after his departure. I was so accustomed to see strange things and such as were contrary to the usual course of nature that nothing now appeared surprising to me.

As the conversation of the Pyglossians was disagreeable and offensive by reason of this natural imperfection, we were willing to get away from thence as soon as possible, and therefore weighed anchor before the time we had appointed. We hastened our departure the more on account of our being invited to supper by one of the principal inhabitants. We all shrugged up our shoulders at this invitation, and nobody would accept of it but upon condition that a general silence should be observed all suppertime. As we were going out of the harbour, the Pyglossians crowded to the shore to wish us a good voyage, but as the wind blew directly from the land, we made all the signs we could by nodding our heads and waving our hands to let them know we would excuse their compliments. I could not help reflecting upon this occasion how very troublesome a man may prove by striving to be overcomplaisant. The chief trade of the Martinians to this country consists in rose water and divers kinds of spices and perfumes.

[I have already remarked that this people, in respect to the form of their bodies, resembled much the human being, except in so far that they spoke with that part whereon we always sit. On our Earth there is no lack of people who, as well in dialect as in shape, perfectly resemble the Pyglossians. Thought I to myself, should Jens Sorensen, Ole Petersen, Andreas Lorensten, and other such like polite characters who, with cynical bluntness, give everything its proper name, and without shame or reserve, even in the company of females, manifest their corrupt and frivolous minds, I say, should these talkers of ribaldry and obscenity come to this country, they would be received with open arms. On account of the affinity of their language they would immediately obtain their burgher-right and be looked upon as natives. For what matters it where the mouth is placed, when that which comes out of it

Is a sounding stink, and a stinking sound,
Which a dunghill discovers in mind and body?]¹

We steered our course from hence to Iceland, a country the most horrid, desert, and inhospitable that ever my eyes beheld. Hardly anything is to be seen but mountains continually covered over with snow. The inhabitants, who are all made of ice, are dispersed here and there amongst the tops of the hills in places where the sun never comes, for all between the summits of the mountains, to speak poetically, is bound up in eternal frost. On this account likewise it is perpetually dark here, or if there is any light it is only what proceeds from the glittering of the hoarfrost. But the valleys which lie between these hills of snow are (full as miraculously) scorched with heat and burnt up by the fiery vapours with which the atmosphere abounds. For this reason the inhabitants never dare venture down into the valleys unless it be in hazy weather or when the sky is overcast. And as soon as ever they perceive the least glimmering of the sun's rays, they either get back into the mountains or plunge directly into some cavern. It often happens that while the inhabitants are upon the road into these valleys they are either melted or come to some other misfortune. The extraordinary heat in these places furnishes them with a ready means of punishing notorious criminals. The executioners take the opportunity of the first cloudy day to carry such criminals down into the plain where they tie them to a stake, and there leave them exposed to the burning rays of the sun, which soon dissolves and melts them. The country produces all kinds of minerals, except gold. These are bought up by foreign merchants in the crude state in which they are digged out of the earth. For the natives, being unable to bear the fire, know nothing of the art of smelting or working up of metals. 'Tis thought that the Iceland trade is the most beneficial of any that is carried on in these parts.

All these countries which I have been hitherto describing are subject to the great Emperor of Mezendoria, properly so called; for which reason these, as well as others which have not been mentioned, are by travellers called by the general name of the Mezendores, or Mezendorian Islands, though they are distinguished from one another by peculiar names, as has been shown in this itinerary.

That empire, which is no less spacious than it is extraordinary, was the end and as it were the center of our voyage. Eight days after we left Iceland, we arrived at the imperial city. Whatever the poets have said about societies of animals or trees we here found to be real. For Mezendoria is a country which is actually possessed in common by animals and trees, who are alike endowed with reason. Any kind of animal or tree whatsoever is allowed to enjoy the privileges of this city, provided he is obedient to the laws and to the established government. One would be apt to think that a mixture of so many creatures of different forms and opposite natures should necessarily create disorder and confusion. But by virtue of prudent laws and constitutions this contrariety is made to produce happy effects. For by means thereof a different office or employment, and such as is suited to his different genius, temper, and abilities, is prudently assigned to each of these miscellaneous subjects. Lions, because of their innate magnanimity, are here made generals of armies; elephants, by reason of their natural sagacity and the soundness of their judgments, are appointed members of the supreme council of the nation. All offices at court are filled up by chameleons, which animals being by nature subject to change can the more readily accommodate themselves to times and circumstances. The land forces are made up of bears and tigers and such warlike animals. Bulls and oxen are admitted into the sea service, for these being simple and well-meaning creatures, and at the same time hardy and obstinate and not overburdened with good breeding, are therefore esteemed the properest inhabitants for that boisterous element. They have likewise a seminary of calves, which are instructed in the art of navigation and trained up for the service of the fleet; these are called sea-calves, and are promoted by degrees to the dignity of captains and admirals. Trees, by reason of their uprightness, are created judges. Geese are advocates in the supreme courts of justice, and magpies have the management of causes in the inferior courts. Foxes are made plenipotentiaries, envoys, consuls, agents, and secretaries to embassies. Rooks are generally appointed administrators to the goods and chattels of such as die intestate. Goats are philosophers, especially grammarians, as well out of regard to their horns with which they are used to push their adversaries upon the slightest provocation as on account of their venerable beards, in which respect they surpass all other animals. Horses are civil magistrates; and vipers, moles, and dormice, farmers and husbandmen. Birds are employed as couriers and postboys. Asses, on account of the loudness of their voices, are made deacons; and nightingales execute the office of singing-men and choristers. Cocks are the watchmen in great towns, and dogs are porters at the gates. Wolves are the superior officers in the treasury and customhouse, and hawks and vultures are their deputies.

By means of these excellent institutions all public offices are duly and faithfully executed, and everything transacted in the most orderly manner. This empire, therefore, ought to be a pattern for all legislators to copy after in the establishment of new forms of government, for that so many worthless wretches get into employments is not owing to any want of persons of abilities to fill them up but solely to an improper choice. But if this matter was taken care of as it ought to be, and wise and able men promoted not on account of their general merits but of their fitness to that particular post, we should see public offices far better managed than they now are, and governments in a more flourishing condition.

What a salutary institution this is which we have been speaking of is evident from the example of this empire. We find in the annals of Mezendoria that about three hundred years ago this law was repealed by the Emperor Lilak and that public employments were conferred upon all sorts of people indifferently, provided they had merit of any kind or had signalized themselves by any extraordinary action. But this promiscuous distribution of places of trust occasioned so many and such great disorders that the government seemed upon the point of being overturned thereby. Thus, for example, a wolf, having acquitted himself with reputation in the management of the public revenues, lays claim on that account to a superior dignity, and becomes a senator; on the other hand a tree, having signalized himself by the integrity of his decisions, was rewarded by an employment in the treasury. By this preposterous promotion two able men at once were rendered absolutely useless to the public. A goat or a philosopher who was extolled to the skies by the scholastics for his keenness and obstinacy in defending an argument, desiring to advance himself, requested the first place that should happen to be vacant at court and obtained it; while a chameleon noted for his good breeding and his compliance with the times obtained by these qualities a professor's chair in the university, which he solicited for the sake of the salary. The effect of this was that the former from an able philosopher became an absurd courtier

163

and the latter from an excellent courtier was transformed into a most empty philosopher. For that perseverance in maintaining his opinions which does a man credit as a philosopher is an imperfection in the other character, since fickleness and inconstancy are cardinal virtues at court, and he that would rise there must regard not so much what is true as what is safe, and must assume a different aspect just as the face of affairs happens to change. What is there a vice is a virtue in the schools, where positiveness and a determined resolution to adhere at all events to the point you have undertaken to defend is a token of a very great man. In short, the subjects in general, even such as were remarkable for very extraordinary abilities, were by this alteration in the constitution rendered useless to their country, and the republic of course began to totter.

In this state of affairs, when everything was running to ruin, an elephant of great prudence named Baccari, at that time a senator, laid this grievance before the Emperor in very pathetic terms. That Prince, being convinced of the truth of what was told him, determined to put an immediate stop to the growing evil. The manner in which a reformation was brought about was this. Such as were in employment were not immediately turned out, for by that means the remedy would have been worse than the disease, but as fast as offices became vacant, such as already were in employments for which they were unfit were removed to others better adapted to their capacities. The good effects of this change soon became visible, and Baccari, for the great service he had done his country, had a statue erected for him, which is to be seen in the great square in Mezendoria at this day. Ever since that time the ancient laws have been religiously observed. Our interpreter affirmed that he had this relation from a certain goose with whom he was very intimate, and who was reckoned one of the most eminent lawyers in the whole city.

Many unusual and even stupendous phenomena are daily

164

offering themselves to view in this country and attracting the eyes of strangers and travellers. The sight alone of so many kinds of animals, to wit, bears, wolves, geese, magpies, etc., walking up and down the different streets and quarters of the city and conversing familiarly with each other cannot fail of exciting admiration and delight in those who are unaccustomed to such kind of sights.

The first person who came on board us was a meager wolf, or customhouse officer; he was attended by four kites, or underofficers, such as in Europe are called searchers. They seized whatever they had a mind to of our cargo, and by that means made it appear that they had learned their lesson perfectly and were very far from being novices in their trade.

The captain, according to his usual civility, always took me along with him when he went ashore. We were met at our landing by a cock who, having asked the usual questions, namely, what our business was and from whence we came, gave notice of our arrival to the chief officer of the customs. We met with a very civil reception and were invited to sup with him. His wife, who, as we were told, was a celebrated beauty among the wolves, did not make her appearance at table. The reason of her absence, we heard afterward, was her husband's jealousy, who did not think it proper to expose a person of her beauty to the view of strangers and especially of sailors, who, by reason of their long abstinence being generally very loving when they come on shore, use little or no distinction in their addresses.

Divers other married females sat down to supper with us. One of our company, a white cow with black spots, was the wife of a sea officer. Next to her sat a black cat who was wife to one of the king's huntsmen and was just come up out of the country. The person that sat next to me at table was a particoloured sow, wife to a gold-finder, all offices of this kind being filled up by such as are of hoggish extraction. She was very sluttish and sat down to table without washing her hands, which is a common thing amongst those of her tribe; but then she was extremely officious and helped me several times with her own hands. Everybody was surprised at her unusual civility, especially as these creatures are by no means remarkable for politeness. For my part I wished she had not been quite so well-bred, since the being helped by such hands was not in the least agreeable to me.

I must here observe that though the inhabitants of Mezendoria resemble brutes as to their shapes, yet they have hands and fingers which grow out of their forefeet, in which respect alone they differ from our quadrupeds. They have no occasion for clothes, as their bodies are covered over with hair or feathers. The rich are distinguished from the poor only by certain ornaments, as collars of gold, or pearls, or garlands wound in a spiral manner round about their horns. The sea officer's lady was so set off with ornaments of this kind that one could scarce see any horns she had. She excused her husband's absence by saying he was detained at home by a lawsuit, a hearing of which was to come on the day following.

After supper was over the particoloured sow whom I have been speaking of took our interpreter aside and had a long conference with him, the purport of which was that she had conceived a violent passion for me. He comforted all he could and, promising her a mutual passion on my part, he next began to make his attack on me. But as he found his words made no impression upon me, he advised me to make my escape as soon as possible, since he knew the lady would leave no stone unturned to gratify her wishes. From that time forward I kept close on board, especially after I heard that a former admirer of Her Ladyship's, a student in philosophy, who was grown jealous of me, had formed a design against my life.

I was scarce secure even on board against the repeated attacks of this inamorata who, sometimes by messages and at other times by billet-doux and love verses, endeavoured to soften my oburate heart. Had not I unfortunately lost these letters when I afterwards suffered shipwreck, I could here have presented the reader with a specimen of piggish poetry. But they are now slipped out of memory, and all that I can at present recollect of them are the following lines in which she thus sets off her beauties.

> 'Tis true, in dread array my bristles rise;
> But let me not for this be hateful to thee.
> What is the steed, without his flowing mane?
> What are the feathered race, without their
>   plumes?
> What is a tree, stripped of its leafy honours?
> What is a mortal man without his beard?
> And what, ye gods! a sow without her bristles?

We made an end of our market with such expedition that we were in a condition to set sail from thence in a few days. Our voyage, however, was retarded some time by a quarrel which happened betwixt our sailors and some of the inhabitants of the country. The occasion of the quarrel was this. As one of our men was passing through the city, a cuckoo who had a mind to be arch upon him called him in derision *Peripom,* which signifies the same as a stage-player amongst us. For as monkeys in this country are commonly rope dancers and comedians, the cuckoo took our Martinian for a player. The sailor, resenting the affront, fell upon him with a cudgel, and repeating his blow, almost maimed him. The cuckoo calling out for help desired the bystanders to bear witness of the assault, and summoned them the next day to give evidence in a court of justice. The witnesses having been examined, the matter was laid before the Senate. The sailor, being ignorant both of the laws and language of the Mezendorians, was forced to fee a pye, or lawyer, to be counsel for him. The cause was thus brought before the Senate, and after a hearing which lasted about an hour, sentence was given

167

to the following purpose: that the cuckoo, as being the aggressor, should undergo the punishment in that case provided and pay the costs of the suit. However, the lawyer's fees had swallowed up all his cash already. The judges who determined this affair were horses, two of which were consuls and the other four senators. An equal number of colts were likewise present who had a right of giving their opinons but not of voting, and were admitted into the court as pupils and candidates to fill up vacancies upon the bench.

Having finished our affairs to our satisfaction and got our loading, which was very valuable, on board, we thought of returning home. Soon after we were out at sea a sudden calm at once put a stop to our course, upon which we fell to our diversions, some to spearing of fishes as they leaped above the surface, others to angling for them. By and by we had a gale of wind, and proceeded on our voyage.

Having long ploughed the ocean with a prosperous gale, we at length came in sight of other sirens who by intervals would set up a most hideous and dismal yell. This struck an uncommon terror into the sailors, who knew by woeful experience that such mournful music portended storms and shipwrecks. Hereupon we immediately took in our sails, and every man was ordered to his post. We had scarce made an end of our work before we saw the heavens covered with black clouds. The waves began to swell, and such a storm followed that the pilot, who had used the subterranean seas for almost forty years, declared he had never known so terrible a one. Everything that happened to be upon deck was immediately washed overboard, partly by means of the waves which were every moment breaking over it and partly by the violent rains which fell at the same time, attended with dreadful lightning and loud claps of thunder, so that all the elements seemed to conspire together for our destruction.

Our mainmast was presently broken short off and carried away, and the rest soon followed it.

We had nothing now but death before our eyes. One was calling out upon his wife and children, another upon his friends and relations, and the whole vessel resounded with their mournful cries. The pilot, though without hope himself, was nevertheless obliged to soothe the rest with hopes and to advise them not to give way to unavailing sorrows. While he was in the midst of this discourse a sudden gust of wind hurried him overboard, and he was quickly swallowed up by the waves. Three others underwent the same fate, namely, the purser and two sailors. I was the only one who bore the general calamity without repining. Life was grown a burden to me, and I had no inclination to return to Martinia, where I had forfeited my liberty and good name. All the compassion I had left was for the captain, who had treated me with so much kindness during our whole voyage. I strove with all the eloquence I was master of to raise his drooping spirits, but in vain; he persisted in his sighs and womanish complaints till a wave came rolling over us and carried him away with it into the ocean.

The storm increasing still, no farther care was taken about the ship. Not a mast, not a rudder, nor even so much as a rope or oar was left, and our vessel floated at random on the waves. We were tossed about in this condition near three whole days, half dead with fear and hunger. The sky appeared serene by intervals, but nevertheless the storm continued with its usual violence. At length we discovered land, the sight of which, though it appeared to be nothing but craggy rocks and precipices, was some comfort to those of the crew who were still left alive. As the wind blew towards the shore, we were in hopes that we should soon be driven thither. But this could not happen without our suffering shipwreck by reason of the cragginess of the coast. It seemed, however, probable that some of us, if not all, by the help of some fragments of the ship might for the present at least escape.

But while we were comforting ourselves with these hopes, we struck upon a rock, which being under water had escaped our notice, with such violence that the vessel was in an instant dashed into a hundred pieces. In the midst of this confusion I laid hold of a plank, being only anxious for my own safety and little minding what became of my companions, whose fate I am yet a stranger to. It is most likely that they were all lost, since I could not hear of the arrival of any of them into that country. I was carried with great rapidity to the shore by the help of the tide and of the waves. This was a means of saving me, for had I continued a little longer in the state I was in I should certainly have perished through hunger and fatigue. After I had doubled the point of a certain promontory, the waves abated and I heard the murmuring of them at a distance only, and that too by degrees grew weaker and weaker till it entirely vanished.

This whole region is mountainous, and hence the frequent windings of the mountains, their overhanging tops, together with the deepness of the vales below, are the occasion of very great echoes here. As soon as I found myself near the shore I hallobed out as loud as I was able, in hopes that some of the inhabitants upon the coasts might hear me and come to my assistance. My first shout was not returned, but after I had repeated it I heard a kind of noise from the shore, and at length saw the inhabitants running out of the woods and coming to meet me with a boat, which was made of osier branches and oaken twigs, a proof that they were not a very improved or civilized people. But the sight of the rowers gave me a transport beyond description, for as to their exterior figure, they did not differ at all from men and were the only creatures of my own species that I had beheld during this whole subterranean tour. They are something like the inhabitants of the Torrid Zone, for they have black

170

beards and short, curled hair, and those who have long flaxen hair are reputed a kind of monsters.

At length they drew near to the broken piece of the ship I was upon and took me into their boat in a dropping condition. They then rowed to shore where, after I had been refreshed with some meat and drink though in a very plain and coarse manner, I soon recovered my vigour and spirits, notwithstanding I had been three whole days and nights in a manner combating with thirst and hunger.

[1] Lewis Holberg, *Journey to the World Under Ground* (1828), pp. 288-289.

CHAPTER XII

The Author's Arrival at Quama

And now a crowd of people surrounded me. They talked to me in their language, of which I was wholly ignorant, and I was at a loss what to answer. They often repeated the word *Dank, Dank,* which sounding like High Dutch I answered first in that language, then in the Danish tongue, and lastly in Latin. But to all this they only shook their heads to intimate that these languages were utterly unknown to them. Then I tried them in the Subterranean languages, namely, the Nazaric and the Martinian, but all to no purpose. This made me conclude that they were an unsociable nation who had no kind of commerce with the rest of the world, and that therefore I should be under a necessity in this country of turning boy and going to school once more to learn my letters.

After we had conversed some time together, but in such a manner that we did not understand one another, they brought me to a cottage made of osiers. There were no seats, benches, or tables in it, for they eat upon the ground, and for want of beds they use only straw, and sleep promiscuously on the floor, which is the more to be admired as they have plenty of timber among them. Their food is milk, cheese, barley-bread, and flesh, which last they broil upon the coals, having no notion of any other sort of cookery. In short, they lived in as plain a manner as the first race of mankind, so that I was forced to live like a Cynic philosopher till I had made such a progress in their language as enabled me to converse with the inhabitants and assist their ignorance.

And indeed, all my orders and directions were observed as so many oracles. Nay, to such a height my reputation rose that they flocked to me in crowds from all the adjacent towns and villages, as to an illustrious doctor, or a teacher sent from heaven. I heard also that a new computation of time was made use of among them which commenced from my arrival. All this, I own, was so much the more grateful to me as in the planet Nazar and at Martinia I had been a public jest, in the former place for my vivacity and quick conception, and in the later for my dullness. And here I experienced the truth of that vulgar saying, "Among the blind, he that squints is a king." For I was now in a country where, with a slender share of knowledge and with ordinary abilities, I could arrive at the highest honours.

And room enough there was here to try my own strength and exercise my talents, for the country abounded to profusion with everything necessary for the use of man. Many things it produced spontaneously, and whatever grain was sowed repaid the husbandman with ample interest. The inhabitants were of a docile disposition, and by no means destitute of wit and understanding; but then, as they had never been taught anything, they remained in the depth of ignorance. When I related to them the circumstances of my family, my country, my shipwreck, and the other accidents that befell me in my travels, nobody could be brought to believe it, for they were positive that I was an inhabitant of the sun and that I descended from that glorious luminary. Agreeably to this conceit, they commonly called me by the name of *Pikil-Su*, that is, "Ambassador of the Sun."

As to their religion, they did not deny the existence of a Supreme Being, but then they did not trouble their heads about the proof of that high point; it was sufficient to them that their fathers before them believed it; and this is their whole system of

173

divinity. As to their morality, they knew nothing except this single precept of "Not doing to others what you would not have done to yourself." They knew no law beside the sole will and pleasure of their emperor, and therefore no crimes but those of a public nature were ever punished. Whatever misdemeanour was otherwise committed, all the revenge the neighbours took was to avoid the company of the offenders, to whom such a general contempt was usually so intolerable that many have died for grief, and as many more have laid violent hands upon themselves through a weariness of life. Chronology they know nothing of, only they compute their years from the eclipse of the sun, which happens by the interposition of the planet Nazar; so that when you inquire how old anyone is, their answer is that he is so many eclipses old. Their physics are excessively barren and absurd; they believe the sun is a golden plate, and the planet Nazar a cheese. When I inquired the reasons why at stated times the planet Nazar increased and decreased, they replied that they knew nothing at all about it.

Their wealth and substance consists chiefly in swine, which they distinguish by some particular mark, and then suffer them to run loose in the woods. They scourge and beat all such trees as bear no fruit from a foolish opinion that their sterility proceeds from malice and envy. Such was the state of this poor miserable people, whom I almost despaired of ever reducing to humanity, but I took courage and employed the whole force of my capacity and abilities in reforming these barbarians. For these my endeavours, and the success which attended them, they regarded me as something above the race of mortals, and so extravagant an opinion did they entertain of my wisdom that they thought nothing was impossible to me. Upon the loss of cattle or goods, they would come at all hours to my hut and implore my assistance. One day I saw a poor peasant prostrate before my door, weeping and wringing his hands, and crying out to me to help him. Upon inquiry into the occasion of his grief, he complained to me of the perverseness and ill nature of his trees, and begged me to interpose my authority to make them bear more acorns.

I was informed that the whole country was in subjection to a monarch, whose residence at that time was about eight days' journey from the place I was now in. I say "at that time," because the metropolis of the empire was movable, that is, His Majesty (whose place of residence was looked upon as the capital) had no palace or fixed habitation, but lived in tents, which he transported, together with his royal family and the whole court, from one province to another. The prince who then swayed the sceptre was a man of years, and was called Casba, which signifies "great emperor." This territory, with respect to the extent of it, merits indeed the name of an empire; but through the ignorance of the inhabitants, who do not know their own strength, it makes no great figure, but is exposed to the insults and ridicule of its neighbours, and is often obliged to become tributary to nations in reality more contemptible than themselves.

Fame had now spread my name and virtues over all the provinces. Nothing of moment was undertaken without first consulting me, and every unsuccessful enterprise was ascribed to my coldness and want of favour. Nay, some had it in their heads to appease my anger with sacrifices. I forbear to recount all the follies of this stupid nation, and shall only give one or two instances by which you may easily judge of the rest. A big-bellied woman came to me to desire she might have a boy. Another entreated me to make his old parents young again. Another begged me to take him with me up to the sun, that he might return from thence with as much gold as he could carry. With these and such unaccountable requests was I continually pestered, though I still reprimanded their folly in a severe tone, for I was afraid lest that absurd conceit of my power might terminate in divine worship.

At length it reached the ears of the monarch that a stranger was arrived in his dominions who called himself the Ambassador of the Sun and who, by giving most wise and divine instructions to the Quamites (so were called the inhabitants of this country, the name of which was Quama), had convinced the people that he was more than man. Upon this he presently dispatched an embassy to me, inviting me to court.

The ambassadors were in number thirty, all clothed with tigers' skins, a dress so much the more honourable in this country as the use thereof is permitted to none but those who have behaved themselves with gallantry in the war against the Tanachites. (These are rational tigers, and implacable enemies to the Quamites.) But during all this time, in the village where I continued, I had run up a stone house of two stories after the manner of the buildings in Europe. The ambassadors beheld it as a stupendous work exceeding human strength, and therefore when they came to me to signify His Imperial Majesty's pleasure, they entered my house with a religious awe, as into a temple of sanctuary. The speech they made to me on this occasion was nearly this:

"Whereas the great Emperor Casba, our sovereign lord and master, derives his origin from the great Spynko, son of the Sun, and founder of the Quamitic Empire, he therefore thinks nothing could be more fortunate or agreeable than your arrival, especially as it must be of the highest advantage to his dominions, and as there is all the reason in the world to hope that under such an illustrious and celestial teacher the kingdom will, in a short time, wear another face. For which reason he hopes you will so much the more willingly honour his court, as the capital of the empire is a more ample field for the exercise of your virtues."

This harangue being ended, I returned my humble thanks to the ambassadors and accompanied them immediately to the palace.

176

Though they had taken up fourteen days in coming, yet in returning we spent only four, which was owing to a contrivance of mine. For as I had observed a vast multitude of horses in this country which were of no manner of use but rather a burden upon the people, inasmuch as they lived in the woods like wild beasts, I laid open to the natives the several advantages which would accrue from the service of those generous brutes, and taught them the art of breaking them. In a short time a great number were tamed, and upon the arrival of the ambassadors, I had as many broken and prepared as would serve us all in our return.

At the sight of the horses thus instructed, the ambassadors were amazed, but were afraid to mount them. But when they saw me and others guiding and turning them which way we pleased by means of the bridle, and that without fear or danger, they took courage, after two or three trials, and ventured upon the journey. And this was the reason that they returned in one third of the time they came.

When we drew near the place where the royal city was supposed to be, we heard that this famous metropolis was removed into another province, which obliged us to bend our course another way.

Upon our approach to the capital, the fright and surprise of the people is not to be expressed. Many, struck with a panic, abandoned the royal city. The Emperor himself kept shuddering in his pavilion, nor dared to go out of it till one of the ambassadors, alighting from his horse, went and explained the mystery to him. I was introduced soon after in great form, and with a train of people behind me, to the Emperor's presence.

Casba was sitting on a carpet, surrounded by his courtiers. Having paid my compliments to His Imperial Highness, he rose and asked me how the Emperor of the Sun did, the founder of the royal family of Quama. To this question, as I conceived it necessary to keep up the popular error, I replied that I was sent from the Monarch of the Sun to reform the savage manners of the Quamites with salutary instructions, and to open a way for them not only to repel the insults of their neighbours, but also to enlarge the bounds of their empire, and that I had orders to end my days among them.

This speech highly pleased the Emperor. He commanded a tent to be erected for me near his own; he also assigned me fifteen domestics to attend on me, and, laying aside the manner of a monarch, behaved to me always like a friend.

CHAPTER XIII

The Rise of the Fifth Monarchy

From that time forward I was wholly taken up in giving a new form to the government and instructing the youth in military discipline.

I began with teaching them the management of horses and training them for war, as I hoped that by our horse alone our neighbours might be kept in awe. The Emperor was soon supplied, through my diligence, with six thousand horse. The Tanachites were at that time preparing for a fresh invasion on account of the delay of the annual tribute, the payment of which had often been solicited in vain.

I was ordered by the Emperor to go and meet the enemy with my new-raised cavalry, to which were added a body of infantry. These were armed with pikes and javelins, with which they might engage the Tanachites at a distance. For the Quamites had hitherto made use of short swords or daggers only, for which reason, being obliged to engage hand to hand with very fierce enemies who were much superior to them in strength, they had always fought upon unequal terms.

Being appointed general in this expedition, as soon as I heard that the Tanachites were drawn up in order of battle not far from the borders of our empire, I marched to meet them with all my forces. The enemy, thunderstruck with the sight of an unexpected army, remained for some time motionless, but our forces, advancing towards them, began to handle their pikes and javelins as soon as the enemy came within reach, and made a heavy slaughter of them. The Tanachites, however, did not lose courage, but made a brisk attack upon our infantry; but the new-raised horse falling upon their flanks, their ranks were quickly broken and they themselves put to flight, so that the fortune of the battle wholly turned on this assault. A terrible slaughter ensued, and the general of the Tanachites and twenty tigers of the first quality were taken prisoners and led in triumph to Quama.

It is scarce to be expressed what joy this extraordinary victory diffused throughout the empire, for the Quamites had generally been routed in all former battles, and forced to beg a peace upon the most dishonourable terms. The Emperor, according to custom, immediately sentenced all the prisoners to be executed; but as I had an abhorrence of this custom, I advised the keeping them in custody, thinking the Tanachites (with whom we could neither be said to be at war nor in peace at that time) would be quiet until they saw what was to become of their prisoners.

And besides, I urged that a truce was necessary for me to put some schemes in execution which I was then projecting. I had before taken notice that the country abounded with saltpeter, and had got together a large quantity of it in order to make gunpowder. I had not, however, communicated my design to anybody but the Emperor, whose authority I stood in need of to erect offices for casting barrels for guns and other kinds of weapons; and I was in hopes that by the help of these instruments all the enemies of this empire might in a short time be subdued.

After I had got some hundreds of muskets made, together with a quantity of ball, I gave a public specimen of my invention, to the great astonishment of everybody. A certain number of men were immediately set aside to be continually exercised in the management of these muskets. After the musketeers came to be pretty ready in their exercises, I was declared *Jachal* by the Emperor, or generalissimo of all his forces, and all the subordinate officers were ordered to receive their commands from me.

While these affairs were transacting, I had frequent conferences with Tomopoloko, the general of the Tanachites, in order to discover the state, the manners, and disposition of that nation. I found him, to my great surprise, to be a person of prudence, learning, and politeness, and was informed by him that literature and arts were in no small esteem in the country of the Tanachites.

He told me likewise that there were a very warlike people eastward of them whom the Tanachites were obliged to be perpetually upon their guard against. The inhabitants were small of stature, and much inferior to the Tanachites in strength of body; but then their understandings were very acute, and they were eminent for their dexterity in managing their javelins, or darts, and for this reason had often compelled the Tanachites to sue for peace. I learned afterward that that nation was composed of cats and that, of all the inhabitants of the Firmament, they were the most remarkable for their able judgment and skill in politics.

It was no small grief to me to be informed that learning, wisdom, and politeness flourished among all the creatures of this subterranean world, man only excepted, and that the Quamites alone were barbarous and uncivilized. I hoped, however, that this reproach would soon be removed and that the Quamites would recover that dominion which Nature has given to man over all other animals.

The Tanachites continued quiet for a long time after their last defeat; but after they had discovered, by means of their spies, the state and disposition of the new body of horse, namely, that those centaurs which had struck such a terror into them were nothing else but horses which had been broken and managed, they resumed new courage and raised fresh forces which the King himself commanded in person. The army consisted of twenty thousand tigers, all veteran troops, except two regiments which had lately been enlisted. These new-raised forces were, however, a nominal and not a real addition to their strength.

This army, flushed with hopes of victory, struck a terror into the whole empire of Quama. Twelve thousand of our foot advanced to meet them, among which were six hundred musketeers, together with four thousand horse. As I had no doubt about the success of the battle, lest the Emperor should be defrauded of the glory of the victory, I entreated the old man to put himself at the head of his forces. I lost nothing of my credit by this feigned modesty, since the whole army looked upon me as their leader.

I thought it most advisable not to let my musketeers have any share in the first assault, having a mind to try whether we could not carry the victory by means of the horse alone. But this piece of management cost me dear. For the Tanachites attacked our foot with so much violence that they obliged them to give way; they stood likewise the shock of our horse so valiantly that for a long time it could not be said to which side the victory inclined.

While we were in the heat of the battle, I led my musketeers on to the attack. At the first discharge of our artillery, the Tanachites were in a manner stupefied. They could not conceive from whence those thunders and lightnings proceeded; but when they saw the dreadful effects thereof, they were seized as it were with a panic. This first salutation laid two hundred tigers prostrate on the ground, amongst which were two chaplains belonging to the camp who were each of them pierced through with a musket ball while they were encouraging the soldiers to do their duty by very pathetic discourses in praise of valour. Their fate was bitterly lamented by all, for they were reckoned admirable orators.

As soon as I perceived the terror our enemies were in, I

ordered a second discharge to be made. This did more execution than the former; great numbers were killed, and among the rest, the King himself. Upon this, the enemy, losing all hopes, turned their backs. Our horse pursued them and made so great a slaughter of them as they fled that the multitude of carcasses with which the field was covered at length put a stop to their pursuit. After the battle was over and we had time to take an account of the number of the slain, they were found to amount to thirteen thousand.

The enemy being thus entirely routed, the victorious army entered the country of the Tanachites, and after a few days' march encamped under the walls of the metropolis. Such a terror had at that time seized all people's minds that though the town was strong and well-secured by its situation, walls, and forts, and well-stored with provisions of all kinds, yet the magistrates came out in the most suppliant manner to meet the conquerors and to offer them the keys of the city.

This city was no less remarkable for its great extent than for the cleanness of its streets and the neatness of its buildings. And it was certainly matter of great wonder that the Quamites, who were encompassed on all sides by nations so polite, should have continued so long in their barbarity. But they were in this respect like some other nations who, though ignorant of what passes in foreign countries, entertain a high conceit of themselves, and who, having no commerce or communication with others, live hugely contented in their own sordidness and ignorance, of which it would be very easy to produce instances among the Europeans.

This defeat became a new era among the Tanachites; and as this decisive battle was fought, according to their computation, upon the third day of the month Torul, they reckon this among the unlucky days. At this season of the year the planet Nazar, whose revolution round the subterranean sun regulates the time and distinguishes the seasons, is at its farthest distance from this part of the firmament. The whole firmament likewise makes its revolution round the sun, but as the planet moves with greater velocity, Nazar seems to increase or decrease according as it is nearer to, or more remote from, this or that hemisphere. The increase or decrease of this planet, as also the eclipses of the sun, is the subject of astronomical observations in this country. I once took the pains, at my hours of leisure, to examine the Tanachitish calendar, and it seemed to me to be an orderly and well-digested thing.

The taking of the capital city was followed by the surrender of the whole kingdom, so that the contempt with which the Quamites had been before stigmatized was changed into renown; and the empire of Quama, by the addition of this conquered nation, became almost twice as powerful as it was before. But as everybody looked upon this success to be owing to my industry and mangement, the esteem which they had for a long time conceived for me was heightened almost into adoration.

The Tanachites being thus subdued, and governors appointed in every city to keep this fierce and warlike people in their duty, I went to work to finish the task I had begun and to root out that barbarity in which the Quamites were as yet involved. It was a matter of great difficulty, however, to introduce the study of the liberal arts at once, for the Latin tongue and a few scraps of Greek which I had learned in Europe would not, I knew, be here of any use. For this reason I caused twelve of the most learned tigers to be sent for out of the enemy's country. These were made professors and commanded to found a university upon the model of those in their own country. I likewise ordered the royal library of Tanachin to be removed to Quama. I was determined, however, that as soon as the Quamites had made such a progress in literature as to be able to stand upon their

184

own legs, I would send these foreigners back into their own country.

I was very desirous of seeing the Tanachitish library because I had been informed by their general Tomopoloko that amongst other manuscripts in the archives of the library there was one composed by an author who had been in our world, and had left a description of its different kingdoms, especially the European ones. He told me likewise that the Tanachites had got possession of this book while they were at war in a very distant country, but that the name of the author was concealed, nor could it ever be learned who he was, nor how he was carried to the superterranean habitations.

Upon looking over the book I found what Tomopoloko had told me concerning the author was true, and therefore I candidly discovered my race and country to him, assuring him at the same time that I had declared the same thing to the Quamites at my first arrival, but that the stupid mortals gave no credit to my narration, but would needs have me to be an ambassador from the sun and still continued to persist obstinately in that error. I added likewise that as I looked upon it to be a crime to keep so vain a title any longer, I was at length determined to discover my origin to the public, by which ingenuous confession I thought my reputation would not in the least suffer, especially as I hoped that the reading of this book would convince everybody how much the Europeans excel all other people in virtue and in knowledge.

The prudent Tomopoloko did not seem pleased with my design and gave me his sentiments upon it, as I remember, in the following terms. "Good sir, before you proceed in your design, it will be necessary for you to see the book, the reading of which may, perhaps, divert you from your purpose; for either the author has misrepresented them, or the manners of the Superterraneans are foolish and absurd, and they are governed by laws and customs more worthy of laughter than regard. But after you have read the book, you may use your own discretion. One piece of advice, however, I will presume to give you, and that is not rashly to reject a title which has rendered you so venerable in the opinion of the Quamites; for nothing serves more effectually to restrain men within the bounds of duty than the opinion which the vulgar entertain of birth and high descent."

I took the advice and determined, with the assistance of Tomopoloko, to read the book. The title of it is this: *Tanian's Journey to the Superterranean World, or a Description of the Kingdoms and Countries upon Earth.* The name of Tanian is thought to be fictitious, and as the book was grown mouldy for want of being taken due care of, and imperfect in several places through length of time, what I wanted most to see, namely, which way the author got up to our world and down again, was missing. These are the contents of what remained of the work.

> *Fragments of Tanian's Journey Above Ground,* translated from the original by the celebrated, noble, and valiant Tomopoloko, general of the Tanachites.
>
> . . . This country (i.e., Germany) goes by the name of the Roman Empire; but this is merely titular, for the Roman monarchy has been extinct for several ages.
>
> The language which the Germans use is with much difficulty to be understood, because the natural order of the words is inverted; for what goes first in other languages comes last in this, so that you may be obliged to read to the end of a page before you can comprehend the meaning of it.
>
> The form of government is strange. The Germans think they have a king, and yet in reality they have none. Germany is said to be one empire, and yet it is divided into many separate principalities, each of which has the sovereign power within itself, so that they often make war upon one another, and have most certainly a right so to do. The empire is said to be "always august," though it is sometimes very much diminished; "holy," though without any holiness; "invincible," though often exposed to the depredations of its neigh-

bours. Nor are the rights and privileges of this nation less
wonderful, since many have rights which they are prohibited
from making any use of. Infinite are the comments which
have been published upon the state of the German Empire,
but so intricate is the subject that in spite of all their labours
they are at every turn as much at a loss as ever concerning
it; for . . .

. . . The capital of this kingdom (France), which is very
large, is called Paris. It may in some sense be styled the
capital of Europe, for it exercises a kind of jurisdiction over
all other European nations. For example, it prescribes rules
to them about their eating and about the fashion of their
clothes, so that let any fashion be as ridiculous and as inconvenient as it will, all other nations are obliged to follow it
whenever the Parisians are pleased to lead the way. How or
what time they acquired this right I could never learn. Their
authority, however, did not, as I understood, extend to other
things, for the rest of the European nations are often at war
with the French, and sometimes force them to accept of
peace upon very severe terms; but the servitude they are under
with regard to dress and the manner of eating is perpetual, so
that whatever fashion is invented at Paris the rest of Europe
are strictly obliged to come into it. The Parisians very much
resemble the Martinians in quickness of apprehension, the
love of novelty, and a fertility of invention.

. . . Having left Bologna, we went to Rome. This city
is subject to a priest who, though his dominions are very
narrow, is reckoned the most powerful of all the European
kings and princes, for other princes exercise dominion only
over the persons and estates of their subjects, but this can
destroy their souls likewise. The Europeans in general believe
that the keys of Heaven are in the custody of this priest. I
was very desirous of seeing so great a curiosity, but I lost my
labour, nor do I know to this day what form they are of, or
in what cabinet they are kept.

The authority which this pontiff exercises, not only over his
own subjects, but over all mankind, chiefly consists in this,
that he can absolve whom God condemns and condemn whom
He absolves. An enormous power indeed! and such a one
as our Subterraneans will never believe can fall to any mortal's

187

share. But it is an easy matter to impose upon the Europeans as one pleases and to make them swallow the greatest absurdities, though they imagine that nobody has any understanding but themselves; and being puffed with this opinion, they look down with contempt upon all other mortals, as if they were barbarians in comparison of them.

For my part, I do not undertake to justify the manners, laws, and customs of our Subterraneans; I will only produce some instances of the customs of the Europeans, in order to make it appear how undeservedly they pass a censure upon the manners of other nations.

It is a custom all over Europe for people to scatter a kind of meal, which is made by grinding the fruits of the earth, and which Nature intended for food, over their hair and clothes. This meal is commonly called "powder," and great care and pains are used to cleanse their hair from it every night with an instrument called a comb, in order to make room for more of the same sort.

They have another custom which appeared to me no less ridiculous, which is this. They have a kind of little cover, or hat, to defend their heads against the cold, which cover they very often wear under one of their arms, even in the very depth of winter. This appeared as absurd to me as it would have been to have seen a man walking through the streets with his coat or his breeches in his hand and leaving his body to be exposed to the inclemencies of the air, from which they were intended to defend it.

The religious opinions of the Europeans are very sound and agreeable to right reason. They are under an injunction carefully to study the books in which the rule of faith and practice is contained, in order to discover their true sense and meaning. These books recommend indulgence to weak brethren and such as happen to be mistaken; but if any should chance to understand a thing in a different sense from the majority, he is punished for this defect of judgment by fines, imprisonment, whipping, and even sometimes by dying at a stake. This seemed to me the same thing as if a man who happened to be short-sighted should undergo the bastinado only because objects which seem square to me appear round to him. I was informed that thousands had been hanged and burned, by order of the magistrate, on this account.

In almost every town and village you see men standing up in places of public resort and severely reprimanding others for those sins which they themselves are daily guilty of; which is just as if one should hear a man in liquor declaiming against drunkenness.

Oftentimes a person who is born humpbacked, crooked, or lame shall be ambitious of being thought handsome, and another sprung from the dregs of the people shall be ambitious of a coat of arms, or a title, which is full as absurd as if a dwarf should affect to be called a giant, or an old man, young.

It is a custom in great towns for friends and acquaintances to visit one another after dinner in order to drink a kind of black broth made of burned beans. This broth is commonly called "coffee." When they make these visits, they are shut up in a box which is fixed upon four wheels and drawn to the place of rendezvous by two beasts of very great strength, for the Europeans think it a disgrace to use their legs.

Upon the first day of the year the Europeans are seized with a disease which we have no knowledge of amongst us. The symptoms of it are strange commotions and agitations of mind and an inability to sit still in any place. They run about at such times from one house to another as if they were distracted, without knowing why they do it. The disease sometimes lasts for fourteen days. At length, when they are quite fatigued and spent with continually running about, they come to themselves again and recover their former health.

As the Europeans have innumerable diseases of mind, so they have innumerable remedies. Some are seized with a strange passion of walking in such a manner as that the left sides of their bodies may be turned towards the right sides of others. The farther north you go, the stronger you find this humour, which proves that it is all owing to the climate and the intemperature of the air. This disease is cured by certain sealed papers filled with characters of a particular kind. As long as the patient carries these papers about him by way of talisman or charm, he grows better and better by degrees till he is quite recovered.

Another raging distemper they have is cured by the sound

of a bell at the noise of which the mind immediately grows calm, and the disorder abates; yet this remedy is by no means effectual, because in two or three hours' time the same raging evil returns.

In Italy, France, and Spain, during the winter season, an epidemic madness prevails for several weeks. They put a stop to it at length by sprinkling the foreheads of the patients with ashes at an appointed time. But in the northern parts of Europe these ashes have no virtue, and the inhabitants of the north recover by the help of Nature only.

Most of the Europeans enter into a solemn covenant with God, which they call "the Communion," three or four times a year, and break it as soon as ever they have made it, so that they seem to make it for no other reason but that they may show that they are resolved not to stand to their agreement.

When they confess their sins and implore the mercy of God, their words are generally set to music. Flutes, trumpets, and drums are sometimes added to the concert, according to the greatness of the crime for which they are suing pardon.

Almost all the European nations are obliged to confess their belief of a doctrine contained in a certain sacred book. But reading this book is totally prohibited in the southern countries, so that people there are laid under a necessity of believing what it is criminal to read or inquire into.

In the same countries, men are forbidden to worship God in any but an unknown tongue, so that such prayers only are thought to be legitimate and agreeable to the Divine Being as are put up by persons who do not understand a word they say.

In the great cities, such as arrive at honours and profitable employments are all paralytic, for they are obliged to be carried along the streets like weak and impotent people on a kind of couch made in the figure of a chest or box.

Most of the Europeans shave their heads and, to conceal their baldness, wear an artificial covering made of other people's hair.

The controversies which are commonly discussed in the schools in Europe are about things the knowledge of which neither concerns mankind, nor is within the reach of their comprehension. But the most learned subjects of all which the Europeans comment upon are the rings, robes, slippers, shoes, and buskins of certain antiquated people who lived many centuries ago. As to the sciences, as well sacred as profane, the generality do not judge for themselves but subscribe implicitly to the opinion of others. Whatever sect they happen to fall into, they stick to it with all imaginable firmness. As to what they say of pinning their faith upon the sleeve of others who are wiser than themselves, I should approve of it, were the vulgar and illiterate proper judges of this matter, for to be able to distinguish who is this wise man that may be relied upon requires the greatest wisdom.

In the southern countries, a sort of little cakes or wafers are carried about the streets, which the priests say are gods; but what is most surprising, the very bakers themselves who show you the flour of which they were made will take their oaths upon it that the world was created by these wafers.

The English are very fond of liberty and are subject to nobody but their wives. As to their religion, it is hard to say what it is, for they take up an opinion one day and throw it aside the next. I imputed this fickle disposition to the situation of the country, for the English live upon an island, and being a maritime people, partake much of the nature of the inconstant element that surrounds them.

The English are very solicitous about the health of everyone they meet, so that a man would take them all to be physicians. But that common question "How do you do?" I found to be only an empty form of speech, and a sound without any sense or meaning in it. Many of these islanders take so much pains to improve their minds and polish their understandings that at length they entirely lose them.

Towards the north there is a republic consisting of seven provinces. These go by the name of the United Provinces, though there is but little sign of concord or unity amongst them. The people here boast of their power as if the whole authority of the republic were lodged in their hands; and yet the populace are nowhere more excluded from public employments, and the supreme power is vested in a very few families. The inhabitants of these provinces are deeply attentive upon heaping up riches, which they make no use of, so that while their purses are full, their bellies are empty. They seem to live upon smoke only, which they suck in through a tube or pipe which is made of clay. It must be allowed, however, for the honour of this nation, that they are the neatest of all people, for they take great care to wash everything except their hands.

In the cities and great towns in Europe, a watch is kept in the street by night. The watchmen go their rounds every hour and wake people out of their sleep by wishing them a good night.

Every country has its peculiar laws, and its peculiar customs likewise, which are ofttimes diametrically opposite to those laws. For example: a wife, according to the laws, ought to be subject to her husband; but according to custom, she has a right to govern him.

Those who live most luxuriously and consume the greatest quantity of the products of the earth are held in most esteem in Europe, and only husbandmen and such as supply materials for the luxury of the great are treated with contempt.

The great number of gibbets, gallows, and places of execution which are everywhere to be seen show the Europeans to be people of very bad dispositions and subject to many kinds of vices. There is a public executioner in every city. The English are an exception to this rule, amongst whom, I believe, there are no executioners, for the people in that country hang themselves.

One would suspect the Europeans to be Anthropophagi, or man-eaters, for it is a custom amongst them to shut up a great number of able-bodied men in cloisters, which they call monasteries, for no other end but that they may grow sleek and fat; and while they are kept in these cells, they are utterly exempted from all labour and have nothing to do but eat and drink.

The Europeans have a custom of drinking water every morning to moderate the heat of their stomachs; but before they are well grown cool by this means, they go to work to warm them again by swallowing down draughts of fiery liquors, which they call "drams."

The religion of the Europeans is divided into two principal sects, one of which are called Protestants, and the other Papists. The former worship one god only; but the latter adore several, for they have as many gods and goddesses as there are towns and villages. All these gods and goddesses are made by the Roman pontiff, or high priest. This pontiff himself is made by presbyters, commonly called "cardinals." Hence it appears how great the power of these cardinals must be, since they can make him who makes the gods.

The ancient inhabitants of Italy conquered the whole world and were subject only to their wives, but the modern ones tyrannize over their wives and are slaves to all mankind besides.

The animals in Europe are divided into terrestrial and aquatic. There are some amphibious ones likewise, as frogs, dolphins, and Dutchmen. The last dwell in a marshy soil and live upon land or water indifferently.

The Europeans use much the same food that we do, but a Spaniard will live upon air.

Trade flourishes much in every part of Europe, and many commodities are sold there in which we never traffic; thus, for example, the Romish church sells heaven; the Swiss sell themselves; and in . . . crowns, sceptres, and the royal authority itself are set to sale.

In Spain, laziness is the token of a gentleman, and nothing is a greater recommendation of nobility than sleeping much. Those are called good men and true believers who believe what they do not understand and never think it worth their while to examine what they hear. Some have even been reckoned saints merely for their slothfulness, their want of curiosity, and their neglecting to inquire into religious matters. But those who are solicitous about their own salvation and happen, through a diligent and accurate inquiry, to dissent from any reigning opinion are said to be damned to all eternity.

It is a prevailing opinion in Europe that future happiness or misery does not depend upon good works or the exercise of virtue and religion, but upon the place of a man's nativity. For all agree that if they had been born in another place, or of other parents, they should have been of a different religion. Hence they in reality condemn people not so much on account of their religion as the place or other circumstances of their birth. But how this opinion is reconcilable with the divine justice or goodness, I cannot comprehend.

Amongst the men of letters, those are most esteemed whose business it is to invert the natural order of words and render that obscure and perplexed which before was plain and easy. These are called poets, and this art of disjointing words goes by the name of poetry. But poetry does not consist in this perversity of style only, because to deserve that name a composition must likewise be extremely full of lies. An ancient poet, Homer by name, is held in high esteem and almost adoration, because he excelled in both these arts. Many have imitated him, but nobody ever yet came up to him either in confounding the order of words or perverting the truth.

The literati of Europe are very fond of buying books, but in this point they do not so much regard the matter they contain as they do the form and neatness of them. The booksellers, who are well aware of this and know that their learned customers had rather feast their eyes than their minds, are perpetually reprinting their books in a different size and letter and with new decorations, by which means they make an infinite advantage. For in this country the liberal arts are made a trade of, and some authors are reckoned as sharp and cunning as any trader at all.

The universities in Europe are shops where degrees, promotions, dignities, and various kinds of titles and other learned wares are set to sale at reasonable rates, all which are not to be acquired in our Subterranean world without indefatigable pains and study for years together. Those who have reached the summit of all erudition, or (in the European phrase) have got to the top of a certain mountain, called Parnassus, inhabited by nine virgins, are styled doctors. The next to these are masters of arts, who come at their titles at somewhat a less expense, and are therefore thought to be less learned. The good will which these Superterranean schools bear to mankind is evident from their thus rendering the way to learning smooth and easy. The northern seminaries were a little more rigid in this respect, since the highest honours are not there conferred without a previous examination.

The learned are distinguished from the illiterate by their dress and manners, but chiefly by their religion; for the latter worship only one god, but the former pay their devotions to several. The principal deities of the learned are Apollo, Minerva, the Nine Muses, and others of an inferior rank which writers, and especially poets, are wont to invoke at such times as they fall into raptures, or a kind of raving.

The learned, according to the diversity of their studies, are distinguished into various classes, for instance, philosophers, poets, grammarians, naturalists, metaphysicians, etc.

A philosopher is a literary merchant who sets to sale precepts concerning self-denial, temperance, and poverty at a stated price, and spends his time in writing and declaiming against riches till he grows rich himself. The father of these philosophers was one Seneca, who by this method amassed together a princely fortune.

A poet is a person who acquires renown by being thought to be out of his senses. Hence it is usual to speak of all great poets as possessed with a divine fury or distraction, and all who express their thoughts with simplicity and perspicuity are judged unworthy of the laurel.

The grammarians are a sort of militia whose only business is to disturb the public peace. They differ from the other soldiery in this respect, that instead of a coat of mail they wear a gown, and fight with their pens instead of swords. They contend as obstinately for letters and syllables as the others do for their liberties and properties. The reason why they are kept up, I believe, is this, that the European princes are afraid lest people in a time of peace should grow dull and lose their spirits for want of somewhat like a war. Sometimes, however, when these differences begin to threaten bloodshed, the Senate interposes its authority. An accident of this kind happened not long ago at Paris, as I was told. For a dispute concerning the letters Q and K growing to a height among the doctors, the Senate wisely put an end to it by allowing everyone to use the letter he liked best.

A naturalist, or natural philosopher, is a person who diligently inquires into the bowels of the earth, and studies the nature of quadrupeds, reptiles, and insects of all kinds and who is acquainted with everything, except himself.

A metaphysician is one who alone knows those things which are concealed from others; who can describe and define the essence of spirits and of souls, of entities and non-entities; and who, being very sharp-sighted in spying out things at a distance, overlooks such as are almost under his nose.

Such is the state of learning in Europe. I could say more upon this head, but it is sufficient to have touched upon the principal points. The reader will easily judge from hence whether the Europeans are right or wrong in thinking no people have any knowledge but themselves.

It must be confessed, however, that the doctors and masters in Europe are much more dextrous in instructing youth than our Subterraneans are. For they have masters of arts and of languages among them who teach others not only what they have learned themselves, but even what they are utterly unacquainted with. If it is an arduous task to communicate clearly to others what we know ourselves, surely it is much more so to teach them what we are entirely ignorant of.

Amongst the men of learning there are some who apply themselves with equal diligence both to philosophy and divinity. These men, as divines, dare not deny what as philosophers they very much doubt of.

The Europeans apply themselves to letters with as much industry as we do; but they become learned in much less time by means of a certain extraordinary magical invention, "literary journals," by the help whereof they can read over a hundred volumes in a day.

The Superterraneans are very religious and constant at divine service; but their times of worship are not regulated by the motions of the heart, but by the ringing of bells, by clocks, or sundials, so that this devotion seems to be purely mechanical, and to depend upon externals, upon custom, or upon stated times rather than to flow from the dictates of the heart.

Their taste for religious duties appears from their custom of singing hymns or psalms while they are cleaving wood, washing dishes, or employed in any other manual labour.

When I arrived in Italy, I looked upon myself to be lord of the whole country, for everyone I met professed himself my slave. Having a mind to try how far this servility which they made such a show of would extend, I ordered my landlord's wife to be brought to me one night; but he immediately fell into a passion, and commanded me to pack up my baggage and be gone; and as I did not make haste enough, he fairly turned me out of doors.

In the northern countries, people are very fond of titles, though they have not the possessions which belong to them. They are likewise extremely ambitious of the upper hand. Moreover . . .

Thus far I patiently attended, but my indignation was now raised and I would hear no more, declaring that these were fictions of a partial writer, and one who was overrun with spleen. But when my heat a little abated, I began to form a more favourable judgment of this itinerary as I saw that the author, though he appeared in many places to be partial and not to have had the best regard to truth, was not, however, mistaken in his judgment, but had often hit the nail, as we say, on the head.

I now determined with myself to take the advice of Tomopoloko and cherish the error of the Quamites concerning my origin, since I thought it more for my interest to pass for an ambassador extraordinary from the sun than for a citizen of Europe.

Our neighbours had now continued quiet for a long time, and I had taken the advantage of this wished-for peace to settle the republic to my satisfaction. News at length arrived that three very powerful nations had entered into an alliance to invade the Quamites. These were the Arctonians, the Kispucians, and the Alectorians. The Arctonians were a nation of bears who were endowed with speech and reason and were reckoned very fierce and warlike. The Kispucians were cats of an extraordinary size and were in great repute among the Subterraneans for their sagacity and judgment; for this reason they kept some very powerful enemies in awe, not so much by their superior strength as by their artifice and stratagems. The Alectorians fought in the air as well as upon land, and by that means gave their enemies infinite vexation; these were gamecocks armed with bows and arrows dipped in poison, which they managed with wonderful dexterity, and thereby did great execution.

These three nations, alarmed at the unusual success of the Quamites, entered into a league or alliance by which it was agreed to check the growing power of the Quamites with their united force before it spread any further. However, before they declared war, they sent ambassadors to Quama to demand that the liberties of the Tanachites might be restored and to threaten war in case such demands were not complied with.

The ambassadors delivered their commission and received the following answer, which was given them by my advice: That the Tanachites, having broken the peace and violated the faith of treaties, ought to impute the misfortune they were fallen into to their own folly and presumption; that the Emperor was resolved with all his might to defend the territories he had acquired by right of war; and lastly, that he was not to be awed by the threats of the Confederate Nations. The heralds were dismissed with this answer, and we turned our thoughts towards making preparations for the impending war.

In a short time I got together an army of forty thousand men, among which were eight thousand horse and two thousand musketeers. The Emperor, though he was grown decrepit through age, resolved to be present in this expedition and was inflamed with such a thirst of glory that neither I myself nor the Empress and her children, who joined with me in striving to overcome his obstinacy, could divert him from his purpose.

What gave me the most disturbance at that time was my jealousy of the Tanachites, for I was afraid lest they should grow weary of their servitude and lay hold of that occasion to shake off the yoke and join the enemy. Nor was I deceived in my conjecture, for a little while after war had been proclaimed, news was brought us that twelve thousand Tanachites had taken arms and were gone over to the enemy. Hence I saw that we should have four powerful enemies to struggle with at one and the same time.

All necessary preparations being made, the army was commanded to begin their march towards the enemy in the beginning of the month Kilian. As we were upon the road, intelligence was brought us that the Confederate forces had entered the country of the Tanachites and laid siege to the castle of Sibol, which was situated on the borders of the Kispucian territories. The place was attacked with so great a force and with so much violence that the governor was just going to surrender it. But as soon as the enemy were informed of our approach, they broke up the siege and marched against us.

The battle was fought upon a plain not far from the fortress which had been besieged, from whence it was called the Battle of Sibol. The Arctonians, which composed the enemy's left wing, falling upon our horse, made great slaughter of them; and as this attack was supported by the rebel Tanachites, it was very near proving fatal to us. But the musketeers going in to their assistance and having thrown the enemy into disorder by two discharges of their artillery, the face of the battle was quite changed, so that they who but just now had borne down our horse and were almost conquerors, being now borne down themselves, began to give way, and at last to turn their backs. In the meantime the Kispucians briskly attacked our foot, and shot their arrows with so much art and with such success that six hundred Quamites were, in a very little time, either shot dead or desperately wounded. But the horse, together with the musketeers, coming to their assistance, the enemy were obliged to save themselves by flight; which they did, however, in so good order, without once breaking their ranks, that they might be rather said to yield than fly. This was owing to the conduct of Monsonius, general of the Kispucians, who at that time was thought to excel all the Subterranean generals in the art of war.

The Alectorians yet remained, whom it was no easy matter to

subdue; for as oft as our musketeers fired upon them, the enemy sprung up all at once into the air, and thence discharged a shower of arrows, which were so well aimed that few of them fell to the ground without doing execution. The reason these arrows seldom missed their aim was that it is easier to hit an object when you are above than when you are below it. Our men often missed their mark because the enemy were so volatile, and perpetually shifting places.

In the midst of the engagement, while the Emperor was in the very heat of action, his neck was pierced through with a poisoned arrow. He fell from his horse immediately and was carried out of the battle to his tent, where he expired soon after. In this ticklish situation of affairs I thought it most advisable to enjoin all such as had been witnesses of this unhappy accident to keep it secret, lest the ardour of the soldiers should abate upon hearing the Emperor was dead. I bade them take courage, and told them that the King indeed was stunned with the sudden stroke, but that the arrow had not entered deep, that the wound had been searched and taken due care of, that everything would go well, and that they might expect to see their Emperor again very soon. By this means most of the army were kept in ignorance of what had happened, and the battle was prolonged till night. At length the Alectorians, quite spent with labour and the wounds they had received, retired into their camp, and a truce of a few days' continuance was agreed upon in order to bury the dead bodies.

In the meantime, as I found that there was need of some other stratagem to subdue the Alectorians, I ordered our musket ball to be cast into small shot. This project was attended with so good success that at our next encounter the Alectorians came tumbling down apace, and one half of the army perished in a miserable manner. Those that were left, seeing this, threw down their arms and begged for peace. The Arctonians and Kispucians followed their example and committed themselves, their arms, and fortresses to our mercy. Matters being thus brought to a happy issue, I called a council and addressed them in the following harangue.

"Gentlemen and fellow-soldiers, I do not doubt but most of you are well acquainted how earnestly I dissuaded Our Most Serene Emperor from this expedition; but his innate fortitude and magnanimity would not permit him to remain idle at home while his faithful subjects were exposing their lives abroad in his defense. I can truly say that this is the only request which His Imperial Majesty ever refused to grant me. How happy should I have thought myself had he refused me everything besides, and only been indulgent to me in this! For then we should not have known that calamity that now hangs over us, our return into the imperial city would have been truly triumphant, and our joys for our success would have been pure and unmixed.

"I cannot, nor indeed ought I, any longer conceal from you that fatal accident which has thus dashed all our happiness. Attend then to the dreadful news: Your Emperor, while he was gallantly fighting for his subjects, was pierced by an arrow in the battle, and now lies breathless in his tent. What grief, what anguish must not the loss of such a prince occasion? I can easily make a judgment of your sorrows from what I feel myself. But let us not give way to despondency; death, to such a hero, is not the end of life, but only the period of mortality. We have not wholly lost our Emperor, since he has left two princes behind, formed after the example of the best of parents, and who inherit their father's virtues as well as his dominions. You cannot, therefore, be so properly said to change your king, as the bare name of king. And since the elder prince, Timuso, is by right of primogeniture to be promoted to his father's throne, I shall henceforth derive my authority from him. He it is to whom we ought to swear allegiance and to whom we will now pay homage."

CHAPTER XIV

The Author Is Elevated to the Imperial Dignity

At the conclusion of this harangue, the soldiery lifted up their voice and cried, "We will have no Emperor but Pikil-Su." I was all astonishment at this, and with a flood of tears besought them to consider better, to remember the allegiance they owed to the imperial house, and the public as well as private benefits they had received from the departed monarch, which it was not possible to forget without bringing an indelible stain upon their character. To this I added that if ever they had occasion to command my services, I could be of equal use to them in a private capacity.

But all this signified nothing. The officers and soldiers join in the common cry, and the whole camp resounded with the beforementioned acclamation. Upon this, I retired to my tent in confusion and ordered the guards to give entrance to none, because, probably, the soldiers might return to reason when this sudden fit of zeal should cool. But the generals and common soldiers burst into my tent and, in spite of all my reluctance, adorned me with the ensigns of royalty, and conducting me out of the tent with trumpets and drums, proclaimed me Emperor of Quama, King of Tanachin, Arctonia, Alectoria, and Great Duke of the Kispucians. Seeing then how vain was all resistance, I no longer struggled with my fortune, but followed the torrent; and I must own that I was not altogether unwilling to be raised to this elevation, for an empire, with three kingdoms and a great duchy, was too delicious a morsel to be eyed with indifference.

I immediately sent to the Prince to acquaint him with the present situation of affairs, to advise him to insist strenuously upon his natural and hereditary rights, and to declare this new election void, as being contrary to the laws of the realm. But at the same time I had resolved with myself not to relinquish in haste an empire thus spontaneously offered me, so that this advice of mine to His Highness the Prince was rather to feel his pulse upon this occasion. The Prince had an admirable understanding and a very solid judgment, and as he well knew the doubles and disguises of the human heart, and that this modesty of mine was only put on to serve a turn, he wisely yielded to the necessity of the times, and after the example of the army, he himself proclaimed me Emperor in the capital city, to which I was soon after led in triumph, attended by the generals and officers of the army, in the midst of the shouts and acclamations of the populace. In a few days after this I was solemnly crowned and invested with the regal authority. Being thus metamorphosed from a miserable shipwrecked sailor into a monarch, that I might strengthen my interest with the Quamites, who I perceived had still a great veneration for the royal race of Quama, I espoused the daughter of the deceased Emperor, whose name was Ralac.

Having performed these great things, I projected new schemes to raise the empire to a height that should make it formidable to the whole Subterranean world. My first care was to assure myself of the duty and allegiance of the lately conquered nations. To this end I garrisoned all their citadels and fortified places in the strongest manner, treated the conquered with the utmost humanity, and advanced some of them to very great offices in the capital. In particular the captive generals, Tomopoloko and Monsonius, had the highest share in my favour, a circumstance that raised the envy of the Quamites, though they suppressed their dissatisfaction for the present; but in time the spark which had long lain concealed under the ashes burned into an open flame, as shall be related in its proper place.

To return to my domestic affairs. The liberal sciences and the art of war I laboured to bring to the highest perfection; and as this country abounded with very deep woods which could furnish plenty of timber for the building of a fleet after the manner of the Europeans, I pursued this point with such unwearied ardour that though in reality I had a thousand other affairs to perplex me, it seemed as if my whole thoughts were directed to this one view. The Kispucians were of great service to me in this case; they had a tolerable knowledge of maritime affairs, and their general, Monsonius, I appointed Lord High Admiral of the fleet.

And now the timber is felling, the instruments for working it preparing, and with such vehemence I apply myself to the business that in sixty days from the first falling of the wood, a fleet of twenty ships now rides at anchor in the harbour. All this corresponding exactly with my wishes, I looked upon myself as the Alexander of the Subterranean world, and that below I was the author of as great revolutions as he was above. The lust of power is infinite, and never finds the point to stop at. Some few years since, the office of a deacon or that of a writer or clerk was the height of my ambition, nor did I aspire to anything greater; and now four or five kingdoms seem too narrow for me, so that with respect to my desires, which rise in proportion to our wealth and power, I never found myself more indigent than now.

Having made myself acquainted from the accounts and informations of the Kispucian mariners with the nature of the seas and the situation of the kingdoms on the coasts, and understanding that it was very practicable with a fair wind to make the Mezendoric shore in eight days' sail, from whence it would be but a short trip to Martinia, and that over a well-known ocean, I say, being acquainted with all this, I made preparation for the voyage. Indeed, Martinia was the principal object of my designs.

I was spurred on by the immense wealth of that nation, and the information I should gain from a people of their knowledge in maritime affairs, since the lights I might receive from them would be very useful to me in the course of all my great undertakings.

There was also another incentive, namely, a thirst of revenge, which prompted me to subdue this nation. I took the elder of the two royal princes along with me as an associate in this expedition, pretending that a fine occasion offered itself to His Highness of exercising his bravery and martial virtues. But the true meaning of this was that I might keep him as a hostage or pledge of the fidelity of the Quamites. The younger prince indeed remained at home, but the regency of the empire I committed to the Empress, who was then big with child.

The whole fleet consisted of twenty ships, great and small, and were all built after the Martinian model by the direction and superintendency of Monsonius the Kispucian general, to whom the sole management of the navy was entrusted, and who had made draughts and designs of them with his own hand. For the Martinians were among the Subterraneans what the Tyrians and Sidonians were in ancient days, or what the English and Dutch are in our times, that is, sovereigns of the seas. Yet when we arrived at Martinia, I perceived that in the build of our ships we had widely erred from their model.

We set sail about that time of year when the planet Nazar was at its mean distance from us. Having sailed three days, we spied a large island, the conquest of which would be no difficult matter by reason of the feuds and factions into which the inhabitants were split; but (what is remarkable) as they were destitute of arms and were ignorant of the use of them, they fought only with their tongues, and gave all the hard names, curses, and foul language they could invent. This was all we had to fear. The only punishment that in this country was inflicted upon offenders was that they were taken up and imprisoned, and upon full proof of the crime were openly brought into the Forum, there to hear themselves reviled in the bitterest manner. Certain people were appointed for his very purpose, called *Sabuti,* that is, revilers, and are there looked upon in the same light as an executioner amongst us. As to the make of their body, they differed from us in only one or two circumstances, which were that the women had beards and the men none, and that the feet also of them all were turned backwards.

After we had made a descent upon this island, about three hundred Canaliscans (so the islanders were called) met us. They attacked us in a hostile manner with their usual weapons, that is to say, with a volley of curses and hard names. With such exquisite malice and in such a diabolical spirit of bitterness their foul language was conceived and uttered (as we were informed by an Alectorian interpreter of the Canaliscan tongue) that they showed themselves perfect masters of their weapons, and not inferior to the grammarians of our world.

However, knowing that rage alone was insignificant without power, I forbade any violence to be offered to them, but only to spread terror among them. I ordered some guns to be fired, which had this effect, that they fell upon their knees and implored mercy. Presently the several little kings of the island came down and made a formal surrender of themselves and subjects, putting their whole dominions under tribute to me, making me at the same time a compliment, that it was no dishonour to be subdued by him whom it was impiety to resist, nor any disgrace to submit to him whom fortune had raised above all the world.

Thus this island (the conquest of which added something to my power, though little to my glory, by reason of the effeminacy of the inhabitants) becoming tributary to me, we hoisted sail, and after a fair voyage of some few days, arrived at the Mezendoric coast. I then called a council of war to inquire what was best to be done, whether it were advisable immediately to act in a hostile manner, or to send an embassy to the Emperor to know if he would make a peaceable surrender, or whether we must come to an open rupture. The majority were for the latter. Wherefore five persons were commissioned for this embassy, one of each nation, a Quamite, an Arctonian, an Alectorian, a Tanachite, and a Kispucian. Being introduced into the capital, they were asked by the chief magistrate, in the name of the Emperor, the meaning of this unexpected visit to the Mezendoric dominions? The deputies replied that it was not by accident but by design they came there, and forthwith they produced their credentials, and a letter from me to the Emperor, the tenor of which was as follows:

Niels Klim, Ambassador of the Sun, Emperor of Quama, King of Tanachin, Arctonia, and Alectoria, Great Duke of the Kispucians, and Lord of Canalisca, to Miklopolatu, Emperor of Mezendoria, greeting. Be it known unto thee that by the immutable council of Heaven it is ordained that all the empires and kingdoms of the world submit to the Quamitic sovereignty. And since the decrees of Heaven are irrevocable, it is necessary your empire should undergo the common destiny of all. We exhort you therefore to a voluntary surrender, and cordially admonish you not to subject your realms to the chance of war by a rash opposition to our victorious arms. A timely obedience may save the effusion of innocent blood and mend your own condition. Given aboard our fleet, the 3rd day of the month Rimat.

In a few days the ambassadors returned with a fierce and haughty answer. Hereupon all prospect of peace disappearing, we made a descent. Having ranged our troops in order of battle, we sent our spies to explore the condition of the enemy. They soon returned with news that the enemy's army was in readiness, that it consisted of lions, bears, tigers, elephants, and birds of prey, to the number of sixty thousand. Hereupon we posted ourselves on an advantageous piece of ground and waited their coming.

All things being now in readiness, and the signal of battle being given, suddenly there came four ambassadors, all foxes, from the enemy, to renew the negotiations and treat of a peace. But having spent some days in conferences with our generals, they departed without coming to any conclusion. It appeared afterwards that these were spies rather than ambassadors, sent for no other end but to explore the state and condition of our army. They pretended indeed that they would soon return with more ample powers, but as we quickly perceived the whole body of the enemy marching briskly towards us, we hoisted our colours and marched to meet them. An obstinate fight ensued. For though our musketeers made a furious slaughter among them, yet the elephants everywhere kept their rank, the hardness of their hide being proof against our ball. But as soon as our heavy artillery began to thunder upon them and the elephants perceived the horrible effects of it, they were seized with a panic and left the field. In this battle thirty-three thousand Mezendorians were slain and two thousand taken prisoners. Those who escaped fled to the metropolis, a city very well fortified, and filled the inhabitants with terror and consternation.

We pushed our victory, and in three days' march came to the capital, which we besieged by sea and land. At our approach we were saluted by a new embassy, which brought much softer terms of peace. In this the Emperor offered me his daughter in marriage, who was esteemed the most beautiful lioness throughout the whole dominions, together with half his empire in dower with her. These conditions were by no means agreeable to me, especially with respect to the nuptials of his daughter, for it seemed to me neither safe nor honourable to divorce my Empress to marry a lioness. Hereupon the ambassadors were dismissed without any answer.

Presently our great guns began to play against the city walls, which, though composed of stone, were soon torn and shattered in many places. And as this city was full of animals of all species, it was strange to hear the variety of noises upon this occasion, such as roaring, howling, bellowing, braying, bleating, and hissing. The serpents retired into the clefts and fissures of the earth; the birds hovered in the air, and seeing the city so fiercely assaulted, fled off to the rocks and open country. The trees trembled and dropped their leaves all over the city. We heard that twenty maids of honour (these were roses and lilies) upon the first discharge of our cannon shrunk up and withered away through fear. Such a prodigious concourse of animals of all kinds, as well those of the city as those from the neighbourhood, miserably straitened each other; and that very assistance which was so necessary was the cause of diseases and infection. The elephants stood the siege better than the rest, but upon the discharge of the great guns, they abandoned the walls.

Hereupon the Emperor, despairing to hold out much longer, summoned a council to deliberate upon the present posture of affairs. They were all unanimous for a peace upon any terms, and therefore without delay His Imperial Highness made a formal surrender of himself, with all his territories. Thus in one day my power was increased by the addition of an empire, together with nine or ten lesser realms or principalities, for immediately all the petty sovereignties followed the example of the Emperor and strove who should be foremost in their submissions.

After such marvelous success, having first placed a garrison of six hundred musketeers in the capital, I ordered the captive Emperor to be conducted aboard our fleet. I treated him with the most perfect humanity, and upon our return some time after to Quama, I gave him an entire province, the revenues of which enabled the royal prisoner to live with a good degree of splendor.

We now set sail from this place and coasted along the Mezendoric shores. In this voyage we demanded hostages of all the several states and governments subject to the Emperor Miklopolatu, so that in a small time the very Mezendoric name and empire were in a manner extinguished. These people were for the most part the same of which I have formerly given some account in my description of my voyage from Martinia.

Leaving therefore the Mezendoric territories, we steered directly for Martinia, which, after a prosperous though long voyage, we happily arrived at. Never was the sight of any country so highly grateful to me as this, and when I reflected that in times past I had been condemned to the oar in this very place to which I now returned as a puissant conqueror, I was hardly able to conceal the transport of joy I felt. I had at first resolved to declare myself in order to spread the greater terror among the Martinians, but I changed that resolution, and determined to cherish the old error concerning my birth and still to pass for an ambassador of the sun.

I flattered myself that in a short time and with a very little trouble I should be able to make a complete conquest of the Martinians, whose effeminacy I was well acquainted with. For this people have a strong propensity to pleasure and are hurried on to all vicious excesses, not only through a natural bent, but from that affluence and abundance which both sea and land conspire to indulge them in. However, I found by experience that I had an arduous enterprise upon my hands, for by means of that vast commerce carried on by these people, they had amassed such endless riches as enabled them to have always at their devotion the choicest of the most warlike troops among the neighbouring nations who stood ready at their nod to fight their battles for them. Add to this that the Martinians were eminent for their skill in maritime affairs beyond all the Subterraneans, and our vessels were in comparison of theirs extremely rude and very slow of motion. For it is easy to judge what sort of ships ours must be which were run up in haste under the direction and supervision of a Bachelor of Arts, as also what a censure they would undergo were they to be submitted to the criticism of the Dutch, English, or Danes. But this defect my artillery atoned for, a method of fighting hitherto unknown to the Martinians.

Before I attempted anything in a hostile manner, I sent an embassy to the Senate with the same tenders of peace which I had lately offered the Emperor of Mezendoria. But while we waited for an answer, all on a sudden we beheld a fleet of ships coming full sail upon us in order of battle. At sight hereof we ranged our vessels in as much order on our side as the hurry would permit, and immediately gave out the signal for engagement.

The battle was fought with equal bravery and ardour on both sides. The Martinians instead of guns made use of a machine which flung stones of an enormous size and weight, and which grievously galled our sailors. They had also fire ships loaded with pitch, brimstone, sulphur, and other combustible materials. These set fire to our best ship and utterly consumed it. Victory was a long time in suspense, and my forces even began to deliberate whether they had best fight or fly. But at last the explosion of the great guns changed the face of things, and so sank the courage of the Martinians that they retired precipitately into their harbour. Yet we took not one of the enemy's ships because, as they were light sailors, they could at any time escape from us.

After this fight we landed our forces, and with all speed made directly towards the metropolis of Martinia. In our march we met our own ambassadors returning from the Senate, by whom they had been received in a proud and lofty manner and dismissed with much such a message as Neptune gave to the winds: *"Speed your flight and bear this word to your king: Not to him, but to us were given by lot the lordship of the sea and the dread trident. He holds the savage rocks.*"[1] For the Martinians, claiming the sovereignty of the seas, received my offers with all imaginable disdain.

And now they levied a vast body of forces, for besides the mercenary troops, the whole military power of Martinia took the field upon this occasion. We had not marched far before we espied a numerous army composed of different nations advancing directly against us. This confidence and presumption of the enemy, notwithstanding their late defeat at sea, occasioned a good deal of uneasiness on our side. But all this was but a meteor which suddenly appears, and as suddenly vanishes, for at the very first discharge of our artillery, they all turned their backs and fled. We pursued the flying foe and made a prodigious slaughter of them. What the number of the slain were appeared from that of the periwigs, which we collected after the action, and which upon a moderate computation amounted to the number of five thousand. The make of these periwigs was pretty much altered since my time, and I observed above twenty different fashions of them; nor is that at all strange, for so ingenious a nation would give a thousand improvements to any invention whatever.

After this successful battle, or rather carnage, we immediately set about the siege of the capital. But when we had prepared everything for the enterprise and disposed our cannon in proper order, the whole body of senators came in a suppliant manner to our camp and made a voluntary surrender of the city, together with the whole republic. Hereupon, peace being declared, we entered in triumph into this most splendid city. Upon our entrance into the gates there was not that tumult and hurry as is generally observable in conquered towns, but a sorrowful silence, and a universal sadness everywhere prevailed. But when we declared that we would not do the least injury to the citizens, their sadness was changed into joy.

The first thing I did was to make a visit to the public treasury. I was beyond measure astonished at the immense stores of riches deposited there, great part of which I distributed among my soldiers, reserving the rest for my own finances. I left a garrison at Martinia and took several of the senators aboard the fleet by way of hostages. Among these was my old friend the Syndic, together with his wife, who had falsely accused me of the crime for which I was condemned to the galleys. Yet I entertained no thoughts of vengeance, as thinking it beneath an Emperor of Quama to resent an injury done to a chairman.

After this complete conquest of the Martinians, I resolved to reduce the several neighbouring powers. But while I was upon the point of executing this design, the ambassadors of four different realms arrived and made their submissions. I had already so many states and kingdoms under my dominion that I did not so much as give myself the trouble to inquire the names of these four surrendered territories, but was contented to comprehend them under the general name of the Martinian Provinces.

---

[1] English translation from Virgil, *Aeneid,* vol. 1 (Cambridge, Massachusetts: Harvard University Press, 1947), p. 251.
Holberg's Latin version:
>   *"Maturate fugam, Regique haec dicite vestro;*
>   *Non illi imperium Pelagi; saevumq; tridentem,*
>   *Nobis sorte datum: tenet ille immania saxa."*
Book I, lines 137-139, in Virgil, *Aeneid*, Vol. 1, p. 250:
>   *"maturate fugam regique haec dicite vestro:*
>   *non illi imperium pelagi saevumque tridentem,*
>   *sed mihi sorte datum. tenet ille immania saxa."*

CHAPTER XV

The Catastrophe

Having performed such an amazing series of exploits, and our fleet being considerably augmented by the addition of the Martinian ships, we now hoisted sail and returned to Quama, where, upon our arrival, we triumphed with more than Roman magnificence. And in good truth the noble deeds we had achieved deserved the highest pomp of festivals and public rejoicings. For what can be conceived more heroic than to transform a nation the most abject, and the most exposed to the insults of their neighbours, into the lords and sovereigns of the whole Subterranean globe? What can be conceived more glorious, or more for my honour as a man whose fate it happened to be to live among so many heterogeneous creatures, what, I say, could redound more to my glory than to have asserted that dominion which Nature gave mankind over the animal creation?

A description of the splendor of this triumph, the crowds, and the applauses of men of all ranks and ages would of itself make a regular volume, and therefore I shall not attempt it in this short account. I shall only observe that from this time a new era appears in history, and there may now be reckoned five monarchies, namely, the Assyrian, the Persian, the Grecian, the Roman, and the Quamitic, the last of which seems to surpass the rest in power and grandeur. And accordingly I accepted the title of *Koblu,* or Great, which was offered me, as well by the Quamites as by the other vanquished nations. There is, I confess, something excessively vain and arrogant in the name Great;

but yet when you compare me with the Cyruses, the Alexanders, the Pompeys, and the Caesars, the title then seems perfectly humble and modest. Alexander indeed enslaved the East, but with what forces? with hardy veteran troops inured to war, for such were the Macedonians in the time of his father Philip. But I, in a shorter space of time, subdued far more and fiercer nations than the Persians, and that by the help only of a rude and barbarous people whom I myself had formed and instructed. The titles I now used were these: Niels the Great, Emperor of Quama and Mezendoria, King of Tanachin, Alectoria, and Arctonia, Great Duke of Kispucia, Lord of Martinia and Canalisca, etc., etc.

Being thus lifted up to a point of power and success beyond even the wishes of a mortal man, the same thing happened to me as to almost all those who rise to greatness from a sordid original. For, unmindful of my former state, I grew intolerably vain and haughty, and instead of all those winning ways which artful princes use to procure the popular esteem, I became a hot and cruel persecutor of all orders of men, despising as very slaves those subjects whom before I had courted to my interest with all imaginable affability, insomuch that none had access to my person without a ceremony almost like that of adoration, and when they were admitted, were received with a most disdainful air, all of which alienated the minds of the people from me and changed their love into coldness and terror.

This disposition of my subjects I soon experienced, and particularly upon the following occasion. The Empress, my spouse, whom I had left big with child, was in my absence brought to bed of a young prince. Intending to acknowledge this prince for my successor, I assembled the several states of my empire, as well those of the conquered kingdoms as those of Quama, to the solemn inauguration of the infant. As none dared disobey my orders, the ceremony was performed with all possible pomp and grandeur. But is was easy to perceive in the visages of my subjects that all the joy upon this occasion was forced, unnatural, and mixed with hidden discontent.

What helped to confirm my jealousy was that at this time certain libels or pasquinades written by anonymous authors were handed about in which the injury done to Prince Timuso by this inauguration was set forth with much satire and acrimony. This created such disorders in my spirits that I could take no rest till I had got rid of that best of princes. However, I thought it by no means advisable to dispatch this illustrious rival in an arbitrary manner, and therefore I suborned certain witnesses to accuse him of high treason. As sovereigns never want for ministers of darkness to serve their criminal purposes, I quickly found out proper persons to swear that the Prince was projecting a revolution and had a design against my life. Upon this he was thrown into prison and condemned by his judges, the majority of whom I had corrupted. However, he was executed privately for fear of raising disturbances.

As to the second prince, because he was very young, I deferred sacrificing him to my repose yet a while, so that the weakness of his age was his protection. Thus stained with the parricide of his brother, I began now to rule with so much cruelty and rigour and carried my rage to such a height that all persons whose fidelity I suspected, whether Quamites or others, I delivered over to immediate death. Not a day passed but was remarkable for some extraordinary execution, which hastened the rebellion which the nobles had been for a considerable time projecting, as will be related in its proper place.

I own I deserved all those misfortunes which I afterwards experienced. It had doubtless been more glorious and more worthy of a Christian monarch to have guided a gross and barbarous people to the knowledge of the true God rather than to have proceeded from conquest to conquest and to have shed such torrents of innocent blood. And indeed it had been easy for me to have converted the whole empire, for there was a time when all my determinations were revered like oracles. But unmindful of God, and of myself, I dreamed of nothing but the vain splendor of a court and the increase of my power. Moreover, being now given up to a depraved and reprobate mind, I chose to aggravate and inflame these discontents rather than remove them, as if the offenses of my injustice were to be rectified by my cruelty. To all the remonstrances of my friends I still urged "Necessity, the tyrant's hellish plea." So that misfortune on misfortune came thick upon me, and I fell into such disgrace and wretchedness that from my example all mortals may learn what a vicissitude there is in human affairs, and how short is the duration of arbitrary power and violence.

My subjects' aversion increased with the severity of my government, and when they perceived that the vices to which I abandoned myself but ill agreed with the divine original I boasted, and were utterly irreconcilable with my character as Ambassador of the Sun, they began to examine everything with more attention, particularly the circumstance of my arrival into these parts and the condition I was in when I landed upon their coast. They now saw that all the great things I had done were owing more to the savageness of the Quamites than to any extraordinary abilities of my own, especially as they found, after that mist of ignorance was dispelled, that I had actually committed many errors in the course of my government. Above all, my conduct was highly censured by the Kispucians, a judicious and penetrating people. They had observed in my public edict a multitude of things so crude and indigested as betrayed the grossest ignorance in politics. Nor was the censure unjust; for as my academical tutors and instructors never dreamed of crowns and sceptres for me, they gave me an education more adapted to a private station than that of a sovereign; and my studies, which

217

extended no farther than to some little system of divinity and a few metaphysical terms, were by no means equal to my present elevation, where I had the charge of two empires and almost twenty kingdoms upon my hands. The Martinians had also remarked that the ships of war I had built were so rude and clumsy that in an engagement they were of no manner of use against a regular and well-appointed fleet, and that all my naval glory was to be ascribed solely to the invention of cannon.

All these cutting remarks they industriously dispersed, and at the same time called to remembrance the manner of my first appearance in this country, namely, how I had escaped from a shipwreck, and being ready to perish with hunger, was taken up by the inhabitants all in tattered garments, an equipage surely very unsuitable to an Ambassador of the Sun. Add to this that these same Martinians, being excellent natural philosophers, had now given the Quamites a tincture of astronomy, enough to know that the sun was an inanimate body, placed in the centre of the heavens by the Almighty to give light and heat to all creatures, and that as it was a globe of fire, it could of consequence be no proper habitation for a mortal man.

With these and other such unlucky discourses was I from day to day distracted. But they were mere murmurs, since nobody through fear of my power dared talk thus with any degree of openness. And in reality I was a long time ignorant that the malevolence of my subjects had risen to such a pitch as to question my condition, till at length I was convinced of it by a book composed in the Canaliscan tongue and published with this title: *The Happy Shipwreck*. For I observed before that the Canaliscans were perfect artists at satire and reproaches, which were all the weapons they waged war with. The book in question comprehended all those accusations of which I have just now given a detail, and was written in a style the most severe and sarcastical that can well be imagined, according to the genius of the Canaliscans, who excel in this manner of writing.

But such was the weakness of my mind at this juncture, such my vain presumption and confidence of my own power, that no advices or remonstrances whatever could make me change my conduct or bring me to my senses. The most wholesome counsels, instead of checking, contributed only to inflame my cruelty. Wherefore those whom I had most reason to suspect, I put to the torture to discover the author of this libel. But all endured their torture with an astonishing firmness, insomuch that this cruelty produced no other effect than to irritate the spirits of my people still more against me. Thus my fate would have it, and I ran headlong to my destruction.

In this state of affairs I determined to sacrifice the surviving Prince Hicoba. I opened my design to the High Chancellor, Kalac, in whom I placed great confidence. He promised me all obedience and assistance, and straight withdrew on pretense of contriving the means of putting this scheme in execution.

But detesting the villany in his heart, he discovered the plot to the Prince. Both of them retired into the citadel, which was well-fortified, and there the chancellor harangued the guards, and in the most pathetic manner laid open their present condition. His discourse, together with the tears of the young Prince, which added considerable weight to it, produced the desired effect. The soldiers ran to their arms and vowed they would die to save their Prince. Upon this the dexterous chancellor did not give their ardour time to cool but persuaded them immediately to swear allegiance to their Prince, and then out of hand sent private messengers to those whom he knew to be exasperated against me, exhorting them to take arms against a tyrant who attempted the extinction of the whole royal progeny. Upon this all the disaffected rose and joined with the garrison.

While I was expecting the return of the chancellor, a messenger brought me the news of this grand insurrection. My friend Tomopoloko advised me by all means to retreat to Tanachin. "There," says he, "we can quickly raise an army and bring these mutineers to reason." These words produced in me various agitations of mind, and hope and fear alternately governed me each moment. At length, in compliance with his admonition I fled from Quama, and that with little or no difficulty, as the bulk of the Quamites were yet unacquainted with the reasons of this sedition. Soon after this, I returned with an army of forty thousand soldiers, the greatest part of which were Tanachites, expecting a considerable augmentation from such Quamites as continued in their duty. But I deceived myself egregiously, for instead of those auxiliaries I flattered myself with, I met a herald who brought me letters from the Prince to acquaint me that war was declared against me as a usurper and invader, and that my wife and son were prisoners of state. Soon after the departure of the herald, I beheld the Quamitic army advancing with my young rival at their head. As they had a fine artillery, I would not run the risk of an engagement till I was reinforced with fresh troops; therefore I made a stop and entrenched myself in the best manner I could.

But when I perceived that my own soldiers deserted to the enemy, who besides expected hourly new supplies, I took advice of my general officers and resolved to engage directly; nor did Tomopoloko oppose this resolution. We fought upon the same plain where some years ago in a decisive battle the Tanachites were entirely routed. The enemy's cannon now threw our ranks into great disorder, and it grieved me to the soul to be baffled by my own invention and be conquered by those very arms I myself had devised. For a while, however, my soldiers sustained the attack of the rebellious army, till a ball took off Tomopoloko. Then everyone lost his courage, and we all turned our backs and fled to the woods and mountains. I, for my part, climbed to the top of a rock, from whence I descended into the valley on the other side. There I paused a while to curse my fate, or rather my folly, and to pour out my soul in tears and sighs. But, alas! it was all too late. So great was the disorder of my spirits that I forgot to throw off my diadem, which was the very thing that in all likelihood must have discovered me.

After I had sat trembling for half an hour in that valley, I heard the voices of some persons climbing the rock and roaring out vengeance against me if they found me. I then looked all round me for a place to conceal myself in. There was hard by a deep wood overgrown with trees and bushes. I presently entered into it, and having picked out something like a path, I walked on till I came to a cave. Here I stopped some moments to take breath. By and by I crept into the cave like a serpent upon my belly, and as I perceived it to be very deep and shelving, yet of easy descent, I resolved to penetrate to the bottom of it. But I had scarce walked a quarter of a mile when all on a sudden I tumbled down, and as if thunder drove me, was hurried headlong through the thickest darkness, till at last a faint glimmering light dawned in upon me. With the increase of that light the force of my motion was proportionably diminished, so that by little and little, and in the gentlest manner, like a person rising out of the water, I found myself among some mountains, which to my unutterable amazement I observed to be the very same from whence some years ago I was hurried down into the subterranean world.

The reason of that abatement of my motion I found after some reflection to be owing to the quality of our atmosphere, which is much denser and consequently resists more than the subterranean atmosphere. Unless it were so, the same thing would have happened to me in my ascent as in my descent, and in all likelihood I must then have been carried aloft through the air as far as the region of the moon. Yet I submit this hypothesis to the maturer examination of philosophers.

CHAPTER XVI

The Author's Return into His Own Country

I lay for a considerable time among the mountains, almost destitute of sense. For my late violent motion, together with that strange metamorphosis from a founder of a fifth monarchy into a famished Bachelor of Arts had occasioned very great disorders in my brain. And in truth, my adventure was so singular and so poetical that it might well shock the frame of the soundest head. In this condition I began to ask myself whether what I saw was a reality or whether it was not some visionary deception. But my distraction abating, and returning by degrees to my senses, my astonishment gave place to grief and indignation. And indeed, turn over the annals of remote antiquity as well as those of modern date and you will not be able to find a parallel adventure with mine, unless perhaps in the case of Nebuchadnezzar, who from the greatest monarch in the world was transformed into a wild creature and lived like one of the beasts of the field.

Much the same freaks of fortune I experienced. For in a few hours two mighty empires were wrested from me, together with almost twenty kingdoms, the shadows and faint images of which now only remained. Lately I was a monarch, and now the utmost of my hopes was to procure the mastership of some little school for my subsistence. Lately I was called the Ambassador of the Sun, and now I feared necessity would drive me to become the servant of some bishop or dean. But a few days ago glory, hope, victory, and success attended my steps, and now care and misery, tears and lamentation are all my companions. In short, I resembled those summer plants which suddenly spring up and as suddenly die away; and to say all in one word, sorrow, rage, anxiety, disappointment, and despair raised such a conflict in my breast that sometimes I resolved to end my being with my sword, and sometimes I determined to plunge again into the cavern to try if I could not succeed better in a second expedition. But a regard for my immortal soul and the principles of the Christian religion restrained me from these mad attempts.

I now endeavoured to descend the mountain by that narrow path which leads to Sandvik. But my imagination was so disturbed that I stumbled almost every step I took, for the whole powers of my mind were taken up in contemplating upon the Fifth Monarchy. This idea so constantly haunted me that it almost unhinged my understanding. And indeed the loss of so much dignity and power could never be recompensed by any advantages which my own country could bestow. For suppose they should make me Governor of Bergen, or what is more, Lord-Lieutenant of Norway, yet, alas! what compensation, what comfort would this be to the monarch and founder of so many empires and kingdoms? However, I resolved not to refuse a thing of that kind, in case it should be offered me.

After I had got halfway down the hill, I saw at a little distance some children, to whom I beckoned and made signs to come to my assistance, pronouncing aloud at the same time these words, "*Jeru pikal salim*," which in the Quamitic language signifies, "Show me the way." But the boys, at the sight of man clothed in a foreign habit, and with a diadem upon his head embroidered with rays like those of the sun, ran down the mountain as fast as they could, and soon gaining the start of me (for I was forced to drag my weary and wounded feet but slowly after me), they got to Sandvik an hour before me, where they alarmed the whole village, vowing and protesting that they had seen the Wandering Jew among the mountains, his head all glittering with rays, and by his groans expressing great uneasiness of mind. The inhabitants inquiring how they knew it was the Wandering Jew, they readily answered that I myself had told my name and country. This mistake I guessed must proceed from those words of mine misinterpreted, *"Jeru pikal salim,"* which indeed have some affinity in sound to that conceit of the children. All the village was now in an uproar, and nobody doubted the truth of the fact, especially as there had been but very lately a story cooked up about this wanderer, who was said to have appeared not long since at Hamburg.

About evening I arrived at Sandvik, where I found a mob of the inhabitants gathered together from a natural curiosity implanted in all men to see strange sights. They stood at the foot of the mountain to meet me, but as soon as ever they heard me speak, they all took to their heels as if they were seized with a panic, except one old man who, having more courage than the rest, would not move out of his place.

To this man I addressed myself and begged to know if he would have the goodness to entertain a stranger. He asked me who I was? and whence I came? To which I replied with a deep sigh that the day was too far spent to begin my story, but that if he would receive me into his house, I should relate to him such a series of adventures as were not to be paralleled in all history, and which must consequently stagger human belief.

The old man, who was a lover of novelty, took me by the hand and led me to his house, and as we went he rallied the ridiculous fears of the populace, who are frightened at a strange face as much as at a comet.

As soon as I was within the house, I begged the favour of some cold water to assuage my thirst, instead of which a cup of ale was brought me by my host himself, because his wife and maids were all afraid to venture themselves near me. Having drunk off my liquor and slaked my thirst, I spoke to my good host in the following terms: "You see before you a man who has experienced the most cruel reverses of fate, and who has been the bubble and sport of fortune to a degree beyond all mortal men. It is indeed an undoubted truth that in a moment of time the greatest affairs may be disconcerted and thrown into confusion; yet nevertheless what has happened to me surpasses all credibility."

To which my host replied that this must be the condition of those who wander for such a length of time; for, continued he, what vicissitudes, what misfortunes may not happen to a man in a course of sixteen hundred years' peregrination? I could not comprehend the meaning of this, and therefore I asked him what he meant by those sixteen hundred years?

"If," returned he, "any credit is to be given to history, it is now sixteen hundred years since Jerusalem was destroyed. I doubt not, most venerable Sir, but that about the time of that memorable action you were even then something advanced in years, for if what is related concerning you be true, we may refer the date of your nativity to the reign of Tiberius."

At these words I was silent for a considerable time, and thought the old man doted, but at last I told him that his language required an Œdipus to unriddle it. With that he brought me a print of the temple of Jerusalem and asked me whether I thought it differed very much from the original? In spite of all my grief I could not help bursting into a laugh, and asked him the meaning of this odd puzzling discourse.

He replied, "Whether I am in an error or not I cannot say; but the inhabitants of this place aver that you are that famous Jew who ever since the days of Christ has been condemned to wander over the world. But yet methinks the nearer I survey you, the more I discover in your face the features of an old friend of mine, who some twelve years ago perished on the top of this mountain."

At these words the mist before my eyes was dissipated, and I knew my old friend Abeline, whose house in Bergen I used to frequent. I flew into his arms immediately, and tenderly embraced him.

"And do I live to hold thee thus, my Abeline?" said I. "I scarce believe my eyes and senses. Yes, I am Klim, returned in a manner from the grave. I am that very Klim who about twelve years since descended into that cavern."

My friend, confounded at this unexpected turn, stood like one thunderstruck; at length he cried out, "Yes! it is he! I see my Klim! I hear his voice! But though no twin can be more like his brother than you are like my Klim, yet I neither can nor dare believe my senses, for miracles are ceased, and the dead rise not now. I must have therefore stronger and more convincing proofs e'er I can give credit to what you tell me."

Hereupon, at once to conquer his incredulity, I gave him a succinct detail of all that had passed between us formerly. This removed every doubt, and straightway he embraced me with tears of joy and cried out, "It is, it is the very man whose ghost I thought I had seen! But explain to me," pursued he, "in what part of the world you have lost yourself all this time, and in what country you procured that wonderful dress you have on."

Then I proceeded to recount to him every particular which had happened to me, and he heard me with profound attention till I came to that part of my history concerning the planet Nazar, and trees endowed with speech and reason; at this, he lost all patience.

"Not all the absurdities," says he, "which dreams convey to us, not all the follies which madness produces, nor all the nonsense which drunkenness utters can equal these visions of yours. I should rather choose to believe with the vulgar that you must have fallen into the hands of witches or hobgoblins; for how idle soever such tales are, yet they have an appearance of truth, if put in competition with this subterranean journey of yours."

I begged and entreated of him to have but a moment's patience more till I had finished my recital; upon which, as I observed he kept silence, I proceeded to relate all that had happened to me below, the sundry accidents and reverses of fortune I had experienced, and how I had been the founder of the fifth and greatest monarchy that ever was. All these things increased the suspicion he had entertained that I was bewitched or had had some commerce with magicians or evil spirits, and that being abused with their diabolical delusions, I had embraced a cloud instead of Juno. In order to try how far the force of these charms and incantations had spread or to what a length my extravagance would run, my friend began to interrogate me concerning the state of the happy and that of the damned in the other world, concerning the Elysian Fields, and divers other matters of that kind.

I soon perceived the sly design of these questions and told my friend that I, for my part, could hardly blame his incredulity, since my narration appeared too fabulous to command a ready assent; however, it was not my fault, for that in reality my adventures were so marvelous as to baffle all human belief. "I solemnly protest to you," continued I, "that I have not added or supplied one jot or tittle from my own invention, but that I have recounted everything simply and ingenuously in the order it happened to me."

My friend, persisting in his incredulity, desired that I would compose my mind and take a few days' rest and refreshment, in which time he told me he hoped these commotions in my brain would by degrees subside and die away.

After I had reposed myself for full eight days, my friend, now thinking I had taken sufficient rest, was resolved to try if I had recovered my senses, and therefore artfully resumed the conversation concerning my subterranean journey. He was now in hopes that the Fifth Monarchy, together with the twenty conquered kingdoms, was all vanished into smoke and so utterly buried in oblivion that not an idea remained of so much as a single town or village. But when he heard me repeat the very same things in the very same order I had before done, when at the conclusion of my history I upbraided him with his obstinate unbelief, and moreover alleged certain indubitable facts, such as that about twelve years ago it was notorious I had descended into that cavern, and that I was now returned into my own country in a strange and foreign habit, he then began to waver and had not a word to reply. I took the advantage of this his situation of mind and pressed the matter still more home. I demonstrated to him that his hypothesis concerning witchcraft and sorcery was far, infinitely far more absurd than this expedition of mine, for that those were justly to be thrown into the class of old wives' fables; but that on the other hand, he could not but know that several philosophers of reputation were of opinion that the Earth was hollow, and that probably it contained within it a lesser habitable world; and that I, for my part, being convinced of it by experience, could not possibly give up my senses with respect to this article.

Convinced at length by these arguments, "Your constancy," said he, "and your punctuality in affirming these things, the pretense of which could not be the least advantage to you, have at last entirely vanquished my incredulity; I must and do believe you."

My friend, thus persuaded of the facts in question, now begged me to renew my story to him, if possible, in a more full and copious manner; accordingly, I obeyed him. He was quite charmed with my account of the planet Nazar, and the Potuan government, the laws and institutions of which, he said, were such as deserved to be a model to all the kingdoms in the world. He also observed, in justice to me, that a description of so wise and well-regulated a government could not possibly proceed from a disordered head or a confused imagination, for that such principles were rather of divine than human original.

When I found that his conviction was perfectly sincere and well-established, I then thought it high time to talk to him about my own affairs; accordingly, I desired to know of him what he thought I had best do in my present condition, or what I might reasonably expect in my own country after the mighty exploits I had achieved in the subterranean world. To which he answered thus:

"Let me persuade you," says he, "never to discover these things to any mortal. You know the zeal of our priests. You know they persecuted the author of that famous discovery of the Earth's motion round the sun, and all who adhered to that philosophy. And what then do you think will become of you for asserting the existence of a subterranean sun and planets? You will be declared a heretic, and as such unworthy to live in a Christian community. How will Master Rupert thunder against you? He who but a year ago sentenced a man to do public penance for asserting the doctrine of the Antipodes. Certainly so holy a person will condemn to the flames the author of so new a system as that of a world underground. I give it you therefore as my best advice that you suffer these things to lie buried in eternal oblivion, and that you live privately in my house for a time."

He then made me throw aside my Subterranean habit and equipped me according to the fashion of my own country. Moreover, he drove away all those crowds of people from the door who came out of curiosity to see the Wandering Jew, assuring them that he disappeared all at once. However, the affair was noised all over the country, and in a short time all the pulpits rang with predictions and prophecies of the evils and misfortunes that must follow upon this apparition. It was said at Sandvik that the Wandering Jew was come, publishing everywhere the approaching vengeance of Heaven, and exhorting the people to repentance. And this story (as stories always gain in telling) was presently enriched with various additions and interpolations. Accordingly some said that the Wandering Jew had foretold the end of the world, and that the next St. John's Day would be the day of the general conflagration, unless they would prevent it by a very sincere repentance, with abundance of other things in the same style. Nay, these predictions had occasioned such troubles in a certain parish that the farmers all gave off plowing and sowing, because as the world was soon to be at an end, there would certainly be no harvest. Hereupon Master Niels, the minister of the parish, fearing he should fall short in his tithes and other articles of his income, told his congregation that to his certain knowledge the day of judgment was put off to the next year. The stratagem took, and they all returned to their wonted labours. As the origin of all this folly and supersitition was known only to my friend and me, it afforded us plentiful matter of mirth and laughter from time to time.

At length, as I did not care to continue longer in a house that was not my own, and as I was under a necessity of coming abroad one time or other in order to procure myself a competent livelihood, I thought it was now high time to begin. Accordingly, we both went to Bergen, and my friend made me pass for a student of Trondheim and a relation of his who came to spend some time in that capital. Soon after he recommended me so earnestly to the Bishop of Bergen, sometimes by letters and sometimes in conversation, that that venerable prelate promised me the first vacant mastership of any school or college he had in his gift. This was an office to my palate, inasmuch as it seemed to be something akin to the elevation I was lately fallen from. For the government of a school is the shadow or image of imperial power; the ferule is the sceptre, and the chair a throne.

But as no vacancy happened in a long time, and as it was necessary something should be done for my present subsistence, I was resolved to embrace the first offer that should be made me. Luckily the curate of St. Cross now died, and the bishop appointed me to succeed him. This promotion seemed ridiculous enough for the monarch of so many empires and kingdoms. But as nothing makes men more ridiculous than poverty, and as it is too high a strain of niceness to refuse muddy water when a man is parched with thirst, I accepted the gracious offer, and am now spending the residue of my days in this office with the contentedness of a philosopher.

A little after this promotion, a match was proposed to me with the daughter of a merchant of Bergen whose name was Magdalen. The lady pleased me highly, but as it was very likely that the Empress of Quama was still alive, I was afraid lest by this marriage with Magdalen I should be guilty of bigamy. But my friend Abeline, to whom I unbosomed myself on this occasion, ridiculed my fears, and by so many arguments demonstrated the folly of my scruples that I no longer hesitated to conclude the match. I lived six years with this wife in the utmost love and friendship, although in all that time I never once related my subterranean history to her. But as I could never entirely lose the remembrance of that height of glory from which I was fallen, some sudden starts and gestures would now and then escape me which did not seem to agree with my present condition. By this second venter I had three sons, Christian, Jens, and Casper,* so that in the whole I have four, if so be that the Prince of Quama is still alive.

Thus far the manuscript of Niels Klim reaches. What follows is the appendix of Master Abeline.

* One would expect to find mentioned here the son Thomas, whose sons Peter and Andreas supposedly supplied the "Apologetic Preface."

Niels Klim lived to the year 1695. He was beloved and esteemed for the sobriety of his life and the purity of his manners. The rector, however, was now and then displeased at his excessive gravity, which he thought proceeded from pride. But I, who knew the man and knew his history, rather wondered at his exemplary modesty and patience who from the government of so many kingdoms could humbly accommodate himself to such an employment. However, with other men to whom his amazing metamorphosis was unknown, he could not altogether escape the charge of pride. It was his custom, at certain times of the year, while his strength permitted him, to ascend the old mountain and take an earnest view of the famous cavern. His friends observed that he always returned from thence with his eyes swollen and his face all bathed in tears, that he would afterwards shut himself up whole days in his study, and seemed to shun the conversation of mankind. His wife also assured me that he would often talk in his sleep about land armies and forces at sea. This absence of mind went so far once as to give orders for the governor of Bergen to come immediately before him. His spouse imagined these disorders of his brain proceeded from an excessive application to his studies. His library consisted chiefly of political books, and as such a choice but ill agreed with the office of a curate, he could not avoid some censures upon that head. He himself wrote his own adventures, and his manuscript, which is the only one in being, is at present in my custody. Though I always intended it for the press, yet I have hitherto been hindered from publishing it by very important reasons.

Finis

BIBLIOGRAPHICAL DATA AND A NOTE
ON THE EDITING

There have been three English translations of *Klim,* the first and second the work of anonymous translators, the third made by John Gierlow. The first was published in 1742 (and again in 1746, 1749, 1755, and 1812), the second in 1828, and the third in 1845.

Except for minor changes (discussed below) the text of the present edition follows that of the first English edition. The best of the three, it is clear and accurate, and the characteristic eighteenth-century style is well suited to the subject matter.

The 1828 edition is of value because it contains new matter, mainly the "Apologetic Preface," introduced by Holberg into the second Latin edition of 1745. All of this material has been edited and included in the present edition, and all additions except the "Apologetic Preface" are printed in brackets.

The 1845 edition is abridged and the least interesting, although it has some attractive engravings copied from Baggesen's Danish edition of 1789. The tone of the translation can be gathered from this passage in the preface: "Greater liberties were allowed at that period in literature than would now be permitted. Holberg's humorous productions are not wholly free from a fault, whose existence the taste of any age may explain, but does not excuse."[1]

Holberg, like Robert Burton, had the itch for Latin quotations. His memory for them was not so good as he thought it was, nor, it is universally agreed, was his Latin. He quoted from Ovid, Virgil, Horace, Persius, Juvenal, Petronius, and others without any reference whatsoever to the source or author. The quotations appear untranslated and unidentified in the 1742 edition, translated into English verse and still unidentified in the 1828 edition, and chiefly absorbed into the text in the 1845 edition. I have decided to leave out all those quotations which contribute little or nothing to the story. Any translation or transition required by the deletion of a Latin quotation is printed in italics. The reader who is interested in the quotations will find them printed with their sources in a Latin edition by C. G. Elberling, Copenhagen, 1866, or in a Danish edition by H. C. Broholm and E. Nystrøm, Copenhagen, 1941.

I have changed the Latin names to their Norwegian counterparts. The Latin *Nicolaus Klimius,* which is "Nicholas Klimius" in the 1742 English edition, therefore appears as "Niels Klim," just as in the 1828 and 1845 English editions. I have modernized the spelling, capitalization, and punctuation, and I have replaced some archaic words by more familiar ones. The paragraphing has been altered, especially in conversational exchanges. For a few other minor changes, mostly in the spelling of Subterranean proper names, I have relied on the 1866 Latin edition.

There is an excellent bibliography: Holger Ehrencron-Müller, *Bibliografi over Holbergs Skrifter* (1933-35). I can add only the 1941 Danish edition above and two editions in French, one published in 1944 by Ides et Calendes, Neuchâtel and Paris, and the other published in 1954 by La Nouvelle Bibliothèque, Neuchâtel. Ehrencron-Müller lists fifty-nine editions in thirteen languages: Danish (thirteen), Dutch (five), English (seven), Finnish (one), French (four), German (fifteen), Hungarian (one), Icelandic (one), Italian (one), Latin (six), Polish (one), Russian (one), and Swedish (three).

---

[1] Louis Holberg, *Niels Klim's Journey Under the Ground,* trans. John Gierlow (Boston: Saxton, Pierce & Co., 1845), p. xiv.

ACKNOWLEDGMENTS

I should like to thank the following publishers: The American-Scandinavian Foundation, for permission to quote from an article by Richard B. Vowles in *The American-Scandinavian Review;* Encyclopaedia Britannica, Inc., for permission to quote from an article by Edmund Gosse; the Princeton University Press, for permission to quote from *Gulliver's Travels, a Critical Study,* by William A. Eddy; George Bell and Sons, for permission to quote from *History of Prose Fiction,* by John Colin Dunlop; Basil Blackwell and Mott Ltd., for permission to quote from *Ludvig Holberg, The Founder of Norwegian Literature and an Oxford Student,* by S. C. Hammer; and the Harvard University Press, for permission to quote from the Loeb Classical Library editions of Ovid, Juvenal, and Virgil. Specific sources will be found in the footnotes.

I should like to thank the Harvard College Library for permission to use its copy of the 1742 English edition, Mr. Philip B. Gove for reading the introduction and making valuable suggestions for its improvement, the staff of the Humboldt State College Library, especially Mr. Leland Fetzer and Mr. Richard Press, for their generous assistance, and the Humboldt State College Improvement Foundation for the 1959 Research Award, which has helped to defray expenses.

A NOTE ABOUT THE EDITOR

James I. Mc Nelis, Jr. was born in Centralia, Pennsylvania, in 1917. After taking his A.B. degree at Columbia College in 1942, he served as an officer in the Coast Guard and the South Pacific during the Second World War. While studying for his M.A. at Columbia University, he taught English at Union Junior College (1946-1948) and Brooklyn College (1948-1950). In 1951 he became Instructor of English at Stanford University where he remained until 1956, receiving his Ph.D. from Columbia University in 1954. At present, he is Associate Professor of English at Humboldt State College, Arcata, California.

Dr. Mc Nelis writes the publishers that he lives on "sixteen acres of woods and brambles with wife, son, two Golden Retrievers, one beige cat, ten brown chickens and a white goat." His hobbies are "painting, writing poems, fishing, 'farming,' and the community theatre."